ROCKWELL

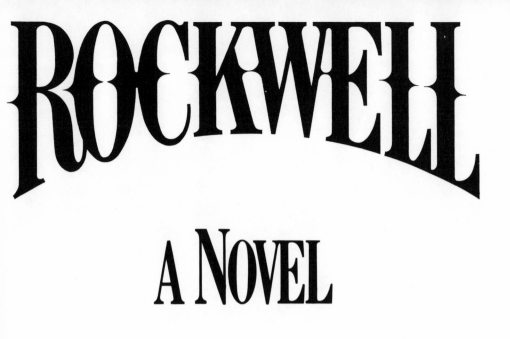

ROCKWELL

A NOVEL

RICHARD LLOYD DEWEY

PARAMOUNT BOOKS • *New York*

ISBN: 0-9616024-2-2

Paramount Books
Box 379
Seaford, New York 11783

November 1987

Printed in the United States of America

*To Lee Scott Dewey and Lynn Dewey Sohm,
not only my brother and sister but my best friends*

Orrin Porter Rockwell
Courtesy of Utah State Historical Society

Acknowledgements

For their remarkable editorial talent and assistance I wish to give special thanks to Dennis R. Lisonbee and Lee Scott Dewey; for additional editorial advice, Dana Wells Watkins and Nik Gasdik; for manuscript preparation, Doris Harrington, Melissa Kalaher, and Laurie Clark; for proofreading, Vernon Ingleton and Lucinda Smith; for research assistance, the numerous individuals whom I credited in *Porter Rockwell: A Biography*; and finally, for the life of the most remarkable man I feel I've ever known, Orrin Porter Rockwell.

PART ONE

THE BETRAYAL

1

Rockwell was surprised to see a mob gathered. They had received word of his coming and were shouting in a frenzy.

James Fox, Deputy Sheriff of St. Louis, had stayed with him from the moment of his arrest in St. Louis to his present transfer to Independence, Missouri authorities, yet even he was more than a little surprised at the outlaw's reception. For a moment Fox feared for his own life as the stagecoach pulled into the midst of the screaming throng.

Rockwell was 29 and tanned, with a chest and arms like a grizzly bear's.

Five dozen men were screaming for his blood. A hangman's noose was passed over their heads, and Fox found himself stepping out of the stage with his revolver cocked. Rockwell gazed through the stage window and eyed the mob. Fox fired a shot in the air. Several men stepped back.

From his office Sheriff Reynolds came forward, grabbed the handcuffed prisoner, and led him into the street.

With Rockwell before him Sheriff Reynolds made his way to the jail, clanged the door shut behind Rockwell, then turned and faced the mob. They glared at their sheriff, but finally dispersed.

Inside the cell, Rockwell found himself in a stone room with a wooden floor and urine-drenched hay.

Flies buzzed loudly, and he pushed the hay aside and sat on moist wood. The room was chilled. Within hours he began shivering. In near darkness he stared at faint rays of moonlight seeping under the door cracks.

He wondered when he would again see Luana.....

Three days passed and the door slammed open. Since he had been fed only small amounts of bread and water, he had to be lifted by Sheriff Reynolds to his feet. He was escorted outside into the blinding light.

The mob had reformed. They shouted and spat at him all the way to the courthouse two blocks away.

Inside, a court convened. The magistrate glared at him, listening to James Fox, Deputy Sheriff of St. Louis.

"Get Governor Boggs here," said Fox.

"What's your purpose?" said the judge.

"Governor Boggs swore to it himself that Rockwell shot him."

"The former governor is still recovering from gunshot wounds.....in the back of his head," added the judge with a sniff. "He obviously never saw the assailant."

"Well Rockwell fessed up to me himself that he shot him," said Fox.

A loud mumble rolled through the courtroom.

"What proof do you have?"

Fox said nothing. The judge studied him; his own small eyes betrayed the impatience with which he was known to rule the court. His dark hair outlined his reddened face. Fox was a tall, lean fellow and at six feet was fully a foot taller than the judge. But he felt intimidated and could not think of a credible response.

Finally Rockwell broke the silence. "I never shot Boggs, your honor."

"And what's your proof?"

Rockwell knew they were aware of his shooting abilities–he had won matches from Missouri to New York. But all he could do was stare at the judge, thinking of an answer.

Deputy Fox darted his eyes across the courtroom, sensing by some a certain halted admiration for the outlaw and by others an outright contempt. All waited for the reply.

"I will repeat my question," said the judge. "What is your proof you did not shoot the former governor?"

"Well, your honor," said Rockwell, "he's still alive, ain't he?"

The courtroom burst into laughter.

As Rockwell was escorted back to the county jail, the jailer confided, "They've found no crime against you."

"Then why am I here?"

"Safekeeping."

"Can you take off the irons?"

"That's up to Sheriff Reynolds."

The jailer was a slight, heavily-mustached, and stoop-shouldered city servant who always carried out his work with clinical precision. Sheriff Reynolds, on the other hand, was an impassioned soul who sought not only law and order for his town but eventual civic aspirations. He had found as the years went on that he truly enjoyed living alone. Many friends however asked him to dinner, not for his position, but because he was worth his salt.

He had always hoped to be appointed to a high-standing, life-long, secure position within the Missouri state government, free from the vacillating whims of voters who could dash him out of office from the damaging rumors or bad press. At 37, he was a large, looming figure, and always seemed to be looking down at you, even if he were sitting. He had a large square head and fat lips.

Inside the cell Rockwell waited a day before food was brought. Then another two days. The iron hobbles were still clamped to his feet and hands.

Another three days passed before he saw the jailer's face. Finally, twelve days later, the sheriff himself arrived.

"I'm half frozen every night," said Rockwell. "Can you build me a fire?"

"Too busy."

"What about the handcuffs?"

"You'll survive."

"Why am I being kept here?"

"Waiting for the judge's decision," said Reynolds.

"How long will that be?"

" 'Long as it takes."

"Then can you loose my hands a little till he decides?" said Rockwell.

"What's the matter– you itch in places you wished you didn't?" Reynolds chuckled and walked to the door.

"What does the judge have to decide?" said Rockwell.

"Nothing. It's up to the prosecuting attorney to find something.

Are you satisfied now? You think it's every day we hold a prize this big?" Reynolds slammed the door behind him.

Rockwell was not only itching, his stomach was cramping and he was aching from his obsession to see Luana.

Luana. He feared he would never see her again. Even if he were released, he knew he had pushed their marriage to the brink. He was faced with the stark agony of his feelings.....

An autumn and a winter had passed since he'd hugged her and the four children. Philadelphia had been the loneliest spot on earth, he had thought. Joseph Smith had sent him East when authorities had announced he and Smith were sought for Boggs' assassination attempt. Unable to find work in Pennsylvania and Ohio, and after basking there in intense loneliness, he chanced to return to Nauvoo, Illinois. On his journey home to Nauvoo–at St. Louis–he'd been snared by a bounty hunter and brought to Independence, Missouri for trial by Deputy James Fox, who had now returned to St. Louis and who Rockwell would never again see. His mind remained riveted to Luana, his four children, his friends, and even his dog.

Rockwell was taken upstairs each day now, and at night would be confined to the dungeon.

The weather warmed the last week of April–he found himself alternately baking from the mid-day heat and shivering in the evenings.

What added to his discomfort was his waste problems; his hands were still cuffed behind his back. The stench was unbearable.

Nevertheless, his arms had ceased to cramp. His stocky frame had begun to take on a skeletal look. Inside, his feelings for Luana were frying his mind. He wondered, since their divorce, if she had yet found another man.....

On the morning of his 30th birthday, June 28th, 1843, Rockwell saw a stranger enter his cell. He was tall and gaunt, about Rockwell's age. He stood directly over Rockwell.

"I've never been in one of these before," said the stranger.

"Neither have I."

"Don't reckon I've been locked up with a criminal before, either."

"Don't reckon I have either," said Rockwell.

The man's name was Watson; he had been arrested for counter-feiting. He was pale in hair, face, arms, and even his eyes. He spoke in a pleasant voice with tones cultivated at a New England univer-sity.

That night neither man slept. The next morning Watson broke the long silence. "Where do you suppose I may find the outhouse?"

"You're layin' in it."

Watson moved across the room and gazed at Rockwell. "Have you perchance considered escaping from this.....hole?"

"Naw, they'll let me out sooner or later."

"Later from what I understand." said Watson.

"What do you understand?"

"If you escape with me I shall tell you."

"No chance," said Rockwell. "I'm gettin' out soon."

"I suppose it is your choice."

The next afternoon Sheriff Reynolds entered and removed Rockwell's cuffs, then led Watson away. Presently Rockwell heard a tap on a window bar–he glanced outside and down and spotted a small black girl on the street below holding a covered basket. She had thrown the rock to get his attention. She now tossed him a whip stock with a long piece of attached twine.

With the "fishing pole" he drew up the basket, uncovered it, and discovered a dozen pieces of freshly fried chicken. He nearly passed out from the aroma. He picked up a warm leg and rotated it in his hand, observing its perfect, flaky, crispness. He could feel the warm meat through the delectably fried bread-crumb skin. He placed it almost worshipfully back in the basket.

He then glared suspiciously outside at the girl. "Where'd you get this?"

"Ain't your business, mister."

"Yeah it is–I'm eatin' it."

"Then do it at your own risk," said the girl, who strutted away.

"Humble child," mumbled Rockwell to himself. He gazed back at the chicken again.

Watson had been in court, but presently returned.

"How was the judge?" said Rockwell.

"Preposterous. I don't know when I'm being released from here.....what's that smell?"

Rockwell produced the basket from behind his back.

Watson's eyes bulged.

Rockwell threw him a piece of chicken.

Watson tore into it, chewed as if he had not eaten in years, and swallowed. Then he noticed Rockwell staring at him. "Well?"

"Well what?"

"What are you staring at?" said Watson.

"Your eyes."

"May I ask why?"

"Sure, go ahead."

Watson gave him an impatient glare. "Why?"

"To see if you're still in there," said Rockwell.

"What the devil are you talking about?"

"Don't talk, just eat." Rockwell threw him another piece.

Watson chewed, glanced up, and beheld Rockwell again staring at him. "Confound it, man, what are you doing?"

"Just trying to see if you're losin' it," said Rockwell.

"Losing it?"

"Yeah, losin' it."

"Losing what?"

"Nevermind."

"No," said Watson, "tell me, what you are looking at to see what I'm losing."

"Life."

"Life?"

"Uh-huh," said Rockwell. "Life. I want to see if this here chicken's poisoned. But so far you seem to be doin' all right."

Watson sighed and glanced down. "You are a genuine gentleman, did you know that?"

"Yep. Who else would share you half his southern fried, fresh, un-poisoned chicken?" And at that Rockwell tore off another piece and threw it at him.

Watson caught it, smiled, and dug in. Rockwell studied him another minute–before Watson caught him again staring. Rockwell winked and began to eat.

The next day Rockwell fastened a hard corn-dodger to the "fishing pole" twine and lowered it below to the street.

Strolling Missourians stopped and stared at it.

"What are you doing?" said Watson to Rockwell.

"Come over here."

Watson moved across the cell and saw below a crowd of eight men and a woman staring up at them, baffled. Rockwell bobbled the corn dodger in front of their faces and laughed. The pedestrians moved on, but soon another group clustered and stared.

Watson returned to his corner of the cell. "You have a strange sense of humor, my friend."

Rockwell glared at him. Watson trembled, fearing he had offended the outlaw. Then Rockwell broke into a smile. "I suppose it is strange, ain't it?"

A lightening storm unleashed with a ferocity Rockwell had rarely seen. He was awakened by a flash and noticed from several more flashes Watson's eyes staring at the ceiling in fright. Moments later thunderous crashes shook the air. After a silence, Watson spoke.

"Could this be a sign of sorts?"

Raindrops dribbled unevenly, and finally formed a hypnotic downpour.

"I know what you're thinkin'," said Rockwell. "So just get the thought out of your head."

"Do you suppose I expect to stay in this trap?"

"You ain't gettin' me in trouble," said Rockwell, "so don't expect me to go along with you."

"If you knew what I did about you–and what they are planning for your friend, Smith–you would realize the extent of your trouble already."

"What're you talkin' about?"

"They came to see Sheriff Reynolds the other day," said Watson.

"When?"

"When I was first incarcerated. They are going to do away with Joseph Smith."

"I've heard that before–everybody's tried–everybody's failed."

"I'm simply telling you what I heard."

"From who?"

"You help me get free–then I'll tell you."

"There's no way to help you break out without going myself," said Rockwell. "And I ain't going. I'll be let out if I don't foul up. So no jail breaks, understand?"

"My friend, you are dreaming."

Rockwell tried dismissing the statement and closed his eyes. The rain came harder. He reopened them. "Who are they?"

"Smith's friends–his own people. You break jail with me, and I'll tell you everything."

Rockwell gave him a troubled look.

Watson re-emphasized his point. "Good behavior won't get you out–I will."

Rockwell thought another minute. Another flash of lightening hit even closer, and the thunder crashed immediately afterwards.

That evening Rockwell and Watson waited for the jailer to return for dishes.

"You shouldn't have ate so much," said Rockwell.

"I'll eat what I please, thank you," said Watson.

They finally heard the jailer clumping up the stairs. As the door opened, the two men sprang to the door, grabbed the jailer, shoved him inside, locked the door, and ran down the stairs.

The jailer's wife downstairs saw them and gasped.

The two men ran outside and Rockwell tossed the key into the garden. Twenty yards ahead was a board fence 12 feet high. They ran towards it and leaped. Rockwell climbed to the top, glanced below, and saw Watson still struggling half way up.

"Go ahead, I'll catch you," said Watson.

"I told you–you shouldn't've ate so much."

"I said I'll catch you!"

Rockwell dropped to the other side and took off running. Across town he heard a shout. He ignored it, turned, and saw Watson's face bobbling above the fence, grunting to get over.

Across town, gathering outside a tavern, were a dozen Missourians. Rockwell picked up his pace, when suddenly he heard from 400 feet back Watson yelling for help.

He stopped. He observed across town that the mob was multiplying. He felt sorry for Watson. They had developed somewhat of a bond. Rockwell ran back to the fence.

"Get me up," shouted Watson.

"Take my hand!"

Watson did and Rockwell pulled him over. On the other side Watson crashed to the ground. Rockwell helped him up and both men took off running.....

Rockwell and Watson glanced back as they neared the woods and saw the mob following, running faster than they and closing, just 50 yards behind.

The weeks of little food and no exercise in captivity began to take their toll on Rockwell. His head began to swim. The treeline ahead lost focus. His pace slackened. "Watson!....." he shouted. Rockwell needed Watson's help now, but Watson kept running.

Rockwell slowed to a standstill. He collapsed to one knee. He panted. Presently a half dozen men surrounded him and the remainder continued pursuing Watson.

They grabbed Rockwell and escorted him back to the jail. In front of the jail, a larger crowd gathered and he heard a voice shout, "Pass the rope–"

Sheriff Reynolds shoved Rockwell from behind, into the mob. "There he is," said Reynolds, "Do what you please with him!"

The rope was passed over their heads when another man suddenly grabbed him–but Rockwell jerked away from the man and pushed him into the mud. The crowd was surprised at Rockwell's sudden strength.

"Stand off or I'll mash your face in," said Rockwell to the mob. He saw by the door a buckskin filled with bullets. He grabbed it and yelled to the mob, "I'll crush any head that takes another step towards me."

Several of the mob drew out bowie knives and advanced on him.....

Sheriff Reynolds stepped in front of the mob with his revolver aimed. The men with knives halted.

The mob dispersed.

Inside the jail Reynolds turned his revolver on Rockwell. Rockwell dropped the buckskin bag, then descended the stairs.

"Watson was caught," said Reynolds from the top of the stairs, watching Rockwell disappear below, into the darkness. "And he's being taken to St. Louis for trial. I reckon you won't see him again unless he happens to get buried in the same cemetary as you."

Rockwell awakened the next morning starving. He had been ironed hand and foot–his right hand to his left foot–where he could not straighten his back. The door opened and Reynolds walked in with a covered dish. Reynolds left the dish and slammed the iron grate behind him. Rockwell uncovered the dish to find a dead mouse.

Twenty-four hours later the jailer entered, saw the mouse, and left without a word. Downstairs he reported it to Reynolds.

Meanwhile, Rockwell could not move. The mouse's odor blended with the dungeon's own, yet the pungent smell nauseated him.

The following day the jailer again entered, gave the mouse a glance, and muttered, "Sheriff says you don't get other food till you eat what's fed you."

Rockwell was by now cramping from hunger. That afternoon, in the stillness of the cell, the jailer peeked inside and saw a plate full of rodent hairs beside the prisoner.....

Rockwell noticed after 18 days that the pain in his wrists had disappeared entirely–the tight irons had loosened enough for him to literally slip them up to his elbows and turn his arms around inside them–he'd lost that much weight.

Lice were embedded deeply in his eyebrows. His color was pale. His eyes were both green and red.

He was dying.

One morning without being given an explanation, Rockwell's irons were unlocked, and he was lifted to his feet.

Through blaring sunlight he was half-carried.

At the courthouse the magistrate bellowed, "A bill has been found against you for breaking jail. However, a grand jury has failed to find a bill against you for shooting Governor Boggs, as charged in the advertisement offering a reward for your apprehension. Do you have a defense?"

Rockwell shook his head no.

"Do you have counsel?"

His answer was barely audible.

"Say that again," said the judge.

Rockwell said nothing.

"Have you any means to employ a counsel?"

Again Rockwell shook his head.

"Here are a number of counselors," said the judge. "If you're acquainted with any of them you can take your choice."

Rockwell's eyes scanned the lawyers; most glanced away but several scowled directly at him. His eyes finally rested on an apathetic face casually addressing his day's chores as he stared out the window. He was Alexander Doniphan, a proven ally to Rockwell's people, the Mormons, years earlier at Far West, Missouri before they had been expelled from the state. The Mormons had fallen into disfavor with the Missourians due to their opposition to slavery and beliefs in aiding the Indians; additionally, many of the Missourians had become incensed at some Mormons' self-righteous attitudes; others were simply jealous of the Mormons' industriousness. To many Missourians, all outsiders were suspect, and if any kind of controversy surrounded them, it was even stronger grounds for rejection: this particularly applied to the Mormons since they had just been forced from Ohio for their untraditional religious beliefs.*

---

*Ohio pastors had worked their congregations into a frenzy over the Mormon belief that challenged the Bible as the sole record of Christian authority. (The Mormons claimed they believed in not only the Bible, but the Book of Mormon, as the word of God. Joseph Smith, their leader, claimed the Book of Mormon was written by ancient prophets in America, and that it had been revealed to him by an angelic messenger; this, local pastors asserted, was heretical since miracles and messengers had ceased at the time of Christ.) Adding further fuel to the fire, some of the pastors' own congregations had defected to the Mormon religion. To retaliate, some ministers claimed the Mormons were not even Christians. (The Mormons defended themselves in public debate, claiming not only that Christ was the head of their church, but that even the church's name was "The Church of Jesus Christ of Latter-day Saints." The Mormons further claimed they embraced Christ as the only literal Son of God. Other ministers asserted Joseph Smith was the being whom the Mormons worshipped; however, the Mormons said they looked upon Smith as merely a prophet–like Moses anciently–who communicated with God and Christ, but that Smith was not a deified being himself. A final theological point that disconcerted most clergymen was the Mormon belief that all people had to believe in Christ plus prove themselves with works of Christian action and obedience–while standard Christian doctrine held that all people were saved by simply believing in Christ.)

An undeniable concern for non-Mormons in Missouri was the fact that Mormons had a political force to be reckoned with; thousands of converts had poured in from Eastern and European missionary harvests, and it frightened their neighbors.

Given this background, Governor Boggs had ordered then-General Doniphan of the state militia to execute Joseph Smith, but Doniphan had refused, claiming it "cold-blooded murder." Because of Doniphan's refusal, Boggs had second thoughts about executing Smith and simply decided to rid his state of the Mormons altogether. As a result, he issued his famous Exterminating Order. All Mormons were to flee Missouri or be shot.

The Mormons complied, fled to Illinois, drained a swamp, and built the largest city in the state, Nauvoo.

The Mormons, while in Missouri, had not been without their allies, however, Including Doniphan.

But today, Doniphan was hesitant to aid Rockwell. "Your honor, I'm crowded with business—here are plenty of young lawyers who could plead for him as well as I."

"Doniphan," said the judge, "that is not sufficient excuse—consider yourself Rockwell's counsel."

Doniphan glared at the prisoner.

"Mr. Rockwell," said the judge, "you will be returned to the jail until your case is again considered."

Doniphan was successful in changing Rockwell's venue to another county, one where he hoped less prejudice would exist. He also demanded that Rockwell be placed on a regular prisoner's diet of fresh meat and corn-dodgers.

However, Rockwell was again ironed hand and foot until the move would transpire, and he was forced to lie in one corner of his cell.

One late afternoon he heard the door swing open. In walked several officers who uncuffed him.

"Get up, boy, we're taking you with us," said the oldest, a tall, skinny deputy with a badge seemingly half the size of his chest.

"But I suggest you wash up and do it in a hurry. A mob's forming outside. They got word we're moving you!"

"Where' we going?"

"You'll learn soon enough." They took him downstairs where he quickly bathed, running a sponge from a bucket across his body in less than 30 seconds.

"Now get me a clean set of clothes," said Rockwell.

"Don't have time."

"You make time—or I ain't moving," said the prisoner.

"It's your neck," said the youngest officer, who disappeared, only to return 10 minutes later with clean clothes. "That mob is beginning to broil." He glanced to the other three officers. They understood his look and in one motion pulled out revolvers.

"Hurry up," said the oldest to Rockwell. "We can't do much to protect you against a mob."

"Then hand me a couple of those guns," said Rockwell, "and I will."

The four men quickly exchanged a glance. The voices outside became louder.

Outside, the officers held their guns on the mob, and in the last remaining rays of sunset tied Rockwell's feet under a dilapidated saddle and his hands behind his back. They led him off on a good round trot, but with only two of the officers accompanying, the tall, skinny one and the floppish-looking younger one, a lad of 19. The only distinguishing feature about either of them, Rockwell noted, was their identical handle-bar mustaches, caked with dried nasal fluid and food particles. Perhaps they were father and son, he mused.

"I hear talk," said the older a mile later, "that some of the more adventurous souls back there plan an ambush before we get to Liberty, maybe even before we get to the Missouri River."

"You believe every scuttlebutt rumor you hear?" said the younger, noticeably nervous nevertheless.

"Sometimes I do," said the older, "especially if it involves my neck."

The night fell and immediately the sky was thick with stars. As they rode, Rockwell realized how easily they could be attacked from the side of the road; he could not actually see the trunks of the trees, but he was vaguely sensible of them against the darkness; among them perhaps were human figures.

A stranger's outline was silhouetted against the stars. He sat horseback directly in front of them. "Mind if I go with you to the river?" said the stranger. "These woods are haunted."

"Yep. Just ride in front of us," said the older officer. "And let me have your gun." The stranger hesitantly complied. He was an aged, wiry soul that resembled a gnarled old tree.

Night creatures were crying and warbling. Rockwell heard a distant owl.

None of Rockwell's party said a word. Six miles later they arrived at the river. They saw on the opposite shore eight men ride off a ferry and take into the woods.

Soon, one of the officers asked the ferry operator, "Where are those eight men ahead going?"

"To hew timber."

But on the opposite shore, after Rockwell's party arrived, they heard no sounds of axes. Three miles into the woods Rockwell heard a crackle behind him. The younger officer turned. "What's that?"

"What?" said the older officer.

"That."

"You're hearing things. There's nothing back there."

"Then you're deaf," said the younger. "I heard it."

Suddenly they all heard it–the crackling of brush and leaves directly behind them.

The two officers cocked their weapons. The older one cleared his throat, clearly concerned. "Move faster, boy, keep your eyes behind you."

Rockwell's eyes went wide. "Unloose my hands and give me a gun."

The two officers stared at him, considering his offer.

"Give him one," said the younger officer.

"No–just keep a look-out," said the older.

Rockwell and the three men came to an opening in the woods. The sounds of crackling brush ceased. They were no longer being followed.

Before dawn, in the cool of a summer evening, they arrived at Liberty, Missouri. Immediately, Rockwell was cast into jail, the same where Joseph Smith had spent several months.

After gazing around the basement dungeon walls–where only a single shaft of light penetrated from a trap door–Rockwell took out a picture locket of Luana and opened it.

He studied for fully a half hour a small, sober picture of Luana Beebee Rockwell, and he wondered if she had by now found another man.....

Ten days passed, and Rockwell found himself before a new

judge, Austin A. King, a short, dark-complexioned Missourian who resembled a mule. He thumbed through papers and spoke with a heavy accent.

"These papers of Mr. Doniphan are too informal, the style too casual; I cannot consider this case, and therefore suggest you return the prisoner to Independence."

Rockwell simply stood, taking the blow, suspecting a plan to keep him in custody forever.

As he and the two officers returned to Independence, he overheard the older officer mutter to the other, "We'll take a different road."

"The first one's shorter."

"I overheard more talk in the tavern–some folk plan to waylay him.....I reckon somebody knew the judge's plan.....I don't know how."

The younger officer gazed at Rockwell and both knew what the other was thinking.....

By taking a little-traveled road the three men arrived at Independence with no encounters.

At Independence jail again, Rockwell was immediately ironed hand and foot. He remained in the dungeon without the use of his hands, only able to eat by leaning on his side and chewing like a dog.

There he remained two months.

Sheriff Reynolds finally came into the dungeon and casually announced that he was leaving for Illinois to capture Joseph Smith.

In addition to Rockwell, Smith was also now sought for the attempted assassination of ex-Governor Boggs, based upon a rumor instigated by an associate of Smith's that Smith had hired Rockwell to kill the ex-governor–in revenge for the exterminating order.

Smith claimed Rockwell was innocent and that Smith had never sent Rockwell to kill Boggs. Smith wrote Sheriff Reynolds to that effect. "The ex-governor had hundreds of business enemies, political enemies, and personal enemies. So why pick on us? Furthermore, you had a non-Mormon suspect for two months who was a fugitive. Then one day you decided you couldn't catch him. Is that why you have chosen Rockwell and me as your new, prime, suspects–without any evidence whatsoever? I demand you release Mr. Rockwell at once."

Instead, Sheriff Reynolds decided to arrest Smith as well. When Rockwell learned of Reynolds' plan, he felt the hackles on the back of his neck rise. Rockwell's hair happened to be the longest ever, greasy and itching from the increasing number of lice infesting it.

Before announcing his intentions, Reynolds replaced Rockwell's water bowl with fresh water and placed an anxious eye on him.

Rockwell knew Reynolds had something on his mind—mainly from the way he kept trying to keep his voice casual—but the attempt was apparent.

"We've got a letter written by Smith himself," said Reynolds, "and it shows his complete confidence in you. We're giving you a once-in-a-lifetime opportunity here. You get Smith into Missouri, and get him here on horseback into our hands, and we'll pay any pile you name. You'll never suffer for want afterwards, I promise."

Rockwell said nothing.

Reynolds cleared his throat. "Am I clear?"

Rockwell blinked, half-conscious.

"I said—"

"I heard what you said."

"Well?"

"I will see you all dead first, and then I won't."

Reynolds slapped him. "You don't understand, do you? We're going to snatch Smith anyway. He has men in his own group who want him replaced."

"Like who—Sidney Rigdon?"

"It don't matter—but they're honorable men."

"I'm sure they are."

Rockwell had always felt there were certain jealous men who wanted to replace Smith as leader. Rockwell had warned Smith in the past about several, but Smith had rarely believed him. He had usually found out only after such "apostates" defected to anti-Mormon newspaper editors with sensational stories. Many men—like William Phelps—had left and blurted out their stories to fuel the flames—then had "repented and returned to the fold." Smith always welcomed such men back with open arms. Rockwell felt they could usually use a good, long probation first. "After all," he once told Smith before they left Missouri, "we wouldn't be leaving if it weren't for their lies. How do you know they're true blue? You shouldn't welcome them back so quick."

"The Lord forgives, I forgive," Smith would say.

Rockwell was skeptical. He knew Smith was right, but he would maintain his suspicions for months. He possessed a protective air towards Smith, for which Smith felt grateful but unnecessary.

Sheriff Reynolds now faced Rockwell with a forced smile. "You're set for life, son. Only thing you gotta do is help the citizens of Jackson County win this time. Help us catch Smith."

Rockwell studied the hidden smirk on Reynold's face, and then he spat in it.

Reynolds wiped the spit from his cheek and forced a smile. "You'll wish you'd never been born, son." And then he left.

Upstairs Reynolds nodded to two men in his office, and they descended to the dungeon. From his desk Reynolds heard muffled groans and smacking of fists, and the sound of boots on flesh. Reynolds leaned back in his chair and lifted his feet to his desk.

While Sheriff Reynolds was gone, hoping to capture Joseph Smith, Rockwell spent his first two weeks semi-conscious. Even then, he worried incessantly over Smith. He wondered if Reynolds would snare him. He was particularly concerned over which Mormons had cooperated in the plot against Smith. Was it Sidney Rigdon? Rockwell mistrusted the man like he did few on the planet.

At one point he began to tremble, worrying over Smith's traitors and the conspiracy with Reynolds. No matter how hard he prayed, and tried to force his mind from the matter, he could not receive comfort. He wished somehow Smith would be alerted to his danger. His own worry began to consume him.....until just after sunset one day a dove flew into his cell. Rockwell watched it walk about, amazed at its presence. He had never seen such a curious occurance. It finally flew and circled the cell, then lit on the window; it left and returned twice more, engaging in the same feat. Rockwell took it as a sign that Smith was safe, and from that point on he ceased worrying.

One morning Rockwell learned from the jailer that Reynolds had returned without Smith. Rockwell's soul rejoiced.

As the story unfolded he learned Reynolds had laid a trap for Smith with the help of not only traitors in Smith's midst, but with the aid of Harmon T. Wilson, a Carthage, Illinois constable–to capture Smith outside Nauvoo on a routine journey.

The conspiratrs had succeeded. Although they had caught him, Smith then outwitted them with a legal writ of habeas corpus, and the two lawmen left empty-handed.

Reynolds of course was furious, and the jailer was afraid Reynolds would now take it out on Rockwell.

But Rockwell was too numb from pain to consciously care.

The following dawn the door crashed open. Rockwell jerked awake with a start and saw Sheriff Reynolds in the framework. Reynolds strutted up to him, stood silently over him, and stared down. Rockwell glanced at the Sheriff's freshly polished boots. His stomach was too sore to take more punishment; he forced the thought from his mind and gazed directly into Reynolds' eyes.

Reynolds flushed with anger. He knelt to one knee, reached his hand to his belt, and pulled out a key. Then unlocked the iron hobbles.

Outside, Rockwell was taken by the same two officers as earlier. He felt relieved to be leaving Reynolds, and he wondered if the transfer were permanent.

Sheriff Reynolds scowled as the two officers led his prisoner away. After bungling his arrest of Joseph Smith, Reynolds was doubly angry that Rockwell was being taken out of his grasp. Rockwell thought he heard the sheriff kick the office wall.

Autumn leaves had faded to a dark, lifeless brown. The chill wind caught Rockwell's face by surprise. He wondered if at Liberty Jail he would again be hobbled in irons.

His escorts seemed anxious to deliver him quickly. By the time he reached Liberty, Missouri his groin and thighs were raw from the rough, creaking saddle. Even his horse seemed anxious to unload him. It was the first time he could ever remember not riding in harmony with an animal.

He was especially grateful to be untied. For the first time in months his legs were unironed, yet he was thrust into another dungeon.

To his dismay his hands were again ironed–although this time in front of him; thus he was able to an extent to use them.

His hopes however of ever being released dwindled. But on the second day, when his eyes caught hold of a stove pipe hole nine feet above the floor, his eyes brightened for the first time in months. He knew he had a legitimate chance to escape.....

That evening, when the jailer left the building, Rockwell removed the stove pipe. At first he thought he would not be able to fit through the pipe. However, he stripped himself of his clothes and pushed them through the stove pipe hole, and finally pulled himself up, with hands still cuffed, to the ceiling space above. He began crawling between the basement ceiling and the floor.

Crawling in this space was difficult. His naked wounds were scratched. He bled. In the darkness he felt spider webs and various-sized insects crawling across him.

He finally found loose boarding–and his fist smashed into the floor above.

Light filtered through the floor and he immediately discovered a large rat's green eyes staring at him, just inches from his nose. He spat at the animal and it turned away. He smashed another floorboard and he crawled out onto the floor and stood.

Rockwell shuffled to the door and found it bolted shut. He glanced about the room and spotted a water pail.

With the bailing wire of the water pail he unbolted the door. He entered another room, one that was small and sparse with an outside door on the far wall. He grabbed his clothes and carried them to the outer door. Before donning his apparel he tried the doorknob.

Locked. He struggled again and realized it was escape-proof.

Back to his cell he crawled, replacing the loose floorboards.

All during the following day he agonized how he could get past that door.

For the first time in months he found himself worrying over something other than Luana and Joseph, and he finally drifted to sleep.....

The next evening he again crawled through the floor, pushed open the loose boards, unbolted the inner door, and found himself standing before the outer door. The process had been more exhausting–he had been fed even less food that day.

He struggled again to unlatch the outer door but again his efforts proved fruitless.

He lay on the floor to think. He would try unbolting the outer door momentarily. Because of his starved and weakened condition, he had a fever caused by unhealed sores and wounds on his body. As his mind wandered among objects of use in the building and how they could be applied to his breaking the door lock, his exhaustion overcame him. He was soon imprisoned in a deep slumber on the floor behind the inner door.....where the jailer would soon be entering just after dawn.....

The outer door swung open. Footsteps seemed like a distant dream. Rockwell jerked awake. Above him stood the jailer and two boys–all three of whom ran to the outer door and yelled for help.

Rockwell struggled to find a weapon. He glanced around, still weak. He donned his trousers. Six men suddenly bolted in and grabbed him.

From his dungeon, now bound hand and foot as in Independence, Rockwell doubted he would ever again see freedom. He wondered if he would die with the vermin crawling over him. He ached from sores, sitting in his dung, his muscles excruciatingly cramped from the irons that kept him perpetually bent neck to foot. But the searing in his mind was even worse. He could not help worrying over Luana and the children.

In this delerium he was visited three days later by Alexander Doniphan.

His attorney was speechless when he saw how wretched the

man looked.

"Are they going to let me die here?"

"Not if you're patient."

"Patient?"

"Fifteen days from now is your trial."

Doniphan left, but that same evening a voice called through the dungeon grate.

"Rockwell, do you want out?"

Rockwell refused to answer, figuring he was being taunted.

"I am honest with you–I can get you out."

"Who are you?"

"Trust me."

Rockwell figured it might be a set up. "What do you want?"

"I'll knock out the jailer when he comes back–I sent him downstreet–I told him his wife needed him. Hurry if you're coming."

Rockwell detected sincerity in the voice, but was uncertain.

"I know what you're thinking–but this is not a trap–can you please trust me?"

"How do you expect me to? I don't even know you."

"Rockwell, you idiot, it's me!"

"Who?"

"Watson!"

"Watson, you fool, you couldn't pull off a jail-break if your life depended on it!"

Rockwell felt a surge of hope and excitement. His blood ran chill. The thought of freedom–yet the chance of another, delayed trial for jail-breaking if he were caught–made his mind swim.

"Hurry up.....I can get you out!"

"I think I'll stay," decided Rockwell. "It's too soon. I'm too close."

"You are insane."

"That's what you said before–and now look at me!" said Rockwell.

"Well at least I'm free."

"How did you get out?"

"I've become rather adept at these matters by now," said Watson, proudly.

"So? How'd you do it?"

"Well, I served a few months time, and they released me."

"Yeah, that's pretty adept all right. You're an exciting escape artist if I've ever seen one."

"Don't be sarcastic, Rockwell. I can do it, I know I can. I can't leave you to rot in there. I left you at the woods and I'm sorry. Give me a chance to free you this time."

"No thanks."

"Rockwell.....are you still there?"

"Of course I'm still here."

"I'll see you later–the jailer's coming."

Rockwell wondered if he should have accepted the offer. The next morning he again heard Watson's voice.

"Take it."

"Take what?" Rockwell looked up and saw a stick entering the ceiling hole. In a cleft of the stick was fastened several dollar bills. Rockwell took them. "Thank you.....where'd you get this?"

"Don't thank me–your mother pooled it together and gave it to me to get to you."

"She trusted a convicted counterfeiter?" joked Rockwell. "She never was much of a judge of character."

"Yes, look what she raised," chided Watson.

"Where'd you find her?"

"I overheard her talking to the jailer, and I followed her down-street and told her what I knew of you."

Rockwell felt torn. He knew his mother in Nauvoo must have tirelessly been trying to free him. He felt ashamed he did not think a hundredth as much about her as she undoubtedly did about him.

"It don't matter," he muttered to himself.

"About what?"

"That she didn't get to see me. She's lucky." Rockwell knew that although most men could make it in half the time, she must have taken a month traveling across state to see him. He fought away the emotions.

"Well," continued Watson, "she said Joseph Smith raised this money for you to fee your attorney. Perhaps it's more than you'll need."

"Yeah, there's a lot to buy down in this place," said Rockwell.

Watson's voice got suddenly grave. "My friend?....."

"Yeah?"

"I don't know what else I can do to help you. You're certain you want me to just leave you there?"

Rockwell paused for a long, reflective moment. "Yeah."

Watson left and never returned.

The next 15 days went agonizingly slow. Rockwell wondered if the court would indeed be convened, or if they had not conjured up even more reasons to keep him incarcerated.

"You there, wake up."

Rockwell opened his eyes and saw Doniphan standing above him.

Soon they were both standing facing Judge Austin King again in the courthouse.

"Mr. Rockwell, you are on trial for breaking Independence Jail."

"Your honor," said Doniphan, "the laws of Missouri state that in order to break jail a man must break a lock, a door, or a wall."

"I interpret that applying to the defendant."

"To walk out when the door is open?" asked Doniphan. Several chuckles came from the jury. "He and Mr. Watson simply walked out of an open door."

Rockwell glanced across the members of the jury.

They retired for a verdict, to decide on the final conviction and imprisonment of Orrin Porter Rockwell.....

The spokesman of the jury stood. "Guilty."

Rockwell's head dropped slowly.

The spokesman continued, "We recommend the defendant be imprisoned five minutes for the misdemeanor."

"Misdemeanor, indeed," snorted Judge King.

"You have our verdict."

Doniphan smiled, triumphant. Rockwell was too stunned to believe it.

On the way back to the jail, Doniphan mumbled to the jailer something of which Rockwell caught only a portion–that half the judges in the state were prejudiced before his case had ever even come to court. In this case, Judge King's own brother-in-law had been killed at Crooked River in a battle with Rockwell's people years earlier.

"However," added Doniphan, "the jurors are considerably less antagonistic towards Rockwell here than in Independence. The judge must have known he could only go so far against him. That's why, I suppose, he concurred with the decision."

Rockwell sat on his dungeon floor another five hours; Doniphan returned after twilight and found him still in jail. Doniphan was furious, castigating the jailer for taking orders from either King or the prosecuting attorney.

"They just want more time to get more charges against him," said Doniphan. "It's illegal, and I've a busy evening. Release this man immediately."

The jailer opened the trap door and Rockwell climbed out to his final steps to freedom. The thrill that surged through him was exhilarating.

"Just get out of the state," Doniphan ordered.

"Thank you, sir."

"Thank me when you're free. You're still a good two weeks' travel to Illinois–and half the rabble in Missouri want to string you up. If you want to make it, stay on backroads–preferably off the roads altogether–except at night."

They arrived outside and Rockwell stared into the dark woods. "What day is it?"

Doniphan was taken back by Rockwell's lost reckoning of time. "Of course.....it's December 13th, 8 o'clock. You have 12 hours of darkness left to travel." He handed Rockwell some flint and steel. "And only use this sparingly."

Rockwell realized it had been nine months since the time he was first imprisoned at Independence. He gazed into the darkness and continued thinking how indescribable it felt to be free.

"Be off with you then," said Doniphan, who watched him step onto the icy street, grab two coarse rags to wrap his feet in for boots, and disappear into the cold Missouri forest.....to begin his race for freedom.

Rockwell heard two men riding ahead; he stopped behind an oak and listened.

"He's smart–we ain't gonna find him."

"Sure we will–keep your eyes peeled."

Rockwell noticed houses north of the road. As he journeyed around them he heard a terrier barking. He quickened his pace. Behind the houses was a stream. The first thing he did was wash off the filth acquired from the dungeons. The water only made him colder. Although his skin was cleaner, his clothes were so encrusted with dirt, sweat, and filth that he was tempted to wash them as well, despite the freezing temperatures. He found nearby a large raggedy wagon canvas, wrapped himself in it, and washed his clothes. Much of the odor remained, but he felt cleaner. After his clothes dried he traveled eastward, beside the road, with the moon in its first quarter, until dawn. After 25 miles he stopped to rest.

The December morning was raw. He awakened with a layer of frost over him. He shivered. The wagon canvas had kept him alive. He walked ten miles, his stomach aching for food. Presently he arrived at Crooked River with the skin worn off his feet. His foot rags were bloody, but he kept them tightly wrapped. Soon he came on a man walking beside the road–the man was frail and possessed a hawkish nose.

"Fancy boots you got there," said the Missourian.

"I'll buy any extra pair you got."

"No chance of that, stranger, ain't got extras; what're you doing with your hair to your shoulders?"

"Been a busy year," said Rockwell. "Forgot to cut it."

"Well," said the Missourian, liking his humor, "I can put you up for the night and give you a decent meal."

"Right kind of you."

"But you gotta walk back a couple miles to my house."

"Walk back?" Rockwell suspected a trap. His feet were in such pain anyway that he doubted he could walk back two miles even if he wanted. Despite the Missourian's affability he could see the invitation as a possible set-up.

"Your choice, stranger."

Rockwell thought about it a moment and sighed. He knew many men were after him, but did this Missourian know his identity? Rockwell glanced at the man's jugular vein. He walked beside him and a step behind. He followed the Missourian to his farmhouse two miles back. Each step was more painful than the previous, and his mind wound tighter around the prospects of facing a trap. What would he do if it were? He would grab a weapon as soon as he saw one–from no matter who possessed it. Suddenly he stopped. He realized he should leave the Missourian immediately and disappear into the woods where he could not be followed.

"Just ahead is food and warmth, stranger," said the Missourian.

Rockwell assessed the fellow's flashing eyes, and decided, against his better judgement, to resume following him. The thought of food and rest–despite the chance this was a trap– drove him on.

When they arrived at the house, Rockwell's eyes darted about for extra horses–none were in sight. Perhaps the man did indeed have no trap intended.

Inside, the Missourian's wife was angry that he had picked up "a ruffian."

"Stranger," jested the man, "are you a ruffian?"

"Not according to my mother," said Rockwell. "But my wife might say different."

The Missourian laughed. His wife scowled and left the room. "As you see," he mumbled, "she's kind of cross. I've got some whiskey–let's drink–and she'll soon have something for us to eat."

Rockwell refreshed himself on whiskey, and they had dinner served. He wasn't certain he had ever partaken of such a feast. Fried potatoes, wheat mush, and eggs–he had seen it many times before–but tonight he ate with unparalleled relish.

Each bite was a royal meal.

He wondered how badly he smelled. He sniffed casually and noticed to his relief that the farmer and his wife smelled like cattle. He smiled and continued eating.

Through the meal, the woman studied his eyes, and though her husband did all the talking, Rockwell smiled gently. A glance at her a couple times told him she was beginning to accept him. Rockwell was amazed that the idiom about married couples growing to look alike was in this case exemplified by her nose–it was as hawkish as her husband's, an odd coincidence.

That night Rockwell was given the rug on which to sleep. He overheard in their bedroom a heated argument over the woman's garden not producing and he complained of her unyielding criticism. It was evident to Rockwell that the Missourian wounded her continually and that she was critical in self-defense.

The next morning Rockwell was invited for breakfast–another feast of wheat mush, bread, freshly whipped butter, and eggs, and he ate heartily.

After breakfast he began wrapping the bloodied rags about his feet when the woman muttered something to her husband.

"Stranger," said the farmer, "my wife says my boy can lead you a few miles east on our horse."

"I'll give you 50 cents," said Rockwell, "if he'll take me till noon."

Rockwell found himself riding eastward, the boy leading the horse and never saying a word.

One of the great joys Rockwell discovered was his simple ability to scratch his itchy, lice-ridden scalp and occasionally wash it in a creek. In fact every time he came across water he took advantage of it.

At about noon the boy stopped the horse to water. Rockwell

dismounted. "Thank you, lad," said Rockwell, and he began plod-
ding forward alone in his red-stained foot rags. The boy watched
him disappear down the road.

Rockwell tried to dismiss the pain in his feet. They were
bleeding. He walked till midnight. He built a fire with the flint and
steel. He heard horsehooves; he snuffed out the fire with dirt and
made his way deeper into the woods.

The horses halted and he heard voices muttering.

"I saw the flames somewhere around here."

"Naw–it was farther on–come on."

He realized how sound Doniphan's advice had been. He should
not have even ridden the farmer's horse–he could easily have been
caught and lynched. He would stay off the road, he figured, until he
arrived in Illinois.

He thought incessantly of Luana. He stared at the stars and
recalled her warm arms on chilled winter nights like these.

Soon he drifted asleep, and by the time he awakened, he realized he'd slept more soundly than he had in months. It was broad
daylight now and though he was slightly shivering, the canvas had
kept out the sting of the evening air.

The sun shone brightly and the air was crisp. He made his way
to a stream and washed the sleep from his face. Now, for the first
time in nine months, he saw his reflection: he looked like an animal.
His eyes, however, were soft and clear, and he began to cry.

He arose and thought again of Luana. All day he thought of her.
He stopped at night near Haun's Mill, where friends had been massacred during the religious strife years earlier. He slept beside the
well where a dozen and a half bodies had been buried by the men's
wives.

The day following he arose at dawn and walked till noon,
concentrating on anything he could think of but his bloodied
feet.....

At noon he came upon a man with a mule. He could see the
fellow was a simple farmer, and read by his movements that he
probably was not harmful.

He struck up a conversation and offered 75 cents to carry him
muleback the remainder of the day.

Hours later they came to a house where years earlier Rockwell
had been acquainted with the family. They did not recognize him,
and he spoke as little as possible. He was certain they would be

alarmed if his name were mentioned; nevertheless he took supper, lodging, and breakfast, then paid them for 12 miles of horseback riding the next morning.

He walked 30 miles; his feet blisters bubbled with blood. He made an encampment in the woods, built a fire, and rested the remainder of the day.

His blisters pained him the following morning such that he could not walk. He ate beef jerky he'd procured from the previous family, and crawled to a nearby stream.

The following day his feet were again too tender to travel. As was the next. He remained by the stream.

His food began running low, and although his feet were far from healed, he was forced again to take his journey.

He came upon another farmer, and hired him for a 25 mile horse ride.

He walked another 25 miles in intense pain. His mind was trained by now to dwell elsewhere.

The next day he walked 40 miles, rested the following day, and engaged a man to carry him horseback three days to Montrose, Iowa.

Finally he saw the Mississippi River. His anticipation of holding Luana and the children made his breaths come faster. He arrived at the Iowa shore and gazed across the water. He saw Nauvoo, Illinois, the home of all his family. He quickly crossed the river in a ferry, and realized the very first thing he would do is warn Joseph Smith.....

Inside the Mansion House, a Christmas Eve party was engaged in dancing, music, and eating, when Rockwell entered.

All eyes turned to him, when suddenly, inexplicably, he felt the dramatist within take over.....

Here he was, looking, smelling, appearing to others like an animal, when it suddenly tickled something prankish in his nature.

"Where's Joe Smith? I'm gonna string him up!"

The crowd hushed with a gasp.

"Le'me at him," shouted Rockwell. "I'm takin' him back to Missouri!"

Several men in suits came forward. Rockwell grabbed one and shoved him aside. Rockwell laid his eyes on Smith and strutted through the crowd towards him. Smith was well-dressed for the occasion. At six feet he was a towering man of the day. Poised, blue-eyed and of a predominantly cheerful disposition, his dark hair receeded from his forehead, giving him a look of ineradicable intellectuality. Women considered him strikingly handsome, men were charmed by his charisma. He decided to put the ruffian outside himself. As he walked towards Rockwell, he rolled up his sleeves, his height lumbering over the intruder.

Smith stopped directly in front of Rockwell, looked him straight in the face, and suddenly broke out laughing.

"Orrin Porter Rockwell!" he shouted.

The two men embraced. The entire company laughed. And the news swept Nauvoo like fire.

At the Nauvoo tavern, Chauncey Higbee winced when he heard the news. He was particularly anguished that–rather than seeing Smith delivered to join Rockwell in jail–both were free now and together again in Illinois. Upon hearing the news, he glanced with chagrin at his brother, Francis, then at Robert Foster, also seated at the table, and then he killed another drink.

These were three of the men who had plotted to replace Smith, and they would just have to do something now about getting rid of Porter Rockwell.

At the Mansion House, Rockwell and Joseph Smith quietly conversed. Rockwell was anxious to warn Smith what he had learned from Watson in jail, but Smith refused to believe in such plots.

"Everyone I know is too trustworthy, but who do you think they are?"

Rockwell sighed and looked down. "I don't know– but I know they're up to something. Maybe it's Rigdon."

"Of that I know you're mistaken. Certainly I've had my problems with him, but I'm certain he would not go this far. These are grave charges, Porter."

"You'll be lying in one if you don't do something about it."

Smith smiled and sat back in a worn but comfortable old chair. "Well, I appreciate your concern, but I think your source is confused."

Rockwell said nothing; he forced his eyes away, not wishing to argue. Though he and Smith had spoken in hushed tones, several members of the party made their way across the room within hearing distance. He would simply have to learn the truth for himself, he figured.

"Porter," said Smith, louder and now with his eyes flashing, "I feel impressed to warn you....."

At that several people stopped their conversation and listened.

"I feel to prophesy–and I do it in the name of the Lord Jesus Christ–that if you do not cut your hair, and if you live faithful, you will be as Samson of old–no bullet or blade will harm you, and no one of this earth will be able to take your life."

Rockwell stared at him. He trembled a little, and could not take his eyes from Smith.

Rockwell bathed upstairs as the party continued. He wore a clean suit of clothes, boots, and cloak donated by Smith's friends, some of whom had gone home and returned with the wardrobe. Rockwell was medium in height for the day, at 5'6". Before the party ended he launched forth a clean, new man into the cold Christmas eve.

Luana lived across town. His anxiousness caused his shivering more than the cold. He arrived at her home, where inside he could see his four children. His heart pounded. He knocked at the door. And when it opened, he gazed inside, stunned.

4

Luana Beebee Rockwell's eyes went from shock to anger. They were pale green, and her skin was milk and roses. Her dark hair was up in a bun. She was even more captivating than he had remembered her. He stared at her with shining eyes, and his lips twitched. Behind her stood a tall figure with his hands on her shoulders. The gentleman was well-dressed. Alpheas Cutler, whom Rockwell had met years earlier at a church conference, was a High Priest. Since Smith's church consisted of a lay ministry, Cutler was an attorney by trade.

Rockwell stared at the two—he simply could not speak and neither could Luana. Cutler, neither recognizing nor remembering Rockwell, broke the silence.

"Can we do something for you, sir?"

"Can I see my children?"

The words came into Cutler like a chisel. He wondered if Luana still had feelings for her former husband, and he felt a surge of insecurity. Cutler did not know how to answer the question and he merely gazed at her.

She replied to Rockwell, "You made your decision long ago."

"Of what?"

"Who we were in your life."

Then she shut the door.

Rockwell stood there in shock. He trudged away from the door, pondering on the irony of his obsession for her for over two years—ever since he had gone into hiding in Iowa, then fleeing to Pennsylvania, and finally spending the next nine months in Missouri jails—only to come home to this.

The shock dissipated on his walk through town. He half- consciously meandered the streets. By the time he reached the Mississippi River his shock had turned to full-fledged frustration.

He kicked loose dirt beside the river, and sat on a rock and began to shiver.....

At dawn he returned to the Mansion House. Smith had remained awake, waiting for him, seated at a fireplace, reading and worrying.

"How long has he been with her?" said Rockwell.

"I'm sorry I didn't tell you. I think they've been courting a half year now—he's quite proper about it and is a good man."

"I always thought he was kind of a proud, aspiring fool," said Rockwell.

"Don't be bitter, Porter."

"You wouldn't be bitter? Those are my young ones he could be raising." Rockwell stared at the fire.

As did Smith. "I'm sorry, Porter."

"I'm sorry—'cause I don't know what to do."

"There's not a lot you can."

"Sure there is. I love them. All of 'em. She might break up with him if I began courting her also."

"Porter, they are betrothed. All she probably feels for you is frustration and anger. Give it time."

"Time for him to take her for good?" said Rockwell.

"Time for the hate to heal."

"Mama says love and hate are very close to each other," said Rockwell. "All it takes is one small spark to touch off one to the other."

"But a very bright spark," said Smith, "and I'm afraid you've lit it. Whatever happened two years ago to cause her to leave you is still obviously on her mind."

Rockwell gazed off.

At the Nauvoo tavern Rockwell sat, swishing whiskey around his teeth before swallowing it. He had just returned from visiting his mother. Their visit had been short. They always were.

He was touched when she had smiled at him at the door. He was also moved, in a nostalgic sort of way, when his old dog had greeted him there as well. The dog was a strange mixture, with the ears of a dachshund, the nose of a terrier, and the body of a great dane; its fur was curly like a poodle's. It was remarkably ugly. Many people laughed when they looked at the thing, but Rockwell had loved it since birth. It had moved with him three times in Missouri and twice in Illinois as his people had been driven, and it had for years never left his side. Now he was back. He petted the creature and it rolled on its back. It yelped and danced around for five minutes, leaping on him and nearly knocking him over. It ran for joy throughout the house, and Rockwell and his mother laughed painfully.

His mother for years had kept herself busy with the other children. Since her husband had died, she was particularly attentive to the needs of her grandchildren. When Rockwell's marriage had dissolved, she had felt relieved that her son was free from what she considered a demanding woman, but she had shed more than a few tears in his behalf. She still suspected his emotional attachment to Luana, though she said nothing about it.

His mother had not related as well to Rockwell as she had to the other children, and had found him since birth a remarkably willful child. But through it all she had somehow loved him the most.

Rockwell had related better, however, to his father, and more especially to his surrogate older brother, Joseph Smith, who had in many ways raised him, the two lads living but two miles apart in Manchester, New York through childhood.

Indeed, Rockwell had chopped firewood and sold berries to help fund the printing of the *Book of Mormon*, such was his commitment to his friend's cause.

He had just left his mother's home, knowing he could not live with her demanding ways. She accepted that, as they had silently agreed to it years previously. As always he would continue visiting her only monthly or so; he was grateful she had the other children and grandchildren to care for. He had spoken little to her of Luana; her admonitions would have been predictable. The dog had followed him of course, and would roam the streets and live almost like a cat, yet always stay near his bed at night and allow him to pet it to sleep, as he had in years past. He was truly attached to the animal.

Inside the tavern the dog sat beside him and watched him sip his whiskey. Rockwell had just been rejected for a job by the chief bartender. He was desperate for employment. Just as he always had in previous years when he visited a tavern, he gave the dog a shot or two, and it shook its head and sneezed.

Three tables away in the soft tavern light Rockwell vaguely discerned the faces of the Higbee brothers, along with William Law, one of the highest ranking Mormons, a member of Smith's First Presidency. Rockwell would never have suspected Law, nor any of the men at the table, as conspirators. Though Rockwell did not know them well enough, he had always thought them likeable, though a bit critical. He still wondered who the conspirators actually were.

He also wondered why the men there engaged in such soft conversation. He lowered himself in his chair to not be seen. The men did not seem to take notice of him or anyone else in the busy tavern, so enthralled were they in their discussion. The room was noisy, and Rockwell could only catch snatches of their conversation. He then overheard something that—although he could not make out the full details of it—enabled him to comprehend their business: the overthrow of Joseph's city!

Rockwell noticed another face—one he had never seen-but of which he quickly learned the identity: the editor of the *Warsaw Signal*, Thomas Sharp.

Rockwell rose casually and strode to the door. A glance back from the doorway allowed him to catch a suspicious, kerosene lamp-reflected glint in one eye of Chauncey Higbee staring at him.

Rockwell quickly turned his face, pulled his hat low, and walked out into the cold.

His dog followed.

Smith was dismayed that Rockwell would even report such an incredible story, much less, in good conscience, give credence to ideas about the infidelity of these men.

"Do you hear what you are saying?" said Smith.

"Yes."

"Did you hear exactly what they were saying?"

"Some of it."

"That's not sufficient."

"It is for me."

Smith gazed out the window. "The Laws have nevertheless

been acting a mite strange of late."

"With good reason."

"I simply can't believe it, Porter."

"Maybe you don't wanna believe it."

Smith stared outside, slowly shaking his head. "I would need much more evidence."

"They could have you dead before you have your evidence. They would love to take over this city and the church."

Smith felt obligated for Rockwell's sacrifices, and soon converted his front room to a tavern for Rockwell's means of employ. But Emma Smith, his wife, returned from a furniture-buying excursion in St. Louis and demanded the bar be dismantled.

"I'm obligated to him," Smith told her. "Especially in light of his wife leaving him."

"And I'm obligated to the children. I will not have them raised under such conditions nor have them mingle with men who frequent such a place. You are at liberty to make your choice; either that bar goes, or we will."

The next day Smith asked Rockwell if he would not mind finding employment elsewhere.

"Well, I've managed so far through my life," smiled Rockwell.

"I suggest you find something not too strenuous, so you can rest. You can take your meals with us a few months, and I'm certain Emma won't mind if you stay with us till you find employment and permanent quarters."

Smith worried about the long-haired, now-scrawny figure who walked out into the cold. Rockwell had lost 50 pounds during his incarceration, although he was slowly regaining weight. Smith rushed to the door. "Porter, I want you to take my horse..... anywhere you like.....at any time.

Rockwell rode on the horse of the prophet towards the temple in the center of town. He stopped his horse and stared up the hill at the majestic building. He would rebuild his muscles if it killed him, he decided. He would rebuild his life. He had too much at stake.

A knock came at the door. Smith answered and saw two teenage lads standing awkwardly.

"Come in."

The two were Dennison L. Harrison and Robert Scott, the latter living as a border with the William Law family. The two entered and Smith wondered about the nature of their visit. They took a seat and got right to business. They apprised Smith of a secret movement to take his life.

Smith was shocked.

"We were invited to the meetings by Mr. Law," said Scott.

"I suggest you go to them," said Smith, after a reflective stare, "but take no part in the proceedings, and report to me."

Smith thanked them and they left. He glanced outside at the temple, and saw Rockwell seated atop his horse on the hill. He suspected what his old friend might be going through emotionally, and could not take his eyes off the man.

Rockwell feared how extensive the assassination plot had developed.

"I want to stay at your side as much as possible," he told Smith.

"You can stay in our home and I'll see you are given meals, clothes, and goods for your trouble—you needn't find other work for awhile. I want you as my bodyguard."

Rockwell nodded. He would carry two loaded pistols, he figured. He felt confidence in his ability to protect Smith.

Over the ensuing days Rockwell spent hours target practicing and working hard in Smith's corral, eating heartily, working physically, and regaining his bear-like form.

The two lads, Harrison and Scott, reported on three meetings they attended; they filled in Smith with the details about a conspiracy by Chauncey Higbee, Francis Higbee, Joseph Jackson, William Law, Jane Law, Wilson Law, Robert Foster, Charles Foster, and Augustine Spencer to assassinate him and take control of the church and the city.

After they left, Smith turned to Rockwell and uttered, "Now it's our turn to fight back."

Rockwell clenched his fists.

On March 24, 1844 Smith publicly indicted Chauncey L. Higbee as one of the enemy in their midst. Smith also excommunicated Wilson and William Law and the latter's wife, Jane, and on April 13th arrested Robert D. Foster for slander and for conspiring against his life. William Law, the best known of the above, was not only the third-highest ranking man in the church but was respected by all men and adored by children.

One day there was a pounding at the door of the Mansion House. Rockwell answered it to discover the Nauvoo city marshal, Thomas Greene, a lanky, likeable, but officious sort, holding a prisoner, Augustine Spencer. Spencer was short, young, intelligent, and well-cultivated.

"What's the trouble?" said Smith, coming to the door.

"He's the trouble," said Augustine Spencer nodding at the marshal, who held Spencer in a tight grip.

"Joseph," said the marshal, "I'm bringing Spencer here into my office to book charges. He just attacked his own brother with his fists—he started the fight and I saw it."

Augustine Spencer struggled to free himself of the marshal's hold on him. "Smith, I'll prepare a lawsuit against the both of you if you don't have him let go of me."

Since Joseph Smith was the mayor of Nauvoo, and the Mansion House was used as the city building for both the mayor's and the marshal's office, Smith unavoidably saw most of the trouble that occured in his city. He wished at times he weren't quite so entrenched in his duties, taking upon himself the presidio of community leadership, but most other men with the ability to help him perform his various roles happened to be overseas. Brigham Young was his senior member of the Council of the Twelve, and was in England performing missionary work, as were most other able assistants. They were needed there to convert others, Smith felt, and export their harvests to Nauvoo to expand the size and strength of the church. Smith accepted the fact he was thus faced with more responsibilities than he cared to face. Brigham Young, in fact, would be a good man to handle such a problem as the one occuring, he figured.

At the door Rockwell then noticed several other men arriving, shouting at Marshal Greene and calling for both Greene and Joseph Smith to release Augustine Spencer. Immediately Rockwell recognized all eight—they were the conspirators! William Law, characteristically, was at the back of the group and attempting to restrain the passions of the rest of the group. Everything he tried, however, failed, as his associates only escalated their anger when they beheld Smith's firmness. William Law then attempted to reason with Smith. He claimed the Spencer brothers always had their little rows, and that they themselves would settle it; Marshal Greene was simply overreacting.

Smith refused his request.

One of the men, Charles Foster, began swearing and drew a revolver from his vest. Immediately Rockwell lunged forward. He grabbed the weapon away from Foster and clenched Foster's neck in a vice-like hold.

Smith then ordered Greene and Rockwell to bring in their two prisoners to be fined. Joseph Smith then also ordered the other seven outside the door to disperse. They walked away, livid with rage, except for Law who walked away simply more determined.

William Law was certain, as he considered the encounter with chagrin, that his own associates were so anxious for a revolution that they were surfacing too quickly with their intentions, allowing their emotions to get the best of them. Law wished to merely see a quiet overthrow of the kingdom.....

Rockwell meanwhile was certain the conspirators would now hasten their plans against Joseph Smith's life.

Later, within days, these men launched their attack against Smith on the legal battlefield; they took their story to a Carthage grand jury. There, they claimed Spencer and Foster had been falsely arrested.

Carthage was the nearest non-Mormon town, twelve miles downroad, and from not only this court incident, but other reports by "apostate" Mormons, the Carthaginians were now becoming increasingly concerned about their Mormon neighbors.

Smith decided to plead his case to the grand jury. He enlisted Hyrum Smith, his brother, John Taylor, Porter Rockwell, and several others to accompany him to Carthage. Hyrum Smith and John Taylor both were tall, spare, grave, and dignified; they were men of thick brown hair and thoughtful demeanor. Both were in their late thirties, likeable, but not particularly handsome. They were undeniably loyal to Smith.

At the courtroom Joseph Smith demanded to the judge, "Investigate the charges!"

"I'll have to delay action on the case until next term, but your case will be heard fairly."

As the Mormon entourage left the court Smith told Rockwell about the conspirators' deeds, particularly those of Joseph Jackson. "He's committed murder, robbery, and perjury, and I can prove it by half-a-dozen witnesses."

Rockwell felt anger at the apparent injustice.

Before leaving Carthage, they stopped at Hamilton's Tavern. Inside, Smith spotted Chauncey Higbee seated at a large table, and ignored him.

Higbee, who was about 40 and tall, had in earlier years been considered somewhat of a street ruffian but more recently had befriended the intelligentsia of the church and had displayed some restraint in his temper.

Therefore, Rockwell was surprised when Higbee spotted them and raised his voice.

"Found any treasure in folks' pockets lately, Joe?"

The crowd turned quiet. Joseph Smith looked at Higbee and said nothing.

Higbee was louder. "Joe, are you still hiding behind your long-haired pet dog, Rockwell?"

Rockwell suddenly spoke up. "Higbee, I don't care what you call me, but you just insulted my best friend."

"Well if your people knew how much your best friend stole from them they'd dump him in the Mississippi with a millstone around his neck."

"Higbee," said Rockwell, softly, "he's done more in one week for the downtrodden folk in these parts than you and all eight of your friends could do in a lifetime. And he hasn't taken one cent."

"Joe," said Higbee, louder, "down deep you know you're nothing more than a gold-digger with empty visions of power, lust, and greed."

Rockwell suddenly walked up to Higbee, reached a hand into his lapel, and grabbed it.

Higbee found himself being pulled from a sitting position to a standing positon and then he found himself being stretched up against the wall. His face suddenly shone with sweat.

Rockwell looked into his large, liquid eyes and his voice quaked, "Apologize to Joseph, Higbee."

Higbee's face began to discompose. He was fearful and embarrassed that a man considerably shorter than himself had him suddenly so intimidated.

Suddenly Rockwell felt a cold piece of metal stuck against his neck. He slowly turned to see Hamilton, the tavern-keeper, leveling a shot-gun into his flesh.

"You fire that thing," said Rockwell, "with that barrel plugged up against me, and it'll back-fire." He turned and glared into

Hamilton's eyes.

Joseph Smith broke the tense silence, "Porter, I think we're finished here."

Hamilton cleared his throat, "Yeah, I think you are."

Rockwell nodded a polite farewell to the men in the tavern, and clopped across the wooden floor and out the door.

Smith sighed, relieved, and followed. He glanced at Higbee and saw hatred like he'd rarely before seen. Higbee's long, horse-like face grew red from the anger he tried to control. He spoke up just as Smith reached the door.

"Joseph, because of tonight, you will live to see your entire city crumbled. And that I swear by the footstool of God."

Days later in Nauvoo, Chauncey Higbee peered admirably at his work of art. The first issue of the *Nauvoo Expositor* flapped off the press, and before the ink was dry he was grabbing a bundle, smelling the crisp, fresh paper, and taking it proudly outside.

Onto the busy mercantile district street he raced, handing out one issue after another, determined not only for every citizen in Nauvoo to receive a copy, but for every person in three counties to read it.

Rockwell happened to be riding past when Higbee spotted him and stared at the back of his head. Rockwell felt the stare and turned back to look. Their eyes met and held.

Rockwell stopped his horse. Higbee disappeared inside a busy general store. Rockwell forced away his anger and resumed riding downstreet. He observed myriads of citizens standing along the road, reading the paper, when he finally overheard one man mumble.

"This could start a war if strangers believe it."

"What's it say?" said his wife.

"They're claiming Joseph is an animal, and hires Rockwell to murder innocent citizens. It looks like the same old press that riled up the mobs against us in Missouri."

Rockwell lay in bed and could not sleep. Thoughts of his children and his wife haunted him, especially of Luana in another's arms; he wondered if Cutler's affections would be as tender as his own.....He petted his dog beside the bed a few moments, then arose. He walked to the window and stared at the moon. He realized he could not endure the uncertainty.....knowing that in later years he might kick himself for not even trying when he had had the chance. He slipped on his trousers and boots......

5

As the four Rockwell children played, their father rode to them and stopped his horse. They glanced at him and vaguely discerned him in the darkness as a long-haired stranger. He dismounted and stood before them. His eldest finally recognized him.

"Father?....."

The other children stopped and stared.

He walked to each one and caressed them, then picked up his youngest, who hugged him.

Rockwell fought the tears. He glanced at the window and perceived a pair of eyes watching. He looked closer and saw the eyes were as beautiful and intense as he had always known them–even more so on this particular night–and they were the eyes he had loved and never been able to release from his mind. He found his breathing uneasy and his chest pounding. His eyes could not leave hers, and apparently she was also glued to him. He wondered if she were feeling even a particle of his passion–and more especially if she were actually yet reconsidering......

Luana disappeared from the glass.

Rockwell set down the child and strode to the front door. There, he tapped gently. The door opened and he walked inside.

Luana stared at Rockwell as he strode to the fireplace, picked up a rod, and began jabbing hot embers. He shifted from one foot to the other. He recalled so many memories that he did not know which–if any–would be appealing to her. He suspected that any recalling of memories could backfire anyway–she could counter it with some negative memory–so he said nothing. He became suddenly aware that the dominant sound in the room was a loud wall clock.

She finally broke the awkward silence. "What do you want?"

"You."

She gave him a long, searching look. "We've been through this," she said. "You had your chance for a decade."

"And I want it back."

"It's too late."

"Who says?"

"Me," came Cutler's voice as he entered from the kitchen. "Can't you see she wishes to be left alone?"

Rockwell was surprised Cutler was present. His horse must have been hitched in the rear of the house. Rockwell decided to disarm the man's anger. He stepped forward and extended his hand. Cutler eased his emotions and took on a gentlemanly air and returned the handshake. "Sorry to bother you, Cutler, I just wanted a little talk with her if you don't mind."

Cutler nonetheless refused to leave the room. Rockwell ignored him but still did not know what to say to Luana. He finally shoved the rod into the embers and left it there.

"Luana, what do you want from me?"

"Just what Alpheas said."

"Can't you give us another try?"

Luana merely stared at him.

Cutler spoke up again, "Rockwell, I really think you should leave."

Rockwell ignored him and kept his gaze on Luana.

She finally walked up to Cutler and rested her hand on his shoulder.

"Alpheas and I have plans to discuss, Porter, if you don't mind."

Rockwell raised his voice for the first time in two years and found himself trembling. "Luana, don't touch him when you're talking to me. Can you have enough respect for me to do that?"

"Porter," she said, "I want you to leave. Everything's been said."

"Everything except one thing," added Rockwell.

"What's that?"

"What I feel for you."

"Alpheas–get him out of here," she said.

Rockwell glared at him and Cutler did not move. "Luana, I want you and the children to know....." But he could not finish it. He could see it in her eyes. Her love had completely vanished. He looked away.

She read his mind. She thought for a moment and chose her words carefully. "It didn't happen all at once–you know that."

Rockwell stared at the floor a minute, and nodded.

Cutler realized his security with Luana and returned to the kitchen alone.

Luana's voice softened, "Was it that hard? Jail?"

Rockwell could not look into her face. He slowly turned, without saying a word, and went outside, leaving her to stare after him.

In the yard he glanced at his children, who had resumed playing. But as he tried not to make eye contact with them, the eldest called out, "Are you back now, Father?"

Rockwell could not look at them either. He slowly trod beside his horse and down the road, giving no reply, wishing he'd never gone to see them.

Editor Thomas Sharp of the *Warsaw Signal* sat at his desk, listening. He was an affable man who bore himself without a trace of self-consciousness. He was amused by the story of Chauncey and Francis Higbee, Robert Foster, Augustine Spencer, and William and Wilson Law.

"We got the first issue published of the *Nauvoo Expositor* and three days later the city council decided to destroy it," said Chauncey Higbee. "They claimed under the Illinois Constitution, Article B, that freedom of the press was not an issue."

"Then what the devil was the issue?" said Sharp, smirking.

"The local populace being stirred into a frenzy," replied Higbee. "But we can publish anything we please. So we took it to court in Nauvoo. We claimed Smith's people started a riot. Witnesses there claimed there was no riot, and the court decided our suit was malicious and they even made us pay the court costs."

"Who did you sue?"

"All the city councilmen and the principals–Joseph Smith and the man he sent to head the posse's destruction of the press, Porter Rockwell."

Sharp knew a hot story when he saw one, and he knew this time he was going to make the most of it. He did not particularly dislike the Mormons' viewpoint against slavery, nor did he care one way or the other about their other doctrines, but he thought Joseph Smith had too much power, and he clearly saw an opportunity to effectually double his circulation. Although his father and brothers in Kentucky were more successful thus far than he, a family tradition among his pioneering newspaper ancestry was one of which he was proud–the ability to jump into an opportunity and exploit a profit out of it. His wife was a kindly woman, his three children obedient and thrifty. He had asked for them to sacrifice long enough. He loved his wife and had stewed silently at the family gatherings when his wife would stare wide-eyed at his brothers' fine apparel and stately horses. Sharp knew she was silently envious of their wives, but through eighteen years of marriage she had said nothing. And she was a woman of such quality, Sharp realized, that her love for him was not conditional on his financial success. He was determined that one day she be proud of him. Today his light autumn eyebrows were a shade lighter than his bushy dark red sideburns and balding head, but they starkly highlighted his intense, blue eyes. He reflected on the story of the several men before him.

"I want you gentlemen to assist me," he finally said to them. "After I print my story, I want you to take copies to every paper in the state, and I want in writing from every editor that my paper gets the by-line. Is that clear?"

The party waited in the Warsaw Tavern downstreet while Sharp polished the article from his interview notes. He read aloud his favorite paragraph.

"We must put an immediate stop to the career of the mad prophet and his demonic coadjutors. We must not only defend ourselves from this danger, but we must carry the war into the enemy's camp."

Sharp felt a tingle as he hadn't since the early years. He had attempted to build up his paper for so many years on so many schemes, and had tried so many various promotions with such negligible results, that something this time told him deep down this might be his last opportunity to really do something big.

Meanwhile, Rockwell felt a yearning still eating away at his heart. He knew, as utterly absurd as it seemed, he had left certain things unsaid. Luana was the only woman of his life, he realized, the only woman he felt he could ever love.

Though her passions for him appeared dead, they must be alive somewhere within her–she still possessed enough anger to hold some kind of feelings. His mother's adage on love and hate was still playing on his mind. Yet what was killing him was the fact he knew there was no mistaking it–he simply could not live without her. He also loved the children. They were his, and that alone should bind them together. He would also prove to her that he had indeed changed. Rockwell was riding beside Smith, unable to stop thinking of Luana's remarkable beauty and charm. He and Smith were returning from a court proceeding where they had just been exonerated from shutting down the *Expositor* newspaper. The court had taken place in an adjacent county where they had hoped less prejudice and more objectivity might exist. But, upon returning, they feared Nauvoo might now be attacked because of the proceeding.

Rockwell thought of the irony: he and Smith saw what they were certain they would never again see. They thought they had left behind all their troubles in Missouri. Tonight, however, riding back to Nauvoo, in every town they passed, they found copies of the *Warsaw Signal*–and of Sharp's article calling for arms to be raised against the citizens of Nauvoo, Illinois. What was more frightening was the response: citizens were meeting under torch-light in courtyard squares, and organizing themselves into vigilante groups. Rockwell and Smith traveled beside the road under the cover of trees, their faces dappled by the moonlight, and they said not a word, both thinking what the other was thinking–and seeing the same old cycle of violence re-forming. Added to Rockwell's concerns was his inability to shake Luana's image from his mind.

Under the moonlight on the woodland road, as they re-entered Nauvoo, Rockwell beheld Pisces brightly lighting the firmament. He found the city still quiet and unscathed. Without a word to his companion, he turned his horse another direction to see Luana once again and to clarify those things that had gone unsaid.

Before he had ridden three blocks, however, Rockwell passed the Nauvoo tavern and spotted Chauncey Higbee exiting. He moved his eyes to the road that led to Luana's, but at the same time his soul ached with curiosity over Higbee's plans. Higbee, without seeing Rockwell, mounted up and rode the opposite direction.

Rockwell glanced again down Luana's road, then gazed back at Higbee. He sighed and decided to follow the man.

Twelve miles later in Carthage, Higbee dismounted. Rockwell followed him into Hamilton's Tavern and spotted him across the room. Higbee had seated himself with several of the conspirators.

Rockwell advanced carefully through the crowded room in order to not be seen; his long hair was tucked under a high collar and he kept his hat pulled low. He seated himself within ear-shot of a loud Robert Foster, whose voice boomed from a bit much whiskey.

Rockwell did not catch all the details, but enough to send a shiver across his neck: he heard pieces of plans about a lynch mob. This was different than what Smith had been expecting–the mob would attack from the river shore and hit the Mansion House first. It would take Smith prisoner even before the Nauvoo Legion could be alerted.

Stunned, Rockwell eased his way through the standing, talking bodies, and hurried out the doorway.

Before Rockwell closed the door, however, Chauncey Higbee caught sight of him. Higbee whispered to five men at an adjacent table.

The five men quickly arose.

Rockwell rode as the wind. He was two miles outside Carthage when he heard horsehooves pounding behind. At first he figured the mob was advancing on Nauvoo.....until he realized.....they were after him!

His horse tired.

It slowed.

His pursuers gained on him.

He returned his horse to a gallop. His pursuers were a hundred yards back now and closing.

Then his horse lost a shoe. He bolted from the horse and ran into the woods. He hid in thick brush and heard the mob advancing. They trotted on either side of him, not seeing his humped figure in the brush.

Rockwell then took off running to his left, judging by the moonlight, towards Nauvoo. He heard horses just behind him. He jumped behind a fallen tree and crawled to one end.

His pursuers–he counted five–scanned the woodland and

slowly advanced to him. He wondered if they had spotted him.

He slid into one end of the hollow tree. He noticed beside him—rather he smelled beside him–a rotting odor.....and quickly realized.....it was a skunk.

A live skunk.

He strained his eyes outside the log for other cover but saw none. He glanced back at the skunk. The animal's dark eyes regarded him, then waddled away to the other end of the log.

Rockwell sighed with relief. Then he heard two horses pass directly over him. Others passed around the log. The last horseman passed just as the skunk exited. A horsehoof caught the skunk by surprise–and it reared its tail.

The other horsemen, now 30 yards ahead, heard a simultaneous horse whinney and human scream. The horse presently passed them in a thunderous gallop.

All the horsemen, curious, trotted back and found their comrade on the ground, sitting upright, receiving intermittent spurts of scented liquid. The man swore. The other four burst into laughter.

Rockwell meanwhile ran, fully a quarter mile away, directly towards Nauvoo.....

Still breathless, Rockwell stood in Smith's study, having just warned Smith of the lynch mob. Smith turned to his brother Hyrum, and ordered him to call out the legion to protect the city. If ever a loyalty existed between two men, Rockwell thought, it existed between Hyrum and Joseph Smith. They had never spoken harshly to one another in all the years Rockwell had known them and their mutual respect was intransigent. Hyrum had never seemed to mind his brother's tendency to order him about when Joseph was excited, either, and today was no exception. By contrast, Rockwell noted, Rigdon, the Laws, and others generally flinched at Smith's commands. Other, less-ranking souls in the kingdom never questioned Smith. Just those very competent, very charismatic, articulate fellows Smith surrounded himself with who could get things accomplished better than others but whom Rockwell suspected as being too proud for their own good, and, as events were bearing out, actually vying for leadership–complete leadership–with Smith out of the way. It was said that the Smith brothers had a bond that was unbreakable, which Rockwell appreciated, and Rockwell also was proud that both brothers accepted him as another brother, albeit a younger one whose counsels were not always regarded as highly as he would like; nevertheless, he was aware of the roles men retain since childhood, and he was grateful to be a part of the brotherhood.

That night, Rockwell wanted to talk to Joseph Smith about Rockwell's inability to give up on Luana. But Smith's mind was elsewhere, so Rockwell left the Mansion House, deciding to see the lynch mob for himself.

The woods surrounding Nauvoo provided natural cover for the several hundred Nauvoo Legionnaires guarding the city that night.

Under the moonlight Rockwell, dressed in uniform, seemed out-of-form as his long hair swirled in the breeze. He rode a new horse given him by Smith, and took position in the brigade south of the city. The excitement of an impending confrontation took some of the bite out of his emotional obsession over Luana, and for that he was almost relieved. He strode to his commanding officer and requested an assignment as forward guard.

"Are you loco?" said his commander.

"Maybe."

Rockwell found himself 200 yards in front of the infantry, and here in tall grass he waited.

The stars shone brightly when–through the woods–he observed the lynch mob moving near the river. They were already directly on him!

He took out his pistol and cocked it. He knew he could not retreat in time to sound a warning–the mob would see him. He decided to watch them for a moment. He saw in their faces the same belligerent, prejudiced, narrow-minded expressions he had seen in half a hundred mobs' faces in Missouri. He quickly realized what he desired: an all-out battle. Suddenly he found himself wanting to see the legionnaires' rifles cut them to bloody shreds. He wanted to slaughter them and release the anger and injustice he had felt because of their bigotry, and take out on them what he had lived through at the Independence and Liberty jails. He could tell from their sounds that half of them were fairly soused. The others were eating as they walked, The Nauvoo Legion could have a field day.

His lower lip quivered. He could launch the massacre by shooting the point man 50 yards ahead–Frank Worrell–then take off running back to his lines, leading the frenzied, mob into a trap.

But from that thought he realized the consequences: an army combined from several states could march on Nauvoo within days, and Smith's peace strategy, although Rockwell disagreed with parts of it, would be thwarted. Then again he could show the mob what they're really made of and perhaps win some respect–and some second thoughts–on giving his people future problems.

The lynch mob came closer–Rockwell saw over 300 men–and he arose.

The mob spotted him and stopped. He heard mutterings, but Frank Worrell held them at bay. Worrell finally called out, "Soldier, you alone?"

"Come forward and find out," said Rockwell.

6

Frank Worrell was considered an outstanding Carthage citizen. He was tall, masculine, and charming. He owned the largest tool manufacturing company in the county. He was 47 and looked as though he'd never seen a day's illness.

Frank Worrell did not know Rockwell by identity but had heard from Chauncey Higbee about the long hair. Worrell gazed back over his men, many of whom yelled to "attack the woman in uniform." Another of Worrell's men yelled, "What have we got to lose?"

"Just step forward," shouted Rockwell. "And you'll find out."

Suddenly 600 rifle bolts shattered the air in unison–rifles were cocked and made ready to fire–it was the Nauvoo Legion behind Rockwell. They had heard the commotion and advanced to his position without his knowing it.

From the sudden, terrifying clash of metal, Worrell's eyes went wide, and he shouted to his men, "Retreat!"

"Hold fire!" a legionnaire officer yelled.

Rockwell watched as the mob slowly retreated into the woods and disappeared.

At the Mansion House, Rockwell reported the episode to Joseph Smith. And he reported of another of Higbee's plans that he had overheard in the tavern–to burn the *Nauvoo Neighbor*, Smith's official news organ, before morning.

Rockwell wanted to confide in Smith of his concerns about Luana, but realized the moment was not appropriate–Smith was still consumed with the affairs of state and the state of survival. As Joseph Smith met with several gentlemen in the room, including Hyrum Smith and John Taylor, he planned how to combat the combined strategies of the *Warsaw Signal* and the conspirators. Rockwell decided to join them. He chose instinctively a high-backed Jacobean chair that had somewhat the air of a throne.

Visiting observers to the Mansion House all agreed that the furniture gave one a feeling of solidity. Partly because of that, Rockwell unconsciously enjoyed returning to Smith's study whenever occasion would permit. Emma, of course, would just as soon see Rockwell up in his room with his dog. The dog, incidentally, had been spending its days lounging lazily along the Mississippi River bank. Emma had the unfortunate task of feeding it whenever Rockwell was gone for the day, and at this Rockwell was amused. He had trained the dog to fend for itself; Emma was overly concerned, he felt.

Emma in fact soon entered, and with her usual royal composure she presented all the gentlemen with tea.

(Years later, tobacco, tea and alcohol would be shunned by active Mormons generally, but as long as consumption of such beverages remained moderate, most church leaders for years, including this night, partook freely, until church policy would change.)

Emma glared at Rockwell, not particularly pleased that he always chose her favorite chair, especially in his usually scruffy condition. "At least he bathes often," she would confide privately to Smith, searching for something positive, but for some reason she did not particularly care for the man, nor for his ugly dog.

Rockwell meanwhile cast a gaze on her, thinking she was very beautiful but in a hardly human way.....Certainly not in any way he would want a woman.

He wanted only his own woman. As he studied the gracious manner in which Emma carried herself out of the room, he realized how Luana was indeed, although in a far less refined form, the most beautiful woman on earth. He yearned to feel her arms around him again, to bask in her light and warmth. He loved her. And that's all he could think of. Despite the warning from his inner sensibilities, he decided he would have to go see her again and clarify the things he had planned to say before he had followed Higbee. He grabbed his hat and rose, but then changed his mind. He sat down again. As the conversation of the men in the smoke- filled room droned on, he changed his mind still again. He could use the fresh air, he told himself.

He left the room without a word, unhitched his roan, and rode off to finally see her.

Meanwhile, at the *Warsaw Signal*, Thomas Sharp sat at his desk to proofread. He glanced up and saw Chauncey Higbee and William Law entering with drawn faces.

"Smith knows more than we think he knows," said Higbee. "He got tipped off to our plans and we couldn't set fire to the *Nauvoo Neighbor*."

Sharp smiled, "Worrell just told me of the lynch mob and their "attack" on Nauvoo. You gentlemen are disappointing me."

Higbee picked up a glass paperweight from Sharp's desk.

Sharp noticed it, concerned. "What we need is something to galvanize the community against Joseph Smith– I'm sorry, did I say community? I mean communities–every community in three counties in fact–even more–even the counties of Eastern Missouri." Sharp realized if he could set up a cost-effective circulation in such a broad area, he would be taking major steps at achieving his goals. "And if they were all moved to action simultaneously," continued Sharp, "Joe Smith's force would pale by comparison."

"What could do it?" said Higbee, holding the paperweight to his eye and examining it closely.

"The appropriate article"about the appropriate incident," said Sharp, now standing, beaming, feeling actually exhilarated.

At the Nauvoo tavern Rockwell stopped for a couple of drinks; he could use a bit more courage, he figured, before resuming his journey to Luana's.

He found Luana alone. The children were napping and Cutler was away at work.

Luana's mouth trembled when she again saw Rockwell.

"I can't give up this easy," he said.

"That's fairly obvious."

"I can't leave the children to be raised by Cutler."

"He's a wonderful man.....We're getting married, I suppose you knew that."

"Joseph figured as much."

Luana discovered Rockwell trembling. "You still spend all your time with him?"

"He needs me," said Rockwell.

"Always has."

"Now especially," he said, "what with things the way they are."

"What things?"

"Mobs."

"There always have been mobs," she said.

"Not like this, it's different."

"I guess a lot of things are different."

He understood the inference and confronted it. "I won't leave you again."

"You said that five years ago."

"It was you who got rid of me two years ago," he said.

"And where were you five years ago? Ten? You weren't around here."

"Well just don't blame Joseph," said Rockwell.

"Who says I am?"

"You really think I'll let you go through this thing with Cutler?"

"Do you really think you can stop it?"

Rockwell felt his neck heating. "I'm them children's father."

"Physically only."

"Eternally."

"Alpheas and I are having the children sealed to us," she said, "and that's all there is to it." It was the belief of Mormons that marriage in their temple could be performed not just for this life but for the hereafter. "Sealing" was the term used for such marriages. Rockwell sickened at the prospect of losing his children even for this life.

"The devil you are," he said. "They ain't being sealed to nobody else."

"You gave up that privilege," said Luana.

"Who says?"

"The divorce says. I'm free now and they're free."

"Ask them who they want as their father."

"You divorced them also, Porter. All of us."

"Not forever. They can't be sealed to him."

"You can leave the house now."

"When I'm finished," he said.

"Can't you see? We are for the hundredth time!"

"Ask them–see what they think–see what they wanna do!"

"Porter, the issue is dead!"

"It ain't–ask them!"

"Do you want me to call the marshal?"

"Answer my question!" he shouted.

"I've answered it! There is no question–we're all free from you– no matter who they want–they go with me! Is that clear? Do you understand?"

"Well I've changed my mind–Cutler don't get them!"

"It's too late, Porter. It's over. It's.....all.....over."

Rockwell was crushed. He forced himself to look out the window at the peaceful farmland, and finally his breathing slowed.

"Luana, I love you. I know you once loved me...I know you can again."

Her words were carefully stated, "Porter, for once and for all.....I have.....a new.....life."

"I'm left with nothing.....can't you see that?" he said. "The chilren are a part of me."

"I'm sorry," she said, "but again, you made that choice."

"I never told you that was my choice."

"It's not what you said, Porter, it's what you did. You chose to stay away from us day after day and come home only on weekends half our marriage."

"And the other half?"

"You still don't see, do you? Or what you've done to us. You don't think the children suffered from that?"

"Well they never see me now–does that make it better?"

"It does, yes," she said. "They have no expectations."

"But they belong with me!"

Luana trembled with anger. "I raised them, and I decide who they belong with, do you understand? And I decide what they need–and you've proven you are not what they need!"

"I told you before and it's true: I have changed. I will never leave you and them again."

"Only your feelings have changed, Porter. You realize what you've lost, but that doesn't work for us because you are the same man! You're an adventurer. It's as simple as that. My family are farmers. My children will be. We're two different sorts, Porter, and we cannot live together. Go back to Joseph and your causes and your excitement. You have no interest in us. Not real interest. Not in me or my feelings or my concerns or my life in these four walls. And I can't take that. All you have left is an obsession. We've only become something you can't have. You're in love with the yearning, but not with us." She turned her back, walked to her bedroom, stopped, turned, and stared at him sadly from the framework. "Think on what I've said.....it's true as much as you're alive."

He stared at the floor. "You don't understand me.....or what I feel."

"Fine.....can't we just leave it at that?" she said. "We'll never understand each other."

His face flustered with frustration.

"And if you really want to know, Porter.....I simply don't even care anymore. Doesn't that tell you anything?"

Rockwell looked up from the floor to her penetrating eyes.

"If you come by again," she added, "I'm having the marshal arrest you. Is that clear enough?"

Rockwell looked down again, too hurt to see her, and he slowly walked away.

Under a grey sky there was not a breath of wind. Riding horseback Rockwell was lost in thought. He wondered if she were right– if he were indeed what she claimed–an incurable adventurer. He had not thought so anymore, but he wondered.....

He took his ride deeper into the country, craving solitude, feeling hemmed in by civilization. He decided to water his horse. He dismounted at a stream and sat with his back propped against a tree. His mind searched the sky as he recalled his earlier years with Luana.

Two hours later he was again riding, the sun splashing rays through the trees onto him.

Then a slight fog rolled in as the sun lowered. He could smell the warm scent of the soil. The red sun settled behind a faint mist.

He rode through the twilight wondering what he should do. He realized Smith was still consumed by affairs of the city. Rockwell also realized he had never felt such loneliness, not even in the jail– because there he at least had hope. He fought the depression descending on him. No other women could attract him –he rarely met single ladies anyway but when he did they all paled by comparison. His heart seemed hopelessly set on her! When he thought of Cutler's affections it cut him like a knife. Furthermore, the entire church and city seemed in worse straits than ever. Because of his inability to do anything about it, coupled with his longings for Luana, he pondered the possibility of leaving Nauvoo altogether, defecting from his people and protecting himself from probable imprisonment. He could be a bartender in New Orleans. Perhaps he just needed to get away from her and the children for good and start a new life.

An early star twinkled palely close to the horizon. He had heard a distant star up close is really a sun. His concerns scorched his mind. He simply did not know what to do, where to go.

Ahead was a campfire. Perhaps human company is all he needed. He felt intensely lonely. He saw two hundred yards ahead six or eight men engaged in some activity. Through the mist a chill was coming in like a knife. He looked forward to sitting at the fire, listening to the simple chatter of Carthage rurals. Not all were prejudiced and perhaps these were more friendly than most, even if they would recognize him. He tucked his hair under his collar and continued riding forward.

Six men had another man surrounded whom they seemed to be questioning rather vigorously.

Rockwell's curiosity was struck. He dismounted, tied his horse, and walked forward still unobserved. He hesitated behind thick bushes and could barely discern the men but could hear them clearly.

"I told you–I ain't one of Joe Smith's people."

"Well then you can join us," said another–whom Rockwell vaguely recognized through through the bush as Frank Worrell.

"Ain't interested," said the man. He was an older fellow, medium but frail, and he had long bushy sideburns and no hair on top. Rockwell recognized him as Alexander Tillman.

"Look, maybe I ain't clear," continued Worrell, "you don't have a choice."

"And maybe I ain't clear–I ain't interested," said Tillman.

"You will be when we finish with your business."

"Well that's real gentlemanly of you," said Tillman, "But what about the law?"

"What law?"

"You think the law says you can drive innocent folks off their farms?"

"The judges interpret the law." Frank Worrell was satisfied with the judicial system, as he was with most everything regarding the American government and its protection of his way of life. He was proud to be a captain in the city militia. He was fearful of what he had heard on good opinion was detrimental to his ancestors' way of living and believing, namely this strange new cult that had moved into the county and practically taken over. He could not for the life of him understand why otherwise good, loyal citizens like Alexander Tillman would seek to sell merchandise to his avowed enemies just for the almighty dollar.

Tillman scowled at Worrell. Rockwell knew Tillman vaguely as the owner of a merchandizing distributorship who sold to all the Nauvoo general stores. "Well I've seen how the judges interpret the law," said Tillman, "But the Mormons will put up a fight–they will not in a thousand years deliver Joe Smith over to you."

"You're saying," said Worrell, "that their property ain't more valuable to them?"

"Not that valuable."

"They've got a lot of it now," said Worrell.

"Not to give up Smith–you're loco."

"We'll see who's loco."

"Yeah, we will," said Tillman, "especially if you think you can get the old settlers to fight against the Mormons. I ain't gonna fight 'em."

"Well then you can fight for one side or the other, or share the same fate as them."

"Yeah, well we'll see," said Tillman. But if you touch my business, I'm coming after you."

"Who's touching your property? Just sign this contract. The Mormons can buy from somebody else–and nobody will be hurt."

"Nobody else has the merchandise I've got. They need my goods. They'll be hurt without it. I'll be hurt without the sales."

Worrell fumed. He was not used to being crossed. He grabbed

Tillman and shoved him towards the fire.

"When we finish with you," said Worrell, "you'll talk hurt, all right." Worrell had never considered himself a particularly violent man, but for the sake of what he believed in nothing could get in his way, and he was almost daily surprising himself with the extent to which he would operate to accomplish simply what needed to be accomplished.

Rockwell moved instinctively forward, not certain what he was going to do–particularly since he was unarmed–but he was certain of one thing–he was not going to leave old Alex Tillman stranded.....

7

Worrell's five men circled and watched. Worrell lowered Tillman to the fire, the flames within a foot of his back. Tillman began to wince from the pain.....

"Just sign the contract," said Worrell, "isn't that clear enough?"

Tillman was a stubborn old goat. He would rather sizzle than sign anything against his will, and he was determined to not give Worrell the pleasure of hearing him scream. His face contorted as he felt the pain shooting through his back. He was now but inches from the flames and the heat was scorching his nerves.....

Suddenly a body came belting out of the forest and it lunged into Worrell's back. Tillman sprawled to the side and Worrell plunged forward off balance.....directly into the flames. He screamed and scrambled to his feet, his coat ablaze.

Rockwell grabbed Worrell's pistol and whirled it onto the other five stunned men.

"You better help your buddy," said Rockwell. "Or he's gonna be a toasted marshmallow."

But the five men simply stood there in shock while Worrell shouted for help, still in flames.

Rockwell looked them over and gave them a command. "Roll him on the ground, idiots."

One man grabbed Worrell's left arm and flung him to the ground. Two others jumped beside him and rolled him in the dirt, extinguishing the fire on his coat.

Rockwell ordered Tillman to mount his horse. Rockwell then snatched the contract from the ground, stepped up to the fire, and dropped it in. "I don't think you'll be needing this anymore."

As the men watched the burning paper, one poured cold water onto Worrell's back. Rockwell continued, "I reckon you oughta leave Tillman's business alone or you're gonna see these flames on somebody elses property." He then backed away, taking Worrell's gun.

When he disappeared into the woods, Worrell, in pain, leered at him.

"We'll see who's property sees the flames."

Joseph Smith swatted a newspaper against the table. He sauntered to the other side of the room, infuriated.

"Who would ever think," he said, now staring out the window, "that anyone would believe this nonsense?"

"Well it's working," said Rockwell. "I've seen horsemen gathering to Carthage from all over the countryside." Two days had passed since he had saved Tillman; and in the meantime, the *Warsaw Signal* had published a continuous stream of reports about him and Joseph Smith.

"What do we do now?"

Almon Babbitt entered, holding a copy of the *Warsaw Signal*. Babbitt was a friend of Smith's and a Mormon attorney; he was a recent convert who sought more than anything the adulations due him from Smith. He considered Smith almost as bright as himself, perhaps the only man in fact he had ever met with such cerebral heft. Babbitt was an extroverted, short, stocky man, three inches shorter than Rockwell, and he possessed a small fleshy nose with large nostrils. People liked him for his ebullient spirit and gregariousness. He was extremely competent and had a mind, some said, sharper than a bear trap.

"Did you see the article?"

Smith answered by moving his eyes to his own copy on the table.

"So what do you think?" said Babbitt.

"There's only one thing I really can do at this point," said Smith. "Put the whole city under martial law."

Babbitt was frantic. "You're not serious. The press will have a field day."

"They already have," said Smith. "I have no alternative."

Rockwell left the Mansion House again depressed. He was further convinced the persecutions were stepping up with even greater acceleration than they had in Missouri. The whole thing was coming down like a house of cards.

It was only a matter of time before the city would be burned and he and Smith would be apprehended.

To add to his anguish, he felt no hope of ever convincing Luana that she should have him back. He was determined to not even try, despite his feelings. His last visit–of her threatening to call the marshal on him–was a blow. He felt himself, despite his love, actually resenting her. He had no where to go but New Orleans, he decided. He had earlier in the day offered to Smith to accompany him as bodyguard anywhere in or out of the country he wished to move, but he himself would not stay another week. Smith had rejected the offer.

Smith now watched his childhood friend ride up once again to the hill of the temple.

There, Rockwell pondered. He gazed at the temple before him and looked down the hill at the Mansion House, sensing Smith's watching eyes. Rockwell realized how far he had come for his friend. He fought the feelings welling up within him–he simply had no use for life here anymore and there was not much he could do. Yet the harder he fought, the more he realized he could not leave. He was angry with himself. He had tried to leave before–and had felt life in Pennsylvania so empty compared to the friends he had had here–that he had been willing to risk even prison to return. And had paid the price. Had the price been worth it?

His friends. He would just as soon die, he figured, than leave them.

Smith saw him returning, and smiled with glistening eyes.

Rockwell's dog meanwhile had stayed by his side for at least twelve hours; he had seen Rockwell packing his few belongings into saddlebags and sensed that his master was ready to leave. He would go with Rockwell, of course, wherever Rockwell chose.

The dog had remained near the Mansion House, obeying Rockwell's command to "stay" while Rockwell had traveled the countryside much of the past few weeks. Emma had tired of leaving food scraps for the creature; she had finally realized the dog was surviving well enough alone. While she did not allow animals into her home, Joseph Smith demanded that Rockwell's dog was an exception–for a reason she did not understand. In any case the animal had free reign of the place.

When Rockwell had announced to Emma that he was leaving and taking the dog with him, she beamed. As she now saw them out the parlor window, returning, she slunk into her bedroom.

Rockwell dismounted and walked with the dog toward the front door. Joseph Smith's oldest boy, Joseph III, passed them, studied the animal, and muttered to Rockwell, "I'm glad you're not leaving but he sure is an ugly critter."

Rockwell thanked him and continued into the house.

That night, Smith stood in uniform atop the Mansion House. He practically glowed with his characteristic aura that mesmerized his people, and he boomed his voice to two thousand soldiers.

Rockwell meanwhile left the front ranks to stand at a corner of the building and search for enemy spies in their midst. He thought he caught sight of Chauncey Higbee at the back of a crowd of civilians. He feared Higbee might carry a weapon. Higbee made his way through the crowds as Smith spoke with fire in his eyes.

"I call God, angels and all men to witness that we are innocent of the charges heralded forth through the public prints against us by our enemies; and while they assemble together in unlawful mobs to take away our rights and destroy our lives, they think to shield themselves under the refuge of lies which they have fabricated.

"Will you all stand by me to the death, and sustain at the peril of your lives, the laws of our country, and the liberties and privileges which our fathers have transmitted unto us, sealed with their sacred blood?"

The soldiers responded with a thunderous, "Aye!"

Smith drew his sword to the sky. "I call God and angels to witness that I have unsheathed my sword with a firm and unalterable determination that this people shall have their legal rights, and be protected from mob violence, or my blood shall be spilt upon the ground like water, and my body consigned to the silent tomb."

As Joseph Smith closed his remarks, Rockwell closed in on the last spot where he had seen Higbee. As he arrived there, however, Higbee was gone.

He then spotted Higbee's horse galloping downroad, disappearing into the night.

Later that night Thomas Sharp listened to Chauncey Higbee's report of Smith's speech.

"It sounds like they plan a full-scale war," said Higbee.

Sharp's face was sallow and drawn, suffering from little sleep over his increased circulation endeavors. Despite the exhaustion, his paper was a source of subdued pride to him. He sat back and reflected on the potentiality that Smith's speech would have on even greater circulation and advertising revenue.

"I think," said Sharp, "that Smith and his people are going to learn what a full-scale war really looks like."

Beside a stream Rockwell stared at his reflection. Although the animal-like image from his deprivation in prison no longer appeared, a new look in his face revealed an intense, inner burning. However, the pain he felt over the loss of Luana and the children was tempered by an impending, developing war he could smell in the air.

He had come to the woods to think, but now felt a gnawing hunger beckoning him back to the Mansion House. his dog was waiting back there and he missed it.

Despite his feeling of futility, he knew he was still hopelessly in love with Luana, yet he was still determined to never again talk with her. He had achieved some peace of mind over her from the woodland walk.

He climbed upon his horse, trotted through the woods, and found himself cantering down a peaceful country road. A brisk, warm breeze filled his nostrils with rich woodland odors.

Birds chirped happily.

The air cooled quickly. A late afternoon thunder cloud rolled in from the east.

He decided to pick up the horse's gait.

Clouds darkened and Rockwell heard distant thunder. Before he reached Nauvoo, rain began to pour. Soon he heard a different thunder. On adjacent roads across the countryside he heard the roar of hooves–horsehooves–hundreds of horsehooves. He glanced to both sides of the road and realized in a flash that the horsemen were only several rods away–on parallel roads that converged onto his, not more than fifty yards distant.

He rode off the main road into the woods. He spotted a cabin in the clearing, being plundered by a large number of men. The family was fleeing the premises. Rockwell had with him only a small amount of ammunition and he determined it best not to confront the horsemen. He rode deeper into the forest.

Another farm was being attacked. Horsemen tied ropes to the roof and hitched the ends to horses and yanked it off. As the rain poured into the roofless home, a woman cried over her possessions.

Another horseman reined in and informed the rest that reinforcements were coming–2,000 men from Missouri with cannon.

As Rockwell made his way back to the main road, he spotted several dozen others riding to Carthage. He hid off the road. As the mob passed him, he eased onto the road and galloped towards Nauvoo.

Nearing the city he came across other families on the road, hauling their few possessions to town. In anger he rode, the mud flinging high behind his horse's hooves.

Fully drenched from the rain and sweat, he arrived at the Mansion House and rushed inside.

Joseph Smith stood at a window in his study, staring out at the rain.

"I reckon," said Rockwell, "you've heard."

Smith did not hear him, lost in thought.

Hyrum Smith was seated across the room holding a letter; he read it to Rockwell.

It was from Governor Ford, now in Carthage, Illinois, who had come to investigate the *Expositor* issue first-hand. The letter demanded Smith to send representatives to Carthage and declare his side of the story.

"What's wrong with that?" said Rockwell.

"It simply means," said Hyrum, "that the conspirators have reached him with their side of the story first. No telling how many days they've been filling him with lies."

"But at least we have a chance to give our side," said Rockwell.

"It would be useless," said Hyrum. "His aides have made no bones about their animosity towards us. And with the conspirators' affidavits, I'm afraid by now Ford will have made up his mind."

"But at least it's a chance for us," said Rockwell.

"What chance?" said Hyrum. "The man's a consummate politician. He sees what Sharp has done with public opinion, and whether he agrees with it or not is not even the issue. We haven't a chance in Hades."

"The law–what about the law?" said Rockwell. "The Illinois constitution itself supports a city destroying slanderous presses–and your lawyer, Babbitt–you've said he's the best–he says the police do it all the time in New York and that no First Amendment stuff can counter it. Even the district judge here agreed! He's not even a Mormon. So what are you going to do?"

Hyrum turned to his brother, "So what are we going to do?"

Rockwell answered for Joseph Smith, "Fight fire with fire!"

Joseph Smith the next day prepared to send a delegation to Carthage.

Almon Babbitt strolled in the door having overheard them. "Don't send it–I just came from Carthage."

"Why not?" said Hyrum.

"Rabble are threatening death on sight to any one of us who even approaches the city."

Rockwell stood. "Then I'll go! I'll get through alive!"

"Don't send anyone," said Babbit.

Rockwell glowered and Smith continued, "I'm sorry, Almon, but I do have to send a delegation to the governor to explain our side of the story and why the district judge agreed with us."

"Then just don't send Rockwell," said Babbitt, still glaring at him. "The press has made him their favorite target. If he represents us they'll play it to the hilt in the *Warsaw Signal*, and we'll have a full-scale war on our hands."

"What do you think we have on our hands now?" said Rockwell.

Joseph Smith finally decided to send John Taylor, well-known for his diplomacy and peacemaking abilities. Taylor successfully

made it past the mobs, to the governor's temporary office in
Carthage, where he presented the Mormons' side of the *Expositor*
issue.

The next night John Taylor returned to the Mansion House. He
entered Smith's study with the governor's reply. "Governor Ford
has taken sides with the dissenters. The state militia are on their
way to apprehend you."

"What the devil for!" said Rockwell to Smith. "A dozen more of
our homes were unroofed last night! Do they think you did it?"

A gloom fell on the men in the room. Joseph Smith walked to the
window and stared. He turned, his face gleaming from the kerosene light. "We could try to resist the militia with our troops.
However, I see the way opened.....the only way not to be killed and
not precipitate a blood bath. We shall have to look for a new home
for our people.....somewhere in the mountains."

The men looked at him, puzzled.

Joseph Smith and Porter Rockwell walked briskly towards the
Mississippi River. Their two figures were silhouetted against the
twilight sky, and crickets chirped sharply. Rockwell spoke with
excitement, "How far west shall we go?"

"Porter, I'd rather you stay here–I want you to watch our
people. But I need you to prepare a boat for four of us. We'll go in

advance and evade the mobs. Our people will be safe from the mobs–the mobs only want me."

Rockwell, disappointed, nevertheless felt relieved that his family would not be left without him. As soon as the thought crossed his mind he realized he had no confidence whatever in Cutler's ability to protect Luana and the children.

Smith returned to the Mansion House and spoke with his family. As Rockwell prepared the boat, he could see Smith's children outside the house, tears flowing from their faces. Smith returned to the shore and Rockwell could see tears glistening in his eyes.

Hyrum Smith, Willard Richards, and William Phelps met Smith at the shore, and all four men bid Rockwell farewell. Rockwell hugged Smith. Fighting his feelings, Rockwell turned away and walked across town. He knew Smith would escape the mobs yet once again. From New York to Ohio, Smith had been tarred and feathered, beaten, incarcerated at the same Liberty Jail dungeon for even longer than himself, and tried before courts over 40 times, never to be convicted. One mob had attempted pouring lye down his throat, chipping a tooth in the process, causing him to speak with a faint whistle. Rockwell was confident this was yet another chance to escape and another trial for Smith's family.

Rockwell made his way across town to a cabin that had been loaned him just that day by one of Smith's friends.

As Smith watched Rockwell walk away, the four men remaining at the shore discussed their escape. Smith assigned Phelps to take their families to Cincinnati. From there they would be brought West later. Phelps left immediately.

After several hours of deliberating, the three remaining men decided Rockwell should indeed accompany them west. All three knocked at Rockwell's door at 2 A.M., and he groggily greeted them.

"We need you after all," said Smith. "Please come with us."

Rockwell's eyes widened. Despite the concern for his family, he realized Cutler and Luana would probably not let him protect his children alongside him anyway even if it did come to combat with the mobs.

Rockwell smiled at Smith and grabbed his clothes. He knew that he desperately wished to be with Smith.

Joseph Smith, Hyrum Smith, and Willard Richards bailed water out of a leaky boat as Rockwell rowed. The night offered a starlit canopy. No one said a word. Rockwell's dog sat silently at his feet. An hour passed before Joseph Smith finally broke the silence.

"That's the hardest thing I ever did."

"What's that?" said Hyrum Smith.

"Leaving Emma and the children," replied Joseph.

"They'll join us soon enough," said Hyrum, reassuringly.

"Will they?" He suspected Emma's growing frustration for the sacrifices she had endured. She finally possessed an ornate home with furniture and a beautiful city endowed richly in the arts. She had grown more property-conscious of late, he felt, as had many church faithful, and it bothered him.

Rockwell meanwhile listened, fighting not to think of his own family. Forcing them from his mind was more difficult than he had imagined; but he was anxious to reach the Iowa shore.

Dawn's pastel colors turned crimson and glistened across the Mississippi River as the four men pulled the leaky boat from the water.

"Going to be a long walk to the Rocky Mountains," mused Rockwell "unless we have horses. I'll go back for horses if you want."

At the Mansion House Rockwell gathered the horses. Emma stood beside the corral gate with Reynolds Cahoon, a tall, stout, robust man whom Rockwell regarded as *nouveau riche*: in the short time Rockwell had known him, his heart had seemed more inclined to money-consciousness than towards people. Emma Smith stood, poised.

"I insist you take Reynolds back across the river," she said to Rockwell. "He has a letter for Joseph which I wish to have delivered—it's an explanation."

"I can deliever it as good as him," said Rockwell, glaring at Reynolds.

"I insist, Porter," said Emma, "or I'll see you will not leave this city with my property. Those horses stay or you will take Reynolds Cahoon."

"With all due respect, Emma, I'm not sure you can stop me."

"I'll get word to the ferryman that those horses are my property. And that essentially makes you a thief."

"I guess it does, don't it?"

Rockwell walked away with the four horses, his dog following.

Emma glanced at Cahoon and both merely watched Rockwell and the dog depart. Emma finally called after Rockwell, "Will you take my letter to Joseph, please?"

Rockwell did not look back. "If you bring me the letter I'll take it to him."

Emma followed Rockwell to the river. She spoke softer, with different stratagem:

"Please Porter, I'm not sure I put all my meaning into the letter. I've spoken at length with Reynolds Cahoon, and he can convey my concerns to Joseph."

Rockwell studied her a moment, then nodded Cahoon to follow.

Back across the river Rockwell and Cahoon ferried.

"What is it you really want with Joseph?" said Rockwell.

"The matter lies between Joseph and myself," said Cahoon tersely.

When they arrived at the Iowa woodland, Rockwell led Cahoon through thick brush to a campfire. All three men were seated about it, their faces lit luridly by the flames. Joseph Smith was surprised when he saw the face of Reynolds Cahoon.

Cahoon strode straight to Smith and handed him the letter. As Smith read his wife's words silently, Cahoon expounded.

"Joseph, you always said if the church would stick to you, you would stick to the church. Now trouble comes and you are the first to run!"

Rockwell felt like throwing Cahoon into the river, but said nothing.

"Brother Cahoon," said Smith, "What are you really saying?"

"Emma feels as I do—our people are simply too tired of moving, and frankly our property is too valuable. We've built a city that rivals any in America—it's the most prosperous in the state. We can't just leave it."

"What about the mobs?" said Smith.

"You'll be safe in the courts because of your innocence. You've always been released. The mobs will attack us in vengeance, however, if they know you've fled."

"Not if our people will follow me West," said Smith, "They will be safe. That's the Lord's plan, and He has revealed it to me.

"What about our property?" said Cahoon.

Rockwell was flustered and interrupted, "What the devil are

you talking about? Property What good is property?"

"Well, like the fable says," said Cahoon to Smith, "when the wolves came, the shepherd ran from the flock and left the sheep to be devoured."

A silence fell on the group. Smith stood and gazed hard into the flames. All eyes turned to him and waited for a reply.

"If my life is of no value to my friends," said Smith finally, "it is of none to myself."

Reynolds Cahoon rowed Joseph Smith, Hyrum, and Willard Richards back across the river in darkness.

On the ferry, meanwhile, with his dog, Rockwell returned the horses to Nauvoo. He gazed across the rippling waters, fuming that Cahoon had won his way.

At the Illinois shore Rockwell rendezvoused with Smith and they strode to the Mansion House. Smith said he wished to address his people that evening.

"I'll wait for your word," said Rockwell, "if you want me to gather them."

Emma emerged from the house and kissed Joseph. The rest of the family also came out and surrounded him. Smith looked them over longingly, then went inside for the remainder of the night.

Rockwell began walking to his own lodgings when he stopped and gazed back at the Mansion House silhouetted in the starlight. He understood why Smith never sent word to him to gather his people for one last address. It might be the last night he would be with his family for awhile.....

Fourteen hours later–just after 6 P.M.–Rockwell sat by the river, keeping an eye on the Mansion House, when he saw the Illinois state militia arrive. The officer in charge dismounted, strode to the door, and knocked briskly.

Joseph Smith answered it, stared at the officer, and sighed. He bid farewell to his wife, picked up each child, hugged each one goodbye, and trudged out to his horse and slowly mounted.

Rockwell's feelings were mixed with anger and frustration. He remained at the river, watching from a distance, at Smith's orders. Smith foresaw of Rockwell's danger if Rockwell should accompany him to Carthage and had told him not to follow. Because parting with his family was difficult enough, Joseph had asked Rockwell not to even be present. They had bid farewell to each other earlier in the day, after Smith had disarmed the Nauvoo Legion on Governor Ford's orders. Smith sought to cooperate to soothe his enemies' feelings, also desiring every way possible to reassure the governor of Smith's intentions for peace.

Rockwell now sauntered to the road where, hidden by trees, he watched Joseph ride away. Smith turned around several times to gaze at his farm.

With Hyrum at his side, also under arrest, Joseph stood before a Carthage magistrate. They heard bail was denied them. It was then announced the only judge who could grant subpoenas had suddenly disappeared; Hyrum mumbled to Joseph it was obvious the court was intentionally preventing their witnesses from appearing. And outside the courtroom they could hear a mob shouting.

The judge surprised the Smiths.

"You will be housed until further notice at the Carthage Jail."

Hyrum spoke up, "Your honor, the action is illegal. We have not been allowed an examination before a justice of the peace."

"You heard my decision."

John Taylor and Willard Richards decided to stay with the Smiths, fearful of leaving them alone in Carthage. The jailer had agreed to allow the two men to sleep in jail with their leader and his brother.

The four men now walked among armed guards through the mob. Taylor and Richards pounded their canes onto occasional drunks who tried grabbing Joseph and Hyrum. Across the green, Frank Worrell was cleaning his gun. He eyed Joseph, and watched him disappear into the jailhouse.

Worrell then nodded to a contingent of 70 Carthage Grey militiamen behind him, and, on his signal, they dispersed.

Five hours later they were gathered again, no longer in uniform, but riding horseback towards Nauvoo. Worrell pulled out his rifle and began cleaning it.

Unknown to them, Rockwell had gotten wind of the attack by Worrell's group.

The horsemen under Worrell's direction carried torches which they planned to use against 70 buildings, including the temple and Smith's Mansion House. Some had tried surreptitiously to locate Rockwell's cabin, but had failed. Rockwell's lodgings were a well-guarded secret, known only by city hierarchists.

When the 70 Carthagenians reached the outskirts of Nauvoo, they once again found Rockwell at the forefront of a waiting army, and once again they were thwarted.

Angered and frustrated, Worrell waved a white handkerchief and rode forward to the Mormon front line. Rockwell rode forward and greeted him; he wore buckskins, Worrell wool cloth; both men stopped their horses and glared six feet from each other's steel eyes.

"Rockwell, you're a rodent with rabies and I'm gonna remove your head if you stick it in my trap. That's fair warning."

"Yeah, well I'm waiting."

"I'll tell you what," said Worrell. "When I'm finished with this Smith business in Carthage–you're next. And I don't care how many men you've got around you."

Rockwell used every effort to constrain himself from replying. He glanced back at his band of volunteers–the Nauvoo Legion itself was still disarmed but several dozen owned their own weapons and these were the men who had followed him to the perimeters of the city. He gazed across the faces of his men. He knew they were as angry as he was. They had been stripped of their weapons, their uniforms, and their leader, and were following Rockwell to not only defend their city but to perhaps seek a little revenge.

But Rockwell knew any violence he instigated would cause harm to Smith and perhaps precipitate a war–one for which the once proud and formidable Nauvoo Legion was no longer prepared.

He looked back at Worrell and nodded, then turned his horse, showing his back to the man without saying a word.

Worrell, insulted, led his off-duty militiamen back to Carthage.

Rockwell, meanwhile, waited a few hours in case they returned.

Just before dawn he found himself riding in front of Luana's house. He was in a pensive mood, and he halted his horse. Behind the brown curtain, a soft amber glow from a burning candle lit the living room.

He considered dismounting and seeing her again, but knew he would not. He wondered what she and Cutler might be doing at that moment. Especially what she might be feeling in her heart for the other man. Despite the futility he felt, his obsession had rippled back like rings in a river after a rock was thrown–and tonight he was again riveted to her memory. He sat on horseback fully 15 minutes, and finally lowered his head and rode on.

The next morning he received a letter from Joseph Smith.

At the Mansion House he asked William Phelps to read it. Phelps was impressed that Smith had thought enough of Rockwell to write only him and Emma. In the letter Smith gave Rockwell one unequivocal mandate.

"Stay in Nauvoo, and do not suffer yourself to be delivered into the hands of your enemies or to be taken a prisoner by anyone."

Rockwell left the Mansion House, forgetfully leaving his hat.

Joseph Smith meanwhile sat in jail. Two of his visiting friends, Dan Jones and Stephen Markham, repaired the latch on the cell door, preparing it for possible attack.

Smith finally saw a mob forming outside the jail. A guard handed him a note, demanding that he and Hyrum immediately appear before the court.

At their trial, the Smiths' lawyers called for witnesses. The judge's dull brown eyes smiled.

"Since they will have to be brought from Nauvoo, this court will again be adjourned." The judge observed Smith consulting his attorney. He pounded his gavel. "Any subpoenas will not be considered for an additional two days–I have a busy schedule."

Smith's attorney sighed, "Your honor, it appears the court is insuring another delay in the trial. The defendants are placed in a precarious position." He glanced toward the mob in the street.

The judge bellowed, "You heard the decision." He arose and left.

Outside, Joseph and Hyrum Smith stepped onto the street, and Frank Worrell loaded his rifle.

Joseph and Hyrum Smith were escorted by armed court guards back to the jail. The guards noticed Worrell and other uniformed Carthage Greys leaning against a brick building, conversing casually, keeping an eye on Smith's long walk. One guard spotted Worrell's gun, and Worrell put it away.

Rockwell meanwhile stared at the Mississippi River on a sultry June afternoon. It was free-flowing and smooth, yet ripples were forming in the water. He threw a rock at the ripples.

Back in jail all was quiet. Suddenly a gunshot cracked the air. All five in the cell were suddenly jerked awake. Joseph Smith peered out the window and saw nothing. The air again became still, and the men returned to their sleep. Joseph Smith was the only one to speak, just before drifting off.

"I wish I could see Emma again and speak to my people."

Nothing more was said before they fell asleep.

Rockwell was restless. He sat in his cabin and cleaned his guns by kerosene light. He decided there was no rest for his soul until he accomplished a singular mission.....despite what Joseph Smith had warned him, he would simply have to rescue him.

In his cell Smith pulled out a revolver which had been snuck into the jail the day previous, and he loaded it. He then handed Dan Jones, a short, broad, Welshman, a letter.

"Who's it for?"

"O. H. Browning," said Smith. "I need his legal services. Almon Babbitt is already engaged. This could be my last chance."

"I don't know if I can get through the mob."

"How much is it worth to you?" Smith gazed into Dan Jones' eyes and the Welshman gripped the letter.

Outside, as Jones left the jail, Worrell spotted the letter and shouted to the mob, "It's for a rescue–stop him!"

Jones took out running. The mob went after him. Jones ran to a livery stable. A crowd of 40 men followed, some shouting, but before they caught up to him, Jones came galloping out of the stable on a large black stallion.

Two men mounted horses and bolted after him. After a five minute chase they realized he had too strong of a lead, and they returned to report to Worrell.

"Something has to be done," mumbled Worrell, walking through the mob towards the courtyard, "before they attack us– I'm sure that's what Smith has called for."

At Nauvoo Dan Jones rode past Rockwell, who was riding to the Mansion House to recruit men for a rescue.

"How's Joseph?" said Rockwell.

"Worried, but safe." Jones picked up his horse's gait and trotted downstreet to Browning's office. Jones hoped Smith's desire to procure the attorney would be successful; Jones felt grateful to find the distinguished lawyer in his office.

Rockwell arrived at the Mansion House, surprised to see a large contingency of Illinois state militia. Their horses were tied outside under the security of one guard.

"Who's inside?" said Rockwell.

"Governor Ford and some officers," said the guard.

Rockwell went to the door.

"I'm afraid you can't go in," said the guard.

"I'm afraid nobody's stopping me."

The guard pulled out a pistol. "I'd hate to have to use this."

"And I'd hate to see you die trying to," said Rockwell, his hand on his own pistol. "I'd get a good clean shot off, even if you got me straight in the heart. I'm a tough old devil." He smiled, the guard seemed charmed and lowered his weapon.

"Private," said Rockwell, "I only left my hat in here. I'll be all right." Rockwell had indeed left his hat, but he had also hoped to see just who was in the house with Governor Ford. He also wondered why Ford was even there. Ford had promised Smith days earlier that if Ford would leave Carthage he would take Smith with him. Ford had just left Carthage but had decided against taking Smith. He was in Nauvoo to warn the Mormons to keep still.

The guard studied Rockwell and finally nodded him to go inside. "First hand me your pistol." Rockwell did so and entered the house. He climbed the stairs and went inside a room full of officers and civilians talking. Governor Ford was checking his pocket watch. The room fell silent when Rockwell entered.

Rockwell was suspicious–why the sudden quiet and why the attention to a pocket watch?

Ford had possibly participated—perhaps less actively–in accomplishing what Lilburn W. Boggs had failed in Missouri–he elimination of one of America's most powerful religious figures. Rockwell suspected it in a glance–and all the men in the room at once knew that Rockwell suddenly knew. Without a word, Rockwell grabbed his hat and ran down the stairs.

Outside the Mansion House, Rockwell grabbed his gun from the guard and spotted downstreet Gilbert Belnap, a loyal, carefree chap whom Rockwell knew could be called upon for most anything at a moment's notice. Rockwell mounted and rode up to him.

Belnap's blue eyes, square features, and longish hair somewhat matched Rockwell in looks. He looked at Rockwell with uncharacteristic concern.

Rockwell's excitement was catching. He practically shouted to Belnap for help in rescuing Smith. He had all the guns the two of them would need; all he needed was Belnap's help.

Belnap's eyes dilated and his head nodded. Both men took off in a gallop for Carthage.

At the jail, Joseph Smith found his breathing uneasy. Presently he heard his six guards called downstairs.

The guards found themselves outside facing a mob of one hundred men painted as Indians. The sight shook them. Most were Carthage Greys off duty, and they also began screaming like Indians. The guards fired a warning shot over the mob's heads, but were quickly pushed aside.

As the mob rushed up the stairs, Joseph Smith sprang to his coat and grabbed the revolver. Hyrum Smith went for his pistol and John Taylor and Willard Richards for their canes.

They braced themselves against the door and soon heard a shot. The ball smashed through the wood. Several in the mob leaped against the door–it was cracked open and barrels were stuck through. The two men with canes beat away the barrels as best they could, but several weapons were aimed and fired.

Hyrum was shot in the face. Joseph stared at him. Several other shots hit Hyrum's chest, side, and leg, and then he collapsed.

Joseph knelt beside him, held his head, and watched him die. He then jumped to the door and emptied his revolver. Several of the mob were wounded but none were killed.

John Taylor rolled under the bed, nursing a wound, when another flurry of shots came from the doorway and penetrated his body, stopping his watch at 5:16.

Richards meanwhile had backed against the wall, unscathed.

Joseph Smith gave them both a glance, then leaped into the window. From the well below Frank Worrell aimed his rifle directly at Smith's chest–and fired.

Smith was hit. Blood shot from his back. Several more shots came from the doorway. Blood shot from his chest. Then more shots came from outside again, and he toppled through the window and to the ground.

The mob shouted as they gathered around Joseph Smith. Under the overcast sky they watched him die. Suddenly a stillness fell over them, and they all stood as ashen and still as white oaks would in a windless forest.

Six miles outside town Rockwell and Gilbert Belnap noticed a wagon team coming high speed from a hundred yards away.

A quarter mile beyond the wagon were a dozen galloping horsemen. Rockwell recognized the wagon driver, George D. Grant, who slowed to shout.

"They're out to kill me–head into Nauvoo!"

"What about Joseph?" yelled Rockwell.

"He's dead!" Grant snapped his reins and the horses regained speed.

Rockwell glowered at the on-coming horsemen. Belnap stared at him and saw him take from his saddlebags three weapons. He handed one to Belnap. Then they heard, from a hundred yards ahead, gunshots.....

Rockwell lowered his revolver and fired. A horseman flew off his horse and crashed to the mud. Belnap also took aim and fired. Another horseman was hit in the shoulder and his gun flew away. More shots came from Belnap and Rockwell. Two other members of the mob flew from their horses. Then the horsemen opened fire. Belnap leaped behind a tree for cover. Rockwell stood in the road and stared at the on-coming horsemen.

Balls whistled about as the horsemen reopened fire, but no shots struck him. Belnap wondered if Smith's supernatural prophecy were not taking effect. Of that Rockwell felt no doubt and even less fear. He grabbed his other revolvers.

Belnap watched in amazement as Rockwell squeezed off three quick shots—and three men flew off their horses.

The horsemen all came to a halt; they aimed and fired again; mud splattered up beside Rockwell, but no bullets could seem to hit the man.

Rockwell stepped to his saddlebag and took another revolver. Bullets continued hitting around him, richocheting off trees and whistling over Belnap's head. Rockwell, holding both revolvers now, took aim and fired a shot with his first revolver, then another with his second, and repeated the process, firing first with one revolver, then with the other until three more men dropped, and another had the gun shot out of his hand.

The remaining horsemen all stared in wonder. One glanced at the others behind him and suddenly they all made a silent decision they took off galloping in retreat.

Belnap grabbed his hat and waved it in the air, shouting, exultant to even be alive. Rockwell lowered his head. He mounted and slowly rode away, leaving Belnap standing in the road, staring blankly at him.

Rockwell recalled his most recent days with Joseph Smith. He wondered what he could have done to prevent the murder. His mind soared back to his earliest years with Joseph, playing in the woodlands of Manchester, New York.

Rockwell arrived at the city limits; he beheld his people meandering the streets all the way to the river—commerce was unusually heavy and pedestrians and wagons packed the roads. Many seemed anxiously awaiting word from Carthage.....

In their faces he could see their optimistic expectations: they were waiting for their prophet to reappear on horseback as he had countless times before when freed from jails and judges and court proceedings.

Rockwell stopped his horse on the road and he felt a sullenness descend suddenly upon the city. The entire town seemed to feel it. Dozens unexplainably seemed to take notice of him. Hundreds of others slowed or stopped on the road and it seemed to him oddly as though all the city had turned its eyes to him.

By his look they knew what had happened.

The next day Rockwell stood motionless with 10,000 Nauvoo citizens as Joseph's and Hyrum's bodies were driven through town by Willard Richards.

John Taylor had been brought earlier to the city, wounded, and now lay on a bed in intense pain.

Rockwell's face was lost in the throng as he surveyed the sight: the bodies in the open wagon moved slowly past him, and he saw Joseph and Hyrum Smith one last time.....

He turned his head.

Meanwhile, Thomas Sharp wrote at his desk. He had received news of Rockwell's confronting the mob, and his face twitched. In his front page article he reported not only the death of "Joseph Smith, fallen prophet of The Church of Jesus Christ of Latter-day Saints," but of "The rise of a new despot in our midst–the one needing immediately to be crushed–the Destroying Angel, Porter Rockwell!"

PART II

THE
PRESS

10

Porter Rockwell heard Sidney Rigdon address the several-thousand-strong Nauvoo congregation. The point of the discourse was well-taken: Rigdon was Smith's only surviving council member of the church and therefore deserved the reins to the kingdom.

Rockwell disliked him. He knew Smith had sought to release the ever-aspiring, sometimes ingratiating Rigdon from leadership, but for months the Mormons as a body had not allowed it: they had refused to sustain Smith on this issue when he had brought the matter to a vote.

'So here he is,' thought Rockwell to himself, 'without the Council of the Twelve to keep an eye on him. They're all out on church missions–they don't even know of Joseph's death–and Rigdon here is trying to take over as president of the church.' Rockwell felt like taking the platform himself and telling them what he thought.

He would have, in fact, had he not heard whisperings that Brigham Young was returning from England. Young would do a better job of it.

Many of the leading Twelve had reaped a broad harvest in England and were returning with thousands of converts. Soon, enough of them would be back to sustain a new president.

A majority, including Brigham Young, did in fact return before Rigdon could take over–and they heard Young deliver a most unusual sermon. On August 8, 1844, Rockwell, Anson Call, George Cannon, and others thought they saw Brigham Young take on both the appearance and the voice of Joseph Smith! Rockwell heard others beside him mumble that this was a heavenly sign–the mantle of Joseph Smith belonged to Brigham Young, they asserted, and not to Sidney Rigdon. Young was in reality a far different physical specimen than Joseph Smith. He was stocky, square-jawed, and to some people resembled a pit bull with a continual smile in his eyes.

And Young was chosen the new leader, not necessarily from the heavenly "sign," but from his seniority in the council of the twelve.

Rockwell was pleased with his new leader. Young had taken two years himself to convert to the kingdom, and had always been considered a methodical, bold, likeable, sometimes tactless, but never-wavering Apostle.....and now he would be their leader.

Young did not care much for small talk and he was not given to general reflections. That's why he liked Rockwell. Young further felt he could confide in the man.

Rockwell admired Young in return but as a knight would his king. He did not have the same rapport with Young that he had had with Joseph and Hyrum Smith. Nor had he spent a thousandth as many hours with him. He wasn't sure that he wanted to. Young seemed to be satisfied keeping their relationship a bit formal, and Rockwell was pleased to comply. He could sense that Young trusted him explicitly, but their natural flow of conversation ended with, "Good morning." Young had his own close friends.

Not long after Young's succession, Rockwell rode his horse one day through the Carthage countryside, searching for a lost horse belonging to his neighbor, Anson Call. Rockwell spotted several men gathered in a field, and from the woodland's edge he listened, unseen, to snatches of conversation.

He reported what he had heard back to Brigham Young: plans of "wolf-hunts"–mob parties to burn out rural church members and eventually attack Nauvoo itself.

In reaction, Young turned to several aides.

"You heard Rockwell's report–don't just stand there like a collection of sleeping orangutangs–call out the Nauvoo Legion for drills!"

Several days later at a torchlit meeting in Warsaw, Illinois, Thomas Sharp addressed a mob in front of the *Warsaw Signal* office.

"Brigham Young is raising an army. Although the Nauvoo Legion is supposed to be disarmed, some have armed themselves. Frank Worrell has learned Brigham Young will use this army to attack us unless we attack them first!"

"Where is Worrell?" called out a voice. "He can tell us himself!"

Worrell stood at the back of the mob. "He tells the truth–get your arms, and meet on the public square in one hour!"

Rockwell watched from the shadows of an adjacent stable. He was surprised at what he saw, and especially when several hundred men gathered from neighboring communities within the hour. He glanced at the standard above the building beside Worrell, which read, *Warsaw Signal and Agricultural, Literary, and Commercial Register*. The power of Thomas Sharp was becoming manifest.

Before the moon arose, Rockwell followed Worrell's mob to Nauvoo. Some of them were drinking and becoming louder. Rockwell watched from 30 yards to the side of the road.

They passed several Mormon farms. Families were fleeing before them, but Worrell never bothered to stop them. Rockwell considered by-passing the mob to warn Young and defend the city, but he relied with confidence on the huge guard Young had posted. If a battle would ensue, Rockwell figured, he could by pick off mob leaders from the rear. Again he suspected it would not come to that–the mob would again be surprised at the formidability of the Nauvoo guard, and would again probably turn away.

But half way to Nauvoo the mob was met with a surprise: Brigadier General J.J. Hardin and 500 men–non-Mormon allies to Brigham Young–faced Worrell, and the two armies stopped in the middle of the road.

Rockwell continued watching from cover.

"You plan a little trouble, Worrell?" said General Hardin.

"No, sir, I plan to straighten out a little trouble."

"What trouble's that?"

"The Mormons are the trouble," said Worrell. "Join us and we'll free ourselves of the trouble."

Hardin smiled, "I suppose you mean that." He lit his pipe casually. "But if you take another step forward, your troubles will just begin."

Worrell squinted at him and took on an assumed smile. He realized he was being defeated once again, and it only added to his resolve to smash Porter Rockwell for good.

When Frank Worrell reported the incident to Thomas Sharp, the editor smiled.

"What're you smiling at?" said Worrell, angry.

"We'll only put something else into effect–something that will impassion the populace like the good general has never seen– and he won't be able to stop it."

Worrell looked at him curiously.

"You'll see soon enough," said Sharp, answering his silent question. "But first just make sure tomorrow's paper gets in the hands of the *Burlington Hawkeye*, the *Iowa Patriot*, the *Alton Telegraph*, and the *Quincy Whig*. Am I clear?"

Brigham Young held up several newspapers as he spoke.

"Outsiders and low-lifes have invaded our city. They've begun thieving against Mormons and non-Mormons, but the newspapers claim we are the ones committing the crimes to strike our enemies. And because of these articles, even our former allies–like General Hardin–are questioning us. And the newspapers here," Young pointed to a stack on the table before Rockwell, "claim you're the leader of the thieves! My guess is if you're sighted you'll be shot on sight."

"So what else is new?"

"I'm calling 500 police," continued Young, "to guard the city day and night, and especially to protect the non-Mormons near the city. The press has got to stop this."

Frank Worrell was exhilarated. He strode into Sharp's office with his voice booming.

"Governor Ford has read your article about Brigham Young's call for 500 police–and Ford sees it as a major threat! He has jerked away the Nauvoo city charter!"

Sharp restrained his excitement. "You know what this means?"

"Means they ain't a city anymore."

"What it really means?"

Worrell squinted at him curiously.

"What it really means is Young can't protect his people anymore. Not from arrest. Not with his overused writs of habeas corpus. And not even from the sheriffs of old Missouri. Any legal entity can waltz into Nauvoo now anytime they want and drag off whoever they please."

"How's that going to get rid of 30,000 devils?" said Worrell.

"It's my move. Just read Thursday's paper."

At the Mansion House Brigham Young turned to Rockwell, "All I can do is resist the sheriffs if they try to arrest anyone."

"You can't refuse to turn folks over to the sheriffs," said Rockwell.

"Do I have a choice? I'm not going to let innocent men be hauled off to jail. Some of these sheriffs are already demanding me to turn in everyone on their lists."

"What are you going to do?"

"I'll send them on church missions out of state before I turn any of them over to the witch-hunts."

Rockwell was surprised at his boldness. "Won't the press attack you for disregarding the sheriffs' orders?"

Young simply stared at Rockwell. Rockwell was liking him more by the minute.

Thomas Sharp held up his newspaper. The smell of fresh ink permeated the office, and he gloated. The front page detailed, "Brigham Young's clash with law and order."

Sharp turned to Worrell and smiled. "The ironic thing is–he knew this was going to happen. But I got him in a position where he's stuck. Then again, he's playing with a master."

Brigham Young heard a knock at the door. He opened it to find the Quincy sheriff, Eli McPhearson. "Where's Lot Smith?"

Young shook his head as if he didn't know.

"Cyrus Wheelock? I've also got a warrant for him."

"What for?" said Young.

"Ain't your business. Where is he?"

Another shrug from Young.

"Anson Call?"

Silence.

"And Rockwell."

"Who?"

"Porter Rockwell."

Young shrugged with his usual smile behind his eyes.

The sheriff leaned against the doorway and leered at him. He knew Young's game, and spat on a bush and strutted away.

Young watched him walk 50 feet. As Sheriff McPhearson mounted up, he turned to Young.

"We'll find Rockwell. And we'll flay him alive. You can count on that."

Rockwell lay on his bed when he heard noises. His borrowed cabin was at the edge of town. He peered outside into the woods, but no one was in sight. He then spotted deeper in the woods several tied horses.

At the door he heard a kick. He spotted his gun across the room. He had no time to grab it. The door was kicked again and the lock broke.

Rockwell jumped behind the door. It was kicked again and this time flew open.

Sheriff McPhearson entered with one deputy–and both men had guns raised.

Rockwell lunged from behind them and shoved McPhearson into his deputy. He spotted the sheriff's gun on the floor and grabbed it. He aimed at the two men, and with his eyes gestured them outside.

Using the sheriff as cover, Rockwell made his way slowly from the cabin to his horse.

Several deputies behind trees took aim.

"You shoot and this trigger is pulled," said Rockwell. He took his horse and walked with it and the sheriff at gunpoint into the woods. After a few minutes they stopped.

"I reckon this is far enough," said Rockwell, and then he nodded McPhearson to return to his men. After the sherriff turned and began walking, he heard Rockwell speak again. "Hey, you don't mind if I borrow your gun, do you?" Rockwell softly chuckled.

McPhearson didn't bother turning his head–much less reply-ing–he continued walking and disappeared back to his deputies.

That afternoon Rockwell sat at a stream and heard distant dogs barking.

Several yards away three possemen stepped out of thick brush. His eyes met theirs. He glanced at his horse–it was too far to run to–so he darted into the woods with several gunshots trailing.

Through the woods he ran and finally came to thick trees and stopped. He panted and heard the dogs coming closer. He spotted across the clearing a horseman. He took off again and spotted ahead a shallow creek.

He splashed into the creek and ran upstream. When the dogs arrived they lost his scent.

Then the lead horseman spotted a man running in the shallow creek 300 yards ahead and disappearing around a bend.

Rockwell ran breathlessly. He heard the dogs barking louder, closer. His foot caught a rock and he stumbled. He splashed and struggled his way up and resumed running.

To the shore he ran and into a meadow.

The dogs lost his trail.

Then one picked up the scent, and ran after his pursuer and the others followed.

The dogs, horses, and possemen all kept pace with the new lead hound, and finally arrived at the far edge of the meadow. There, the dogs stopped and yapped. The horsemen dismounted and surrounded their prey.

Protruding out of thick brush were Rockwell's feet. His boots barely visible.

The possemen glanced at one another, satisfied. They opened fire into the form, expending more than enough rounds to kill their victim.

A deputy whacked away at the weeds to inspect the corpse–and finally exposed him: first his trousers, his belt, and finally they pulled the weeds from over his chest.....and beheld what they had shot to ribbons.....

Rockwell's clothes stuffed with weeds.

Rockwell had escaped by diving into the river ahead.

Rockwell swam in his longjohns. A half mile downstream he emerged from the rapids, exhausted. He staggered ashore and began walking.

He walked as fast as his lungs would allow. The sun beamed through tall trees and a warm breeze cooled his wet underclothes.

Birds chirped peacefully, and he finally came to a cabin.

Here he beheld, standing in the framework of the open door, the figure of a voluptuous yet trim-waisted young woman. She backed into the house and squinted at his wet, tight-fitting longjohns.

He was the first to break the strained silence.

"Ain't you gonna invite me in?" They stared at one another fully fifteen seconds.

Inside the cabin he sat, eating like a bear. He shoveled the food into his mouth in enormous mouthfuls. The young woman studied his large arms and chest, and particularly his large blue eyes.

"What're you starin' at?" he said.

She didn't answer.

"Ain't you ever seen a man in his underwear? What's the matter with you?"

She smiled and he kept eating. The banquet before him consisted of thick chowder and freshly-churned butter and warm bread.

"Not bad," he said after the last bite. "Got any more?"

"You have some nerve," she muttered.

"What's that?" he said, not hearing her clearly.

"I said you have some nerve," she said.

"Some nerve, eh? Don't insult me, woman. What do you mean some nerve? You think I always enter young, beautiful womens' homes in my underwear? That's more than some nerve."

"Do you do this often?" she said with a smile behind her question.

"As often as I can."

Despite Rockwell's demeanor she suspected he was, deep down, very embarrassed. She studied him in silence for a minute.

"So is this all the grub you've got?" he said.

"It's all you can have."

"I reckon I better be on my way then," he said, rising.

"You don't sound very grateful."

"Grateful? Yeah. Hungry? That, too. I gotta be going."

"Wait a minute." She disappeared to the other room and returned with a wool blanket and handed it to him. He draped it over himself.

"Just don't go anywhere public," she advised.

He smiled. He liked her. Standing a foot from her face he noticed her light blue eyes sparkling and he felt a long-forgotten attraction. Her dark blonde hair fell over her front shoulders and he lifted it away.

He sat and stared at her, amazed at the freshness of youth still in her cheeks, and he noted the contrast to Luana.

"The man of this house will be here any second," she announced.

He studied her face another moment and his eyes slowly widened. "So how old are you, woman?"

"Seventeen." She saw his surprise and laughed. The bubble in her laughter was the kind that made you want to laugh, too.

"How long 'you been married?" he said.

Before she could answer, he heard horsehooves outside. He immediately bounded out the back door. He took one last look back and took off running.

The man of the house meanwhile came to the front porch and confronted her. "I saw him leaving."

But Rockwell was a hundred yards into the woods by the time the words were uttered.

At Green Plains, Illinois that same night, Frank Worrell stood with others, listening, and watching by torch-light to a speaker.

"Why can't the Destroying Angel just get caught once and for good? I ask you– is it the power of the devil that supports him? I say we show his people what happens when they don't cooperate with the law!"

The mob shouted in agreement.

Gunshots suddenly shattered the air. Two horsemen galloped past and fired again–this time directly into the mob. Balls whistled over the speaker, but no one was hit.

Nevertheless, the signal was clear to those gathered: Young was fighting back.....and, as Worrell now shouted to the group, "If ever a war has been declared, this is it!"

At the Mansion House Young confided to his aides.

"The affair at Green Plains was staged by *agent provocateurs*. Our people had no part in the shooting into the mob last night. Our enemies staged it for two reasons–because Rockwell escaped them and they want to retaliate, and because it's their newest strategy to rile up our neighbors even further."

Rockwell made his way through the woods and recalled with wonder the beauty of the young woman.

He found himself day-dreaming about her, and he noted it felt good to ponder on a different woman. He wondered however if he'd ever see her again.....he wished she hadn't been married.....he wondered what it would have been like to kiss her.....

North of Nauvoo he entered a thicket of woods. With a hatchet he began constructing a lean-to.

The next morning he was awakened by raucous, cacophanous crowing. He arose and saw several hundred birds descending on the woodland grove; then, as suddenly as the birds had appeared, they left, flapping their large black wings and cawing.

Although still exhausted, Rockwell was fully awake. The forest's rich odors filled his spirit.

He decided to return to Nauvoo—even in a blanket and long-johns if necessary—but he would not stay away from the city another hour. He worried about his people. He would have to sneak to his cabin for clothes and a horse. He hoped the posse would no longer be searching.

And he was in luck. Although several horsemen rode past on the road, he moved along the trees in the shadows of moonlight and arrived at his cabin unseen.

His dog ambled up, wagging its tail. He rubbed the animal and played with it. As always, it was his finest friend.

The next morning, Sheriff Jacob Backenstos from Carthage, Illinois learned that plans had been laid to kill him. Backenstos was to be eliminated for trying to recruit citizens of Carthage and Warsaw to protect the Mormons. One hundred Mormon families had been burned out in the southern part of the county in retaliation for the Green Plains incident.

Sheriff Backenstos thanked a friend for the warning, parted with him, and rode his buggy straight towards Nauvoo. He sought not only his own safety now but to raise a posse, even from among the Mormons if necessary, to protect the Mormon settlers in other parts of the county.

Backenstos was tall and stout. He had fair hair, still thick, and possessed a rough cordiality. Just recently elected, he had this very week come to his first crossroads—of either performing his job dutifully or using it to catapult himself into the political arena where his deepest aspirations lay. Despite his better judgement, he was helping the Mormons. This was career suicide, but he could not stop himself.

As he rode down the road pondering on his position, he heard horsehooves behind him.....and he broke his buggy into a gallop.

Frank Worrell was in the forefront of several men out to "take care of" Backenstos.

At Simpson's Creek, Rockwell and John Redding refreshed their horses. The two were on an errand for Brigham Young to bring in some of the burned-out families who were also afflicted with disease.

Rockwell glanced up and saw Backenstos coming down the hill full speed.

"What's the matter!" shouted Rockwell.

"The mob's after me!"

"Don't worry, I've got 50 rounds. No mob's going to touch you!" Rockwell noticed the man at the forefront of the pack.....and he wondered if this would be his long-awaited confrontation with his old enemy.

Frank Worrell had always exercised discretion through his life, and his last several meetings with Rockwell had proved no exception. When he saw Rockwell this day, however, standing with only one other Mormon on the roadside, he knew this was the moment for which he had been passionately waiting. He glanced at his men, now 150 yards back, and he pulled out his revolver. He would see Rockwell in his grave this very day.

11

Porter Rockwell pulled out two fifteen-shooter rifles plus revolvers. John Redding took two pistols. Both men took position at the side of the road.

The five horsemen came galloping down the hill straight for them, Worrell far in the forefront.

Sheriff Backenstos commanded Worrell to halt.

Worrell kept coming. He cocked his weapon and finally stopped his horse about 100 feet from Rockwell. He took aim directly at Rockwell's chest–and fired.

He missed. He fired again. And again. Dust splattered around Rockwell and Worrell was furious. He fired twice more.

Backenstos shouted to Rockwell, "Go ahead–fire!"

Worrell, now out of ammunition, galloped straight towards Rockwell, intending to club him with the revolver.

Rockwell took aim at the clasp of Worrell's belt. All the consequences of his action suddenly dawned on him. He was not sure if he should fire. The press reports about killing Worrell might even rival the Boggs affair–Worrell was high-ranking and would be made a martyr for the Carthage cause; the *Warsaw Signal* would capitalize on it to instigate innumerable problems. Then he thought of Worrell's boastful tirade at him in front of the disbanded Nauvoo Legion.....and he recalled the death of Joseph Smith. He realized for the first time just whose bullets likely did end his friend's life.

He again saw Worrell's belt buckle in his aim, and finally he pulled the trigger.

Worrell was hit dead center. The bullet penetrated his belt buckle and the man flew several feet into the air. He crashed to the dust, blood geysering from his wound, and Rockwell looked at the man with eyes agape. He saw him writhe on the ground a moment, and fell limp.

Meanwhile the other four horsemen had halted up the hill, but now slowly trotted down to Worrell. Cautiously they held their pistols out.

"Which one of you wants to be next"' said Rockwell cooly.

The four men gazed at him.

"I suggest you uncock your weapons, then, and put 'em away. You can take that dog back where he belongs and bury him."

"He ain't dead yet," one mumbled.

"He will be," said Rockwell. "I got a good aim on him."

John Redding stared, astonished at Rockwell's simple, direct answer.

As did Sheriff Backenstos. "How'd you do that in one shot?"

"Luck," said Rockwell.

When Thomas Sharp received word of Worrell's death, he was stunned. He leaned over his desk, seeking to gain composure. He felt nauseous. Since his best friend and newspaper business partner had died five years previously, he had spent many an afternoon in the tavern drinking away the world's problems with Worrell, and now he would have to face them alone.

He turned to Chauncey Higbee, the messenger with the news, and his reply did not come easily.

"Everything I've written about Rockwell so far," said Sharp, "is nothing compared to what I have yet to report on the man."

Governor Thomas Ford sat at his desk in Springfield, Illinois, holding a copy of the *Warsaw Signal*. His face flushed with anger.

Rockwell rode in the dark, moonless eve past Luana's home. Despite his intentions of seeing her, hr felt an uncontrollable urge to see his children. Perhaps it was the foreboding odor of real or imagined gunpowder he smelled in the breeze.....

He saw his children playing in the backyard. They could not

discern the details of his darkened outline, and, frightened, retreated into the house.

He slowly rode past. He glanced back and noticed Luana appearing in the kerosene-lit doorway. She did not know for certain
who the foreboding stranger was.....but she did have her suspicions.

Brigham Young rode the next morning to the edge of a field.
There, General J.J. Hardin waited impatiently. Young dismounted
and faced him sternly.

"May I ask the purpose of your presence?" said Young.

"To find Rockwell and crush the uprising," said General Hardin.

Young gazed across the field at various peaceful city streets,
and mumbled, "What uprising?"

"We have it on good authority that you have an uprising," said
the general.

"That sounds exciting–I'd like to see it."

Hardin scowled at him.

"Who sent you?" said Young.

"The governor himself. He gave me orders to unroof every
house in Nauvoo if I have to. Where's Rockwell?"

"What's he supposed to have done now?"

"Besides the murder of Frank Worrell," said General Hardin,
"the *Signal* says he's leading a band of 300 Mormon fighters,
sweeping down on innocent farmers and threatening their lives."

"That's pretty bold," said Young.

"It's what the Governor read."

"Does the Governor believe everything he reads?"

"You'd have to ask the Governor."

"And you," said Young, "what do you believe?"

Hardin cleared his throat. "Rockwell is on a rampage, but I'll
secure peace in Nauvoo if I have to put the county under martial
law myself."

Young studied him a moment and muttered, "He's even gotten
to you?"

"I beg your pardon?"

"Sharp."

"I repeat.....I have orders from Governor Ford, and–"

Young interrupted, "No need to go through that again, General,
what do you want of me?"

"First I am ordered to search the Mansion House stables for the bodies of two men last seen in Nauvoo, and it is suppposed they are murdered."

Young's eyes twinkled. "You're welcome to search for dead bodies or anything else."

"Do you know anything about them?" said Hardin with a glare.

Young met his glare. "No, but I have reliable information that some one hundred Mormon houses have been burned in the south part of the county. Perhaps if you go there you'll find your murderers."

Birds warbled cheerfully as twilight peacefully ushered onto the Hancock County countryside.

Torches flickered and bounced from the distant eastern horizon, emerging from the darkening twilight with men on horseback. The last faint remnants of day gleamed in the sky.

Fifty men with torches stopped at a farmhouse.

Jason Call, the brother of Anson Call, wore large spectacles yet was strangely unconscious of other people. He was a devoted family man. Generally he kept to himself, and if confronted he would be the first to turn his cheek. However, if his ire were raised enough he could assume the demeanor of a wolverine.

Curiously surprised at all the commotion, Call came to the door. He was grabbed by the horsemen, jerked away from the house, and immediately ushered to a tree. There, he was tied with his arms around it and his wrists lashed together.

His wife and 15 year-old-daughter came outside and saw a bowie knife stuck through the shirt on Call's back. The shirt was then ripped open.

Levi Williams snapped a 16 foot bullwhip and straddled up beside Call. Williams had known Frank Worrell since childhood, and was still livid with rage over Worrell's death. They had in their teenage years caroused and drunk together, like Worrell, Levi Williams believed his anti-Mormon activities were an act of patriotism. He was simply performing what needed to be done, as distasteful as it seemed, to keep his country, community, andfamily safe from those enemies the press reported by the press.

"We can't find your brother," said Levi Williams to Jason Call, "and he's friends with Porter Rockwell, ain't he?"

Call was so surprised over what was happening that he could not even think to reply.

"It looks like the two of 'em are playing fox with us," said Levi

Williams, "but I reckon the hounds have taken all they can take–
you understand me?"

Call said nothing.

"Where's Rockwell?"

Call glanced back at Williams–a shiver passed across Call's
face.

"All right, then where's your brother?"

Call's shock suddenly turned to anger. "I wouldn't tell you if I
knew."

Levi Williams swore at him and walked 10 paces back. He played
with the leather whip a moment, then stared at Call's back. He
asked him again. "Where's Anson, your brother?" Call said nothing. Williams reared back slowly, then came forcefully forward
with the whip. The knotted leather slashed into the flesh and shot
blood from a deep gash.

Call gasped and his wife screamed. Two men grabbed his wife
and daughter and held them.

"Your wife's watching this till you talk–tell us who else knows
where Rockwell's at."

"Any dog worth his salt," said Call, "should be able to sniff him
out on his own."

"You'll feel salt all right–we'll throw it on your back when we
finish!" Williams lashed him again. The leather entered the first
wound and cut next to the bone. Call trembled.

"You gonna talk, boy? Or die on that tree?"

"I don't know where Rockwell's at–I told you!"

Williams nodded to another horseman holding a torch. The
man tossed it into the barn. As the building went up in flames,
Williams glanced at Call's wife, and suddenly reared back and
lashed again.

Call gasped.

"Then tell us who else knows Rockwell."

"Everybody knows him."

"Who else close?"

"Nobody."

"Just give me one name who might know where he's at!"

"You ain't puttin' that leather to nobody you don't need to,"
said Call.

Williams was enraged. He reared back and snapped again.

Call collapsed and was held by the rope around the tree, his
arms hanging stiff, his legs limp.

The barn became an inferno. The red flames flickered off Call's red-streamed back. "My horse is in there–get him out," said Call.

The horse whined and screamed–but soon was silent. Call pled for the animal's sake. Levi Williams stood motionless.

"Let my wife let it out–he's my only horse!" said Call.

"You know what you gotta do," said Williams.

Call stared at the fire consuming the barn. He scowled at the faces surrounding him; he glanced back at Williams. "If Rockwell hears of this, you're dead meat," said Call.

"We'll see who's dead meat." Williams reared back and lashed him the hardest yet.

Call shouted with pain.

"You open up, boy, or I'm gonna open you up....."

Call remained silent.

Another 20 lashes came slowly, and Call's wife passed out. Call meanwhile dangled and writhed, but was silent with each blow.

Williams finally turned to Call's daughter, "Tell your papa he's gonna die on that tree unless he talks."

She was in shock and said nothing.

Williams turned and lashed again. And again. And again.....

At Jason Call's funeral forty souls gathered in the blistering heat. Rockwell and a dozen others were among the last to arrive. The meadow was green and hazy. Songbirds chittered and the sun filtered through thin clouds.

Most of the people at the funeral knew why Call was dead. Rockwell was not one of them. He had been in the woods surrounding Nauvoo for two days before joining the funeral procession while it was already in progress. He soon descried a certain, familiar-looking young woman and her male companion appearing over the hill. He was slightly shaken. He had thought of her and had attempted erasing her, albeit unsuccessfully, from his mind. He figured she was not only married but was likely sided ideologically with the anti-Mormon community anyway; that community was growing daily because of the continuous outpour of bad press. Now, however, it was apparent she was one of his people. And the gentleman beside her was obviously her husband.

Rockwell was torn. He wondered if she had told her husband or anyone else about their previous meeting in his longjohns. He turned his head, embarrassed not only for that fact but especially that he found himself attracted to a married woman.

As the opening hymn began, the young woman walked beside him and stopped. It became apparent she had not recognized him. He made it a point to keep his face turned from her.

Several minutes into the eulogy, she became suspicous of his odd behaviour. Curiously, she glanced in his direction. She could not discern his face. She stepped forward a step for a better angle, and glanced back at him. She softly blurted, "It's you!"

12

Rockwell's knees felt shaky. He forced a quick smile.

He then overheard news that astonished him, as the man beside her whispered, "Is that the man Call was killed over?"

"What do you mean?" said Rockwell audibly.

Several people turned and glowered at him for the disruption.

The man beside the girl spoke quietly but firm, "Call wouldn't tell the mob where you were at–so they killed him."

Rockwell was dumbstruck. He gaped at Jason Call's widow across the funeral gathering and felt deep remorse and anguish for his friend. No one had told him he was part of the reason Call had died.

Suddenly, from over the hill, they heard the thundering of horsehooves. The sermon stopped. Rockwell gazed atop the vale surrounding the meadow and saw a hundred horsemen appearing.

All forty members of the funeral service stared in disbelief. Rockwell finally shouted.

"To the woods!"

He broke the crowd from their trance. Some ran to their horses and others scrambled to the forest. He noticed the male escort with the girl now running to his horse alone, shouting instructions to the girl to stay with Rockwell.

Rockwell was taken back, but he grabbed the girl's arm and began running.

Only two members of the funeral service had weapons in their saddlebags. As they reached for them they were shot and wounded. Meanwhile the others who reached their horses were also fired upon, but only three men were hit and none mortally. Those Mormons rode off and escaped over the vale. The other 35 had no where to escape but the forest.

Rockwell noticed that the girl's escort fled unscathed, but he was still uncertain why the man had left her. She ran beside Rockwell and they approached the woods.

The Illinois horsemen put away their guns, and now came thundering down the hill.....

Many held bullwhips, and they swarmed on the funeral party like cattle.

Rockwell turned and saw Levi Williams lash his whip at the ankles of the first man he came upon, tripping him into the earth. Then a dozen others were whipped across their backs and faces while running.

Several of the funeral party escaped on horseback–but most of the Mormons on horseback were lashed repeatedly before they rode out of the vale. The others panicked and continued stampeding for the woods.

Several older women screamed, and were tripped by bullwhips and lashed before they could struggle up and away.

Rockwell and the girl made it to the forest. A horseman rode past and reared back to snap him with his whip, but the whip got caught in a branch.

Rockwell lept onto the horse, grabbed the man, and they toppled over. On the ground Rockwell reached for the man's knife–but the man caught his wrist. Rockwell was stronger, however, and took the knife and moved it slowly toward his throat.

Suddenly they heard a gun cocked. Rockwell glanced up and saw Levi Williams aiming directly at him. Rockwell dove to the side and Williams fired.

The shot struck a tree. The horse panicked and reared. Rockwell grabbed a stick. Williams struggled to turn and aim–but Rockwell clouted him across the back. Williams fell to the ground.

The girl meanwhile grabbed a whip on the ground. She reared back and lashed Williams on the face. He swore at her, and she lashed again.

Williams ran to his horse, mounted, and took off galloping. He glared back at the girl and wiped the blood from his cheek.

The other man on the ground ran for his horse also and galloped away.

The horsemen were chasing others in the woods. Several put away whips and pulled out guns. They aimed at various figures running through thick brush, and opened fire.

Balls whistled toward their targets. One Mormon was struck in the thigh, another in the arm, and both were helped away by comrades.

Another horseman approached Rockwell and the girl–but the couple hid against a thick oak. The horseman rode slowly towards them and circled the oak. Rockwell and the girl backed around the other side of it, but the man never saw them and soon rode away.

Rockwell and the girl breathed heavily. In the distance they heard occasional gunshots. They wondered if any were finding their targets. A half hour later they heard the last two shots–a minute or two apart–and finally all the shots ceased.

Soon Rockwell and the girl came to a clearing. They could see in the distance a half dozen cabins burning. They could also see two groups of a dozen horsemen each with torches rendezvousing on a country road.

Without a word of where he was walking, Rockwell disappeared into the woods.

Curious, the girl followed for twenty minutes and neither said a word. Finally she spoke.

"Where are we going?"

He didn't answer. Because of a peculiar intensity in his face, she felt it best to remain silent.

When they arrived at his cabin, they found it in ashes. Under a loose brick in the house he pulled out a pistol. He heard whining. He strode around the cabin's remains and saw his dog on the ground, bleeding from a bullet wound.

He knelt beside the animal and petted its forehead. He stood and stared at it a moment, then pulled out his pistol. He cocked it and the girl turned her head.

Rockwell aimed but could not fire. He recalled the years he had spent with the animal, and for a moment saw it as a puppy. Fully fifteen seconds passed as he held the gun to the dog's head–and finally the girl heard the gunshot.

Rockwell turned his head. She saw his eyes moist. With a shovel blade he then dug a shallow grave and buried the animal. He said not a word.

Soon they heard horses galloping. He grabbed her arm and they dashed into the cover of trees.

At his neighbors' barn he untied and saddled two horses, then he and the girl mounted up.

Within minutes Rockwell glanced back and saw they were being pursued by horsemen. He nodded to the girl to follow, and they began galloping.

Ahead was a road-crossing, where they turned. Before them– 100 yards distant–were a dozen horsemen approaching. Rockwell glanced back and saw they were still being followed by other horsemen, thus they were caught between two on-coming parties. Rockwell glanced both directions again and saw the forces coming closer, hemming them in. He finally gazed at the girl and she read his look.

They were trapped.

Rockwell studied the fence to their side–he gave her a nod and they spurred their horses.....they galloped 30 yards and leaped the fence.

Their pursuers broke into a gallop and rode around both sides of the fence.

Rockwell and the girl rode faster, however, and they came to a river. They splashed into it and swam their horses to the other side.

When their pursuers arrived at the river, they discovered horseshoe prints in the mud, and decided to cross the river. Little did they know, but Rockwell and the girl had already, upstream, circled back and re-crossed the river.....

Under a starlit sky the girl sat beside Rockwell at the water's edge.

"I bet he's worried," she said.

Rockwell glanced at her curiously. "I reckon he's more than worried–he's prob'ly half dead with worry. How come your man left you anyhow?"

"I don't have a man."

"You mean I imagined that fellow with you?"

"No."

"Then who is he?" said Rockwell.

"Papa?"

"You're unwed?"

"Reckon so," she said.

A smile enveloped him–he tried containing his feelings. All this time he had felt anxiety for the interest he had felt in her, and now all he could do was think about it a few minutes. Finally he felt, for some unexplainable reason, like teasing her.

"You'll be an old maid in another year."

"I'll be a young maid in another year. Who wants to get wed?"

"It's certain no man will want an old maid," said Rockwell. "So you have nothin' to worry about."

"That's the last thing on earth I wanna do anyway."

"I don't blame you," he added.

The girl scrutinized him.

Rockwell stared at the stars. "So how come your fool papa took off and left you?" he said.

"He ain't a fool and he told me he was going for help in Nauvoo. He figured I woulda slowed him up if I had gone with him–so he told me to stick by you 'cause you was safe."

"I heard that part," said Rockwell. "He ain't only a fool, he's a bad judge of character."

"I'm beginning to realize that," she said, holding back a smirk.

"Yeah, I'm about as safe as a dog with rabies."

"I'd take my chances more with the dog," she said.

He assumed an air of insouciance and gazed at the heavens. They both stared at the sky awhile before he spoke again. "Tell me your name."

She burst into laughter.

"What's so funny?"

"After all we've been through," she said, "and you don't know my name?"

".....Well?"

"I'll tell you, but it won't do us any good. Papa wouldn't approve if he knew it was you that day in the cabin in your underwear."

Rockwell smiled, and drew his hand to her face, as he had in the cabin, and caressed her hair; then with his palm behind her head he drew her face closer to his. She studied his eyes, noticing only a faint tint of midnight blue sparkling from them in the moonlight, and she saw a gentleness in his soul and years of pain, and it brought tears to her own. And then she kissed him.

They caressed their lips as they kissed and she felt a surge of excitement she had not known existed.

Rockwell was enthralled by the feeling pouring from her and they soon locked their kiss and held.

Minutes passed, and Rockwell felt he was reliving a dream. One he had never consciously experienced. He had never felt these feelings with Luana, not this intensely.

Minutes later they were simply staring at the moonlit waves of the water. "I reckon I've never felt much like this," she said.

Although he knew his own feelings, he felt awkward articulating them, so he didn't. He turned and looked into her eyes again.

"Papa is not just going to kill you," she said, "he's going to draw and quarter you alive when he learns what you've done to my lips."

"He oughta barbecue me as well."

"He probably will."

She surveyed his intense eyes, and smiled. She almost said what she was feeling–the exhileration shooting through her soul and what caused it–but instead decided to study his face, and soon she lost her smile. They kissed again and the feelings surged even stronger, impacting Rockwell's soul with a passion that was pounding into his consciousness. He had tokeep reminding himself that she was reality. After a few moments he pulled away. He feared the pit they were digging for each other. He was, in the eyes of all Illinois, a wanton killer, and he could not put on a young woman the label of outlaw's widow before she reached her eighteenth birthday.

But he knew he was losing.....

That night as they slept, he gazed across the campfire and noticed her still awake. She was the most stunning filly he'd ever seen, he thought to himself.

Dawn diffused its softening glow on the forest, and Rockwell arose. The girl was already at the river, washing her face, when he knelt beside her. He studied her innocence, her glowing skin, and then he turned away.

With nothing said between them, they rode their horses an hour before discovering a band of horsemen. Suddenly to their side a gunshot sounded. Other horsemen had been hiding in the brush. In panic, her horse ran away with her. A flurry of shots followed and branches shattered about her head.

Rockwell tried to follow, but she and the horse disappeared in thick underbrush. He wondered if she had been hit or even killed. As he rode searching for her, the horsemen did not pursue Rockwell. He wondered if they had caught her. He circled back to where they had been fired upon. There were no traces of her. He knew for now he would have no way of knowing about her safety. The idea of losing her churned his insides.....

And then he realized.....he still did not know her name.....

As he continued searching he was still unable to find her in the woods. He rode to the river, made his way upstream, and traveled to Nauvoo.

At the Mansion House he learned that the city was under siege. "Where's Brigham?" he asked.

"There," said Lot Smith, pointing to the temple on the hill across town.

To the temple Rockwell galloped.

Inside, he found Young conferring with aides in the foyer. Each greeted Rockwell joyously, and shook his hand firmly.

"We've had a dozen reports from the Illinoisians," said Young, "that you were trapped and killed."

"I probably was," said Rockwell.

The men smiled, but Young remained sober. "Sheriff Backenstos was acquitted. Charges are still on you however. I suggest you not get anywhere near the mobs."

"Afraid I already have. Have you heard any reports of a middle-aged fellow lookin' for his 17 year old daughter?"

"Don't know who that could be–why?"

"Actually....." Rockwell cut the explanation short. ".....Nevermind."

Young regarded him curiously.

"Brother Brigham," came Almon Babbitt's voice, booming with anger as he suddenly entered the foyer, "John Sikes, the federal marshal, is outside waiting to arrest you!"

"On what charges?"

"Passing bogus money."

"Preposterous," said Young. But then he thought a moment. "All right, we'll give them their money' worth."

Young sent William Miller outside wearing Young's cap and cloak. There, U.S. Marshal John Sikes arrested William Miller.

Miller assured the marshal there was some mistake, but Sikes was adamant. Sikes claimed other Mormons had given him the dodge before, but this time Sikes has his man for certain, he assured Miller, and he dragged Miller off to Carthage.

There, Sikes learned that Miller was not Brigham Young.

Miller was promptly released.

At Hamilton's Tavern, despite the fact the crowd also wanted Young captured, they burst into laughter when theyheard of the marshal's mistake.

From his study in the Mansion House Brigham Young informed Rockwell of his most surprising, long-awaited news yet.....their people would be going West.

Between times spent in hiding, Rockwell had in recent weeks participated in the church's 50-man advisory council decision to flee Illinois, but he did not know just when they would leave.

Rockwell went to the upstairs bedroom where Young had recently given him a room, wanting him nearby as his bodyguard.

Later that night as he walked by the river and gazed at the moon, Rockwell wondered if the girl were still alive.

With the advent of the news of them fleeing Illinois, Rockwell felt hopeful that–if he could find her–he would be able to settle down with her away from the mobs. Still, it was possible, as they had joked, that her father really would oppose him taking her to wife. Certainly the fact she was only 17 was not a concern: indeed society perceived youthful marriages–even with wide age differences–a common practice. Rockwell was 33. But his reputation could bother her father if the man believed any of the non-Mormon newspaper reports, which some of the Mormons did, and the fact Rockwell had already been married and that his wife had left him were not in his favor.

That night, as he lay in his bed, he could not sleep. He thought about the girl and the emptiness in his life. He was haunted by the last expression of mixed love and fear he had seen in her. He finally drifted asleep.

In his study several days later Brigham Young confronted Rockwell with news he thought would shatter Rockwell's dreams.

"Luana is getting sealed to Brother Cutler tomorrow."

"Good."

Young was baffled as Rockwell walked past him, whistling, outside to tend the stables.

"Good?" said Young to himself as he stared at the closed door.

That night at dinner, Rockwell learned details that cut away his appetite.

"The children will also be sealed with them," said Brigham Young.

Rockwell retired to his room and wept. Later, unable to sleep, he went to see Young in his study.

"It sinks in, after a few hours, doesn't it?"

"Only about the children."

Brigham Young sat silently while Rockwell collected his thoughts. "I know she had talked of it—but she's really doing it?" said Rockwell.

"The children will choose who they wish as their father in the next life. At least we'll all be associated with the Lord Jesus Christ, so it won't matter anyway, will it?"

Young inspected Rockwell's face a few seconds and felt increasingly sympathetic towards him. "Pray over it, Porter, that's what the Spirit, the Comforter, is for, you know that; you've had experiences in this kingdom as deep as any man."

Rockwell said nothing but retired to his room again and sat. He had already dissolved any hope of reclaiming Luana, but the reality now of not only the children being taken from him but of another man taking her to bed also began to tear at him. He would study the stars all night. Outside he took a walk.

He was still walking the next morning when Luana and Cutler appeared with the four children at the temple entrance.

It was 11 A.M. when Rockwell hid in the shadows of the nearest building. His eyes went from each of his children to the memory of each of their birth's.....

He was still standing, staring at the temple door, when the new family of six emerged an hour later. They seemed elastic, ebullient. He saw Luana place her arms around Cutler's neck and kiss him long and with passion.

Rockwell turned his head. He strolled behind the building and down another street. He found himself staring at the tavern door. He thought for a moment, and glanced upstreet at the temple again. He beheld his family, standing with Cutler, in one final glimpse, and he entered the tavern.

Many drinks and three hours later he emerged. He staggered to the Mansion House and made his way up the stairs.

From his bedroom Brigham Young heard him coming.

Rockwell pulled off his boots and lay on the bed. For the second night in a row he didn't sleep.....he simply gazed at the moon.

13

Within days, the mobs swarmed Nauvoo like hornets. In freezing January evening temperatures, the Mormons were driven from their homes and forced to cross the iced-over Mississippi river.

Dozens died from a blizzard. Others were ill from exposure. Members of the mob fired cannon across the river, panicking hundreds.

Rockwell fled with Young, and both men took few belongings.

During their trek they aided their people night and day. Finally one night in their tent, just before drifting to sleep, Young confided in him that Luana and her family would likely be staying in Iowa.

"I've talked with Brother Cutler," said Young. "He and thousands of others feel the trek will be too hard for 'em. Maybe in later years they'll re-join us. Many are leaving the church. But I don't think Luana will."

"Luana has her weak moments–I worry about her," said Rockwell.

The next day, as Rockwell saw his people constructing 12,000 wagons, Brigham Young approached him at a campfire and gave him an unexpected assignment.

"I want you to return to Nauvoo with a letter for Almon Babbitt. It seems the mob is allowing those who disavow the faith to stay, and letting others stay to wind up the city's official business– Babbit is one of the latter. Whatever you do, stay out of trouble. Just deliver the letter to Babbitt and get out."

Rockwell journeyed for two weeks across Iowa into Nauvoo. He was angry that they had left Nauvoo in the first place. Although Young had remained philosophical, Rockwell could not view it in the same light.

It was evening when he arrived at Nauvoo, and the moon cast an eerie glow on the nearly-deserted, once-teeming city. Soon he happened to spot Chauncey Higbee upstreet on horseback. He followed Higbee to the tavern, curious. Against his better judgement, he allowed his emotions to grip him. He was not sure what he would do with the man, but he found himself thinking of revenge.

At the entrance Rockwell confronted Higbee.

"What do you want of me?" said Higbee.

"I'm not sure yet."

"Sheriff Backenstos promised me protection."

Rockwell glanced up one street and down another. "And I don't happen to see him around at the moment, do you?"

Higbee's huge sallow face went white. "He'll find you and hang you if you touch me."

"As you can see," said Rockwell cooly, "I'm trembling."

Higbee's pitch rose. "You'll be doing worse than that if you touch me."

"I promise I won't touch you." said Rockwell as he pulled out his revolver.

Higbee glared into Rockwell's eyes, horrified. He then looked around for an escape route.

Rockwell's face was stone. "Where can you go, Higbee?" He then aimed at Higbee's face and pulled back the hammer. He fired–just over Higbee's head. Brick chips fell from a stone wall beside Higbee and landed in his hair.

Higbee took off running.

Rockwell mounted his horse and trotted along beside him. He fired another shot–this one at Higbee's foot, and missed it by inches but caused dirt to splatter over his shoes. "You're going to need a new shine, Higbee."

He fired again and shot the heel off his shoe. Rockwell halted his horse, and Higbee hobbled away downstreet.

A half-dozen people across the street stared. Rockwell tipped his hat and rode the opposite direction.

At the tavern's guest room Rockwell slept. Suddenly the door burst open. Sheriff Jacob Backenstos stood above him with a rifle aimed at his face.

"I've got six sharpshooters outside," said Backenstos, "and they're the best the state militia could offer–I suggest you come peaceful."

Rockwell stared at the sheriff, feeling betrayed. It's not every sheriff who gets to have his life saved from a mob, felt Rockwell.

Backenstos could not look at his face. He rode with Rockwell to Carthage.

"Charges are still on you for killing Worrell," mumbled Backenstos, "and I know what you're thinking. I'll vouch for you any way I can. But this business with Higbee–threatening the poor idiot the way you did–I can't do much about that."

They passed through the mobs and Backenstos waved his gun at several men. "Keep back and nobody's head leaves his body..... am I clear?"

Backenstos escorted Rockwell safely into the jailhouse.

Inside the upstairs Carthage cell, Rockwell saw Joseph's and Hyrum's blood stains on the floor.....

The next morning after breakfast Almon Babbitt came to visit him.

"How am I going to get you out of here?" said Babbitt.

Rockwell studied him. Despite the man's narcissistic nature, Babbitt did hold a redeeming asset or two; Rockwell admired his competence and semi-loyalty to church leaders despite his unrivaled conceit.

"If you had to do it over again," said Babbitt, "you'd probably do it anyway, am I right?"

Rockwell faintly nodded.

"I can get the court held outside Hancock County if you'll agree to face a first degree murder charge."

Rockwell's eyes smoldered.

Babbitt read his eyes and continued, "They've piled on other charges to keep you here–even counterfeiting– but I think I can get your case transferred to Galena, 150 miles north."

"Sorry."

"Do you want a fair trial or not?"

Rockwell's expression finally melted.

Babbitt read the change. "There's just one thing. At Galena they'll probably hold you in jail for a few months until the trial."

Rockwell flinched at the words.

At Galena he sat in a dungeon-like cell in chains for what seemed an endless nightmare. The hay–like Liberty and Independence–was filthy and the food horrid. He lost 20 pounds in three weeks.

One morning he awakened to behold–seated across the cell from him–Thomas Sharp.

"And so at last we meet," said Sharp, smiling acidly.

Rockwell gazed on him curiously. "What do you want of me?"

"Reduced to maggots and ants, nothing much."

"No deals?" said Rockwell.

"You wouldn't agree to any if I offered–I know you better than that," smiled Sharp.

Rockwell forced a small smile. "Then why're you here?"

"Maybe to talk about the weather, maybe just to gloat, I'm not sure. Maybe it's because I've always wanted to be a caretaker in a zoo."

"A real animal can turn on any caretaker when he least expects it–even during the night sometime. The caretaker wouldn't find his job so fulfilling anymore, would he?"

Sharp lost his smile. "You go for more than the throat, don't you?"

Rockwell smiled.

Sharp faintly trembled. "I can't lose. I'm the master."

"We'll see," said Rockwell.

Sharp fought to maintain his composure. "How does it feel

knowing everybody in this county wants you lynched?"

Rockwell yawned. "Like who?"

"From the county commissioner's wife to the cheapest whore," said Sharp. "How does it feel to be so popular?"

"I'm flattered."

"There's a time for love, and a time for hate, a time for peace, and a time for war. But the war's about over, isn't it? I drove an entire city out of this state. And my paper is the most successful in five counties. But I haven't even started my final move."

Rockwell smiled, "I think you have."

Sharp regarded him, "No, sir. You'll never get out of this cage alive. Animal's teeth or no animal's teeth."

At that Thomas B. Sharp left the cell, shutting the door cooly behind him.

Rockwell lay on the hay of his cell, watching the week pass, thinking of Sharp's words, and hearing nothing from Almon Babbitt.

One evening he heard leather shoes clopping up the stairs. He heard a key enter the lock. The door opened. And there stood a torch-lit figure. He perceived immediately a long-haired woman..... and he presently recognized her.

Luana.

She placed the torch in a wall holder beside the door and entered the dark cell.

Rockwell distinguished only her dark silhouette against the light of the hallway. "What do you want?" he said.

"Nothing."

For half a minute she stood there, studying him, seeing him chained as an animal, and finally she spoke.

"Alpheas and I are very happy."

"Thanks for telling me."

"Children are doing well," she said.

"Fine. That's fine."

"Brigham's journey West is delayed. The U.S. Army recruited 500 of our strongest men to serve in a battalion with the war at Mexico. That's causing the rest of our people to serve double-duty."

"And you're not going West?" said Rockwell.

"Alpheas feels the Lord doesn't want us to."

Rockwell snorted skeptically.

"He's a good man, Porter."

"Yeah."

"At least we're healthy. Six hundred of Brigham's people have died of malaria, and now they're being hit with starvation. Alpheas says the reason he and I are still healthy is because we've separated ourselves from Brigham's camp."

Rockwell moved his eyes to the floor. "I'm glad to hear how healthy you and your husband are."

"Brigham has negotiated with Omaha tribal chiefs–he's trading plows for food. Alpheas says those who go West with Brigham will all die. Alpheas is a wise man."

"You don't know how happy you've made me, Luana, coming all the way here to tell me that."

Luana saw beyond his expression, attempting to assess him deeply. "Amazing how some folk miss old things already."

Rockwell was surprised, but tried to be disinterested.

"I guess some folks just happen to miss things they didn't think they ever would," she said. "Do you know what I mean?"

He regarded her a moment and understood.

"Like spring in Nauvoo," she added. Her mind was filled with memories of their first arriving in Nauvoo.

"Hard to know if one really misses spring–or just ain't as happy with another season as they thought they'd be," he said, reading her heart.

"It's easy to know what your heart feels, even though it takes awhile," she said.

Rockwell noticed her trembling slightly, and he felt pity for her, despite himself. He wanted to feel anger, but he couldn't. "I think it's hard to recall the season myself sometimes," he said.

"Sometimes?"

"All the time lately. And forever as far as I'm concerned. Especially since I got an early frost-bite one spring; there's just no lookin' back."

"Not ever?" she said.

"The seasons are made to go on, Luana. I would never want it back."

She studied him a moment, her eyes the widest he'd ever seen them. "It's as simple as that?"

He gazed at her and eventually nodded.

Luana stared at him for a full minute, and finally walked out without another word.

Rockwell was left looking at the door with tears in his eyes.

When Rockwell's jury decided he was not guilty of murder, the packed courtroom shouted and booed.

According to some witnesses, Frank Worrell had demonstrated a tendency to violence, and the Galena grand jury believed Backenstos' testimony.

Rockwell strode from the courtroom under escort of the Daviess County Sheriff, Tom Mackelby. Beside them walked Jacob Backenstos of Hancock County. When they arrived at the jail, Mackelby handed Rockwell his revolver and no bullets.

"It's for your own good."

"What about my horse?"

"Keeping it for court expenses."

"Court expenses?"

"Ain't my idea," said Mackelby.

Rockwell glanced at him and then at Sheriff Backenstos. He noticed a glimmer of admiration in their eyes, but no one said a word.

Outside, Backenstos watched Rockwell disappear around the bend of a deserted, country road.

Rain had fallen, and the scent of the air with the breath of freedom in Rockwell's lungs tasted fine. He was free after four months of dungeon life. As he passed a farm, he noted the smell of the freshly turned earth. He felt a determination to never again be captured by enemy–no matter what the reason–yet he was grateful he had played a role in diverting press attention away from its crusade to drive out the last remaining Mormons in Nauvoo to the top-page news his own court case provided. Nevertheless, he knew he was still in danger: no woods were in sight for him to travel in only a meadow for the next several miles–so he felt unusually vulnerable.

Rockwell found himself walking faster than his strength allowed, towards Nauvoo, 160 miles south. His plan was to find a horse there and ride across Iowa to rejoin Brigham Young. Realizing the anticipation he felt, and the possibility of collapsing at his present pace, he forced himself to slow.

While he determined to be of benefit to Young in whatever way possible, he also thought again of settling down with the young girl, if she were still alive.

Not twenty miles from jail, in an open meadow creek beside the road, he stopped to drink. He heard hoofbeats. He glanced up and saw a rider approaching. The man stopped and spoke.

Rockwell saw who it was.

"Must be real proud of yourself," said Thomas Sharp.

"Not particularly."

"Why's that?" said Sharp.

"I shoulda had enough sense to kill Worrell months earlier," said Rockwell, "and you with him."

Sharp smiled and pulled out his gun and began polishing it. "Well, here we are, four months later. I guess they let the animal out of his cage while the keeper was busy with other things."

"I guess so."

"I hear from the county sheriff you have no ammo," said Sharp.

Rockwell nodded.

"Funny," said Sharp. "I always carry mine loaded." He spun the cylinder.

Rockwell squinted at him a moment and turned his back on him.

Sharp, surprised at his gall, watched Rockwell walk away from him; he said nothing until the man was 50 yards away.

"I don't need to deal with you, anyway, Rockwell. 'Cause it's not even worth my time anymore."

Rockwell glanced back and just kept walking.

The next morning ended with only three riders passing him, two of whom peered with unusual interest. Rockwell sensed his danger was increasing, but he also felt no alternative than to continue across the unprotected meadow as fast as possible. The protection of a forest was just ahead.

After noon he arrived at the edge of the forest, only to find a man lying on the road, holding his thigh and groaning.

Rockwell walked up to him.

"Can you help me, mister?" said the stranger.

"What's the matter?"

"I was thrown."

When Rockwell knelt to look him over, the man rolled to his side, pulled from under his belly a pistol, and pointed it straight at Rockwell's neck.

Six more men jumped him from behind–and all held rifles aimed.

At a campfire Rockwell sat with his hands tied. The evening was

cool and he shivered. A guard sat across the fire and stared beyond the thicket. Fifty yards away, through thick trees, were a hundred mob members, holding torches and listening to Levi Williams. Sharp's face was among them.

Through the thicket a hangman's noose was dropped over a
tree. A horse was untied and being brought to him by two men. He
would be placed on it and its rear would be smacked, leaving him
dangling.

He heard the mob, most of whom were half-drunk, shouting for
his death. He glanced across the fire at his guard, staring at the on-
coming horse, and he finally muttered to himself.

"Enough of this."

He jumped up, leaped over the fire, and smashed his head into
the guard's abdomen. Although his hands were tied, his fingers
grasped the knife in the guard's belt. Rockwell clasped the handle
and in a flash sliced the knots loose.

He saw the two men arriving from the thicket with the horse—
and he beheld their astonished looks. He ran straight for the horse
and sliced the reins from its wrangler. He jumped on it and
launched a gallop into the woods.....

Both men stood with mouths agape.

Finally, they pulled pistols and fired—but the shots merely
cracked several branches beside Rockwell—and he galloped away.

Thomas Sharp ran to the clearing and saw Rockwell escaping.
His register of surprise turned to a faint smile of admiration. The
war was over anyway, he thought to himself, and he had decisively
won. The Mormons, he figured, would trail into the desert and die,
much like a comet that flashes in the night and trails into oblivion.
Smith was dead, the renegades like Rockwell and Young would be
butchered by Indians or ravaged by disease and starvation, and
their entire civilization would be vanished within five years, he
figured. Five years at best. Give it three. Of this he felt such a
certainty that he would ride to his office immediately and print a
final epitaph to Porter Rockwell and Brigham Young.

Several dozen mobbers were now on horseback giving him
chase, but Rockwell was miles ahead. He could see their torches
shimmering behind him in the distance.

For the next two days Rockwell hid in woods while riding only
at night. On the third morning he reached Nauvoo.....

The streets of the city were deserted. He did find Anson Call at home, from whom he procured a horse.

"I'll join you in a few days," said Call, who was the brother of the deceased Jason Call. "I've only been hit with the ague."

As Rockwell rode across Nauvoo alone he scanned the city that once teemed with commerce and thousands of families.....and for an instant he pictured Joseph Smith atop his steed beside the Mansion House.....

Rockwell thought he saw a twelve-year old lad beside the Mansion House. He wondered if he were imagining that, too, until he heard the boy's voice calling. Then he recognized Joseph Smith III running towards him and climbing a fence.

Rockwell dismounted and hugged the boy.

"You're not coming West, lad?"

"Our family's staying here."

Rockwell was disgruntled that Emma had not joined Young's people West. He gazed again at the nearly-deserted streets and he felt a bizarre sensation. With a pain in his chest he studied the boy.

"Oh Joseph, Joseph," said Rockwell, "they've killed the only friend I've ever had."

Young Joseph saw tears on Rockwell's face.

"I suppose it will do you no good," he continued, "if anyone sees you with me. It could only get you in trouble. Enemies of our people still hunt me. Be off with you, lad."

Young Joseph walked slowly away, turning back several times to study his father's best childhood friend.

Rockwell led the horse beside the river a few minutes until he stopped. He gazed across the water and could not remove his eyes from the scene. In the hazy September morning he pondered, at once calm and disturbed over who could have seen the boy with him. He feared for Smith's boy.....

He walked to the dock and eyed the ferry that would take him across to Iowa. It was making its way across the river towards him now for its final afternoon run. He turned and gazed at the city. The past in Nauvoo was painful. He imagined his childhood days with Smith in Manchester, New York. He saw the Mansion House, with Joseph Smith on the porch, standing proudly in his legionnaire uniform hailing his hundreds of troops, with Rockwell himself on the front line.

Young Joseph III, now atop the temple hill, stared at the riverboat docked down at shore. His eyes rested upon Rockwell beside the dock, and in his final glimpse of Porter Rockwell, the lad saw him mysteriously salute the Mansion House, and turn away.

PART III

THE TREK

14

Upon crossing the Mississippi River, Porter Rockwell rode across Iowa.

Two weeks later he arrived at the western border at Council Bluffs. There he found Brigham Young and other Mormon leaders in William Clayton's tent. They beheld Rockwell as he entered, and suddenly ceased all conversation. Tears glistened in Young's eyes, as in the eyes of several, and Rockwell knew he was back among friends. He was satisfied to note that a place within Young's heart was growing for him.

Outside the tent Rockwell detailed to him his Galena experience, and then learned from Brigham details of what Luana had mentioned: 500 of their best men had been recruited by the Army for service in the Mexican War, despite their being driven out of Illinois and Missouri, and Brigham Young had cooperated. "The Mormon Battalion will honor us, Porter."

"We oughta march the 500 boys on the Carthage Greys militia that killed Joseph is what we oughta do," said Rockwell, "if you wanna talk about honor."

The Battalion had left weeks earlier and would end their journey in California. Rockwell suspected that it would affect those remaining with additional hardships, and he knew he would be one of those affected. He snorted skeptically.

Weeks later, on December 29, 1846, Rockwell met with 15 leading Council members and was chosen as scout and chief hunter to lead a 147 member advance party to the Rocky Mountains. The main body of Mormons would wait in Iowa and leave several months afterwards.

In March a copy of the *Warsaw Signal* was brought into camp. When Clayton read it aloud, Rockwell listened intently. Thomas Sharp's epitaph to the church included a final statement that "Porter Rockwell just married a prostitute."

That night, the camp found difficulty sleeping, being awakened with Rockwell's intermittent roars of laughter.

On April 14, 1847, Rockwell's advance party moved out. The first two weeks across the plains kept him busy searching for Willard Richards' lost horse. He also delivered mail to the main camp back at Winter Quarters.

On April 26th he was awakened by gunfire. Indians were seen crawling into camp and were chased off by guards.

Soon afterwards, he and three others were chasing down Willard Richard's willful horse again, when they were suddenly confronted by 15 Indians springing to their feet with bows and arrows strung.....

Rockwell pulled his pistol, the other scouts did likewise, and one Indian began yelling, "Bacco! Bacco!"

Understanding the man's request, Rockwell yelled back, "We don't have any tobacco!"

But the same Indian approached John Matthews' horse.

"He's got his eye on your bridle, Matthews," said Rockwell. "Don't let him touch you!"

Matthews cocked his pistol and pointed it straight at the Indian's head.

"I advise you, my friend," said Matthews, "to high-tail it back to your village."

The Indians backed away, not understanding the words but not misunderstanding the gaze in Matthews' and Rockwell's eyes.

Two weeks later the party faced a buffalo herd. Rockwell felt hot blood racing through his veins. He dashed ahead of the other hunters and focused on the most feared of all western wildlife–the bull buffalo.

"He can't be dropped with a ball shot in the head," shouted Matthews. "Don't go for him!"

"Why not?" yelled Rockwell, who then galloped after the beast with merely his pistol. He galloped 20 feet ahead of the bull, turned halfway around to aim at him, and fired.

The bull shook its head, stunned, and stopped. It shook its body, then caught sight of Rockwell. And took out after him.

"Wait a minute!" shouted Rockwell to Matthews. "It's supposed to drop over dead!"

The bull buffalo chased him five continuous minutes, zigzagging with his horse until Rockwell finally escaped. Matthews and the others, upon seeing his predicament, burst into laughter.

Rockwell looked glum. He trotted back to his comrades and no one said a word. When he saw them he glowered. Suddenly he realized what it must have looked like, and he began laughing.

They joined in and laughed loud and long.

Over the next several days Rockwell became more adept at killing buffaloes, learning what does and does not work.

By May 25th he had shot four more bulls before the herds vanished. He had also hunted antelope, and had generally kept the party alive by shooting other game and by fishing.

Morale was high but the expedition had spent too many hours wasting time–playing cards and dancing–for Brigham Young's liking, and he finally told them so as well as castigating them for their excessive lightness and contentiousness.

"If you're not tired enough after a day's travel, then start walking!" said Young. "You're making yourselves unnecessary baggage to the poor animals. Then you will not find so much energy. Dancing once in a while is fine. But you've turned this trek into a carnival."

Rockwell was always too tired to frolic anyway.

The next morning Brigham Young watched Rockwell ride ahead of the party, but this particular day he consciously caught himself thinking that "Port" Rockwell will blend in beautifully with the freedom of the wild.

Young and several others had begun calling him "Port," and the appelation would stick till his dying day. In his earlier years Rockwell had been known simply as "O. P." and "Orrin Porter," but by the time he had settled in Nauvoo, most people were calling him simply "Porter." Orin, with one "r," had been his father's name. Few called him by his first name to avoid the confusion.

His mother, meanwhile, was back in Iowa with the main body of Mormons waiting to go West. Until the trek, Rockwell had visited her monthly, as always, and sometimes weekly, as occasion had permitted. They still held a strong affection for one another, though each pursued different lifestyles. His mother had become known, ironically, as one of the prime peacemakers of the Mormon community.

On June 1st the advance group arrived at Fort Laramie. There, Rockwell traded personally with James Bordeaux, the proprietor.

Then, Rockwell continued leading them westward. Brigham Young soon announced exactly where they were going–he had seen it in a vision–from scouts' reports the place was known as the Great Salt Lake Valley.

Rockwell presently rounded up four mountain men who dined with Young. These seasoned scouts gave conflicting reports of "Salt Lake Valley," as they called it. Jim Bridger was the only one positive.

"If ever there was a promised land, that must be it."

Soon, Sam Brannan came on the scene. To Rockwell, Brannan was a colorful soul. He had led 250 Mormons on the ship *Brooklyn* to San Francisco, had launched a newspaper there, and had set out to convince Brigham Young of where the Promised Land really was.....California. Brannan had always thought rather highly of himself; he was of medium build and had rather small eyes, green in color, and because they were too close they gave him somewhat the look of a shrew.

Brigham Young simply, tactlessly, informed Brannan that he was dead wrong. Brannan felt squelched and left for the California paradise alone.

By June 11th many were discouraged. Rockwell's optimism, however, was irrepressible.

The next day he was chosen to lead a small band of eight men into Salt Lake Valley, facing rockslides, steep ravines, and rattlesnakes until they discovered the Donner-Reed trail.

When they found it, he rode back to Young and the other 139 with the news, then rejoined the small patrol to actually find the valley.

While Orson Pratt and Erastus Snow would be the first and second Mormons to ever see the Great Salt Lake Valley, Rockwell would be the third. Upon sighting it, Pratt threw his hat into the air and shouted with Snow, "Hosannah!"

Rockwell heard them ahead and he galloped up, gazed through the canyon entrance, and beheld a vista that took his breath away.....

PART IV

THE WEST

15

A buggy rolled into the valley one hot afternoon, and the man who stepped out was William W. Drummond. He took one look at the expanding town–named Great Salt Lake City–and exclaimed simply, "Very quaint."

He could not wait to sink his teeth into the territory's judicial concerns, he admitted to his aide, since he was now the valley's *bona fide* federal judge. And whether or not Young and his people wanted him, here he was, with a mandate from the president and the power to perform it.

Drummond had irreconcilable elements co-existing within his soul. He sought to be his own man, but in order to be where he was, he had to compromise certain philosophies. He knew clearly the Eastern mining interests had been watching–drooling, as it were–over Young's great basin kingdom. Gold in California had recently sent thousands of immigrants through the territory, making the Mormons rich, and factories and mills operated 24 hours a day. Great Salt Lake City–also shortened to just Salt Lake City–was teeming with industry. Other precious metals had since been discovered near the city itself. So the large companies, he suspected, were putting pressure on Washington to make things happen for them.

Drummond actually hated taking orders, but his first phase of directives would not be that distasteful. He agreed wholeheartedly with what was expected of him: to cut the powers of Brigham Young and turn them over to the powers that be in the East. He only feared one thing.....the future. He disliked the prospects of being told what to do the rest of his life and even of whom to appoint to his staff.....particularly down the road when he would become Governor of the Territory of Deseret.

No one had told him that would be his reward for carrying the banner during his judicial reign, but the position was implied. He would have to prove to them how invaluable he was and in the meantime make for himself a name that exemplified how deserving he really was of the sceptor.

He had not even met those from whom the directives had come. In fact, all was done by implication. Lower-level aides had spoken with him vaguely, informally, while "happening" to run into him in Washington taverns. At first he had thought they were jostling with him, but after reaching certain informal agreements, he was actually rather surprised one day when he did receive a letter of appointment, transferring his duties as an assistant to a district judge in Washington, D.C. to the federal judgeship in the Territory of Deseret.

Drummond's gift of repartee was celebrated. He was widely traveled, and spoke several languages.

And what he lacked in looks he made up for in presence. As with De Bergerac's plume, he carried a special penache of which only he seemed aware that made him superior to women. Many of them were intrigued by this mystery. And especially by the fact he carried in his eyes a constant sparkle. A sparkle which excited women.

He was short, stout to the point of plumpness, and balding. Women fought over him.

His wife adored him.

He was bored out of his wits with her. In order to have his fun, of their 23 years of marriage he had for 22 of them sent her off to relatives for the summer. Even now he was not particularly looking forward to her arrival in a few months (she had suggested it be in a few weeks, he had talked her into months). He had decided before he even left that once he was far out in the wilderness he would escort any woman he felt like escorting, at any time, with or without his wife around. His promotions had been and would be predicated on performance, not on puritanical morality, and the fact that he happened to be in the hotbed of Mormonism made him smile all the broader at the irony. He would have his fun with the Mormons, he figured. He stopped a stranger on the street.

"Where's Brigham Young?"

" 'Round the corner."

"Get him a message for me."

"You tellin' or askin' me?"

Drummond was surprised at the man's insolence. He had heard the Mormons were sheeplike. Their new-found freedom had made them a bit raw, he thought to himself, but he would match their vituperousness. And, if necessary, raise them one.

"Tell him I'm not interested in meeting him," said Drummond, "nor in being interferred with. But tell him his hey-days are over." Drummond then explained who he was. What he did not explain was his intention: to step on Brigham Young like a snail in his garden.

The stanger nodded with a scowl and shuffled toward Young's office with the message.

Drummond's concerns were those which he had been briefed on by the secretive aides. In addition to various documents, he had been given newspaper clippings from the Mormons' last area of residence, the *Warsaw Signal*. He knew fully what to expect of these people. And he would establish an office and courtroom a stone's throw from Brigham Young's high command, just to make a statement.

His most enjoyable moments, however, would be found in the tavern. Most active Mormons shunned the place, as the decree had recently come down from Brigham Young to abstain from liquor–although it would take decades for some active Mormons to catch onto the practice–but inactives and non-Mormons alike flocked to it. Here, Drummond would be esteemed more as a hero to the non-Mormons than he would be even in the courtroom.

And soon he became the respectful recipient of an increasing number of tavern toasts.

It was on one such hot afternoon, after a day's deliberating, that Judge Drummond strutted into the tavern with his aide, Simon W. Lefevre, and overheard for the first time complaints of "Brigham's

Destroying Angel."

"I've heard the stories," said Lefevre, when Drummond asked him what they were talking about.

"Who are they speaking of?" said Drummond.

"Porter Rockwell."

"The Porter Rockwell?"

"The Porter Rockwell."

"Certain people assured me he would've been killed in brawls with the Indians by now," said Drummond. "Where is he?"

"Mostly out trekking outlaws."

"What for?"

"He's the U.S. Deputy Marshal."

Drummond was amazed. "How could a bloody outlaw become a U.S. Deputy Marshal?"

"I don't know."

"What else do you know about him?"

"Just the stories."

"He should've been lynched in Missouri. Find out what you can about him by Monday."

"Judge, I've got a busy weekend ahead."

"Drop it–go find out everything you can about him." Drummond knew he needed an angle–something convincing and heavy which could crumble the frontier power structure under Brigham's feet–and he knew it just might be this–the expose of the church's most notorious desperado. "And find out how close he is to Brigham Young and the rest of the hierarchy here."

Simon Lefevre was not pleased with the assignment. Having worked as a legal aide in Denver, and before that in Boston, he had been highly recommended to certain parties of which he was not even aware, who in turn had recruited him to assist Drummond at this new post.

Lefevre was by nature an obsessive worker. His vitality was immense. But having just met an interesting single woman at the tavern the day before, he had plans to spend it with her this weekend, and was, upset by this intrusion on his social life.

As to his feelings about Drummond in only several weeks of service, he both disliked and respected him.

Lefevre was but 27, yet was considered to possess wide-ranging interests and a dry wit. He also communicated well to older people, possessing the ability to converse on most any topic. This gave him a solidity and an air of maturity that were of service to him.

As a college man six years previously he had been something of an athlete, and had courted women with position and wealth, despite the fact his own family was middle class and had trouble financing his education. He had received scholarships from unknown benefactors.

Drummond theorized to himself that Lefevre's mind had been discovered and hoped to be used by those same benefactors who owned the gigantic mining interests. Drummond additionally suspected–which caused a rather uncomfortable pressure–that they would both have to produce.

Lefevre's ambition was hard to define. He wanted to work his way up, but to what he was not certain. He seemed to enjoy utilizing his investigative abilities, and even taxing them when possible just for the fun of it. He rarely found women he could enjoy, since he considered them his intellectual inferior. He generally became quickly bored with them, and sought to lose himself in his work, hoping that one day the perfect one might appear.

He stood from his table, forced himself to thank Drummond for the drink, and left.

Porter Rockwell rode to the ranch of John Neff. He had heard that John Neff had an interest in securing the first canyon south of Mill Creek for lumber, and he also had heard the man was looking for a partner.

"Come in," said Neff, repairing the corral gate, "and have refreshment." Neff knew well of Rockwell, but Rockwell could not place him. Rockwell may have had a difficult time recognizing him even if they had been better acquainted. John Neff was now almost totally grey. His hair was grey, his face, his eyes; he looked as though the desert sun had baked the color out of him. Even his voice was grey. "My daughter will get us some drinks."

Rockwell's hair was braided, as he now often kept it, and he also wore a beard.

Upon entering the cabin, Rockwell caught sight of an attractive young woman and immediately recognized her. She was fuller in the face and an inch taller but was just as trim and every bit as beautiful. The years had been good to her.

She looked at him, surprised, and said nothing.

Rockwell noted a faint tremble.

John Neff noticed nothing. He had heard of his daughter talk of

Rockwell years earlier, after her escape from Levi Williams and his men, but he had no idea any sort of feelings had developed between them. Since then, Neff had wondered why she could not bring herself to marry any of the eligible young men she had since courted.

Unknown to her father, Rockwell had been in her mind continually, and now, upon seeing her, he flushed.

John Neff did not see that either. He was busy watching his wife setting the dinner table. Neff had remarried while crossing the plains. His new wife was dark and comely, part Indian it was said, and only five years older than his daughter. This woman had seen her own parents and brother ravaged by cholera before the migration West. She had not particularly loved John Neff, nor Neff her, but it was a marriage of convenience. However, they had been surprisingly compatible. Over the years since, he had caught himself often watching her, as he was today.

John Neff then gave a glance to his daughter, wondering what the devil all this silence was about.

"Honey," he said to his daughter, "Do you remember Porter Rockwell?"

She practically whispered. "Sorta."

"Rockwell, this is my daughter, Mary Ann."

So Rockwell finally had her name. He observed that she had, with several more years on her, attained more character to her face, and even a great beauty, but none of the coldness of great beauty.

Mary Ann's smile turned to a warm gaze.

Rockwell's smile also turned into a gaze–a clear, piercing glint, and the senior Neff cast his eyes back and forth between the two. He was surprised at what he was discovering.

Judge William Drummond sat in his courtroom waiting for the day to end. It was an unseasonably hot afternoon when Simon Lefevre entered a side door to wait for the judge to slam his gavel.

An hour later the two sat at the sweltering bar, cooled by an open door to the dark, windy alley, finding the hot autumn air still more comfortable here than anywhere else in town. Drummond noted that Lefevre wore his clothes well and his clothes were well cut. Drummond had not seen him in 10 days. During that time, Lefevre had poured himself into his research of Rockwell.

"I learned everything."

"Everything?"

"Yeah, but they're mostly rumors," said Lefevre.

"Any facts?"

"Some."

"Start with the facts."

Lefevre was self-possessed. He marshalled his facts well and was able to state them with precision. He sat back and began an account which mesmerized the judge. He told of Rockwell's arrival in the valley and of his activities since.

"Rockwell first explored the valley, and then went part way East again to help the main body of Mormons reach the valley. In November, 1847, four months after he first arrived, he went to California and on the way he almost died of thirst. But he survived and brought back from California 135 mules and 25 discharged Mormon Battalion soldiers from the Mexican War.

After he returned, Brigham Young offered him free land but he refused it—he wanted to live away from everybody."

"Did he become a recluse?" said Drummond.

"No, he socialized regularly, dining with at least one family who invited him for dinner often. But he also wanted to be alone, building his ranch."

"What happened to him then?"

"He helped kill some 15,000 predators to cattle and then he scouted Utah Valley, 50 miles south. By March, 1849 he was appointed an officer in the Nauvoo Legion that was just reorganized. Then on the 12th of March he was appointed U.S. Deputy Marshal in the first public election of the valley."

Simon Lefevre sat with a certain apprehension. He did not wish anyone to overhear this. So, at his request the two left the bar and strode across the room to the privacy of a corner table. There, he continued.

"Brigham Young next sent him to Utah Valley to pacify Ute Indian chiefs who were harassing the Mormons there."

Lefevre was interrupted. The proprietor to the tavern came up and informed them he was closing, but Drummond, in his indefatigable way, talked the owner into performing paperwork in the back room until they left, as they still had a few drinks to finish over important conversation. Drummond tipped him generously. When the two were alone again, Drummond gulped another drink and spoke softly.

"So what has Rockwell done since?"

"Primarily tracked cattle and horse thieves."

"Who has he killed?"

"Church enemies claim he's an assassin for Brigham Young."

"I know that, but what's the proof?"

"I don't know–people talk."

"What do you think?"

Lefevre regarded the empty room. "Everyone who drinks here thinks so. But then they only talk to each other."

"So find me the proof."

"I'll find what I can."

"What else do you know about him?"

Lefevre sat back and took another swig before resuming.

"Brigham Young sent him again to California. This time with Amasa Lyman and 30 others to teach the church gospel to California Mormons and gather up tithing.

"While there they saw Sam Brannan. Now Brannan was no idiot. He had been collecting church tithes from the people to build his own mansion in San Francisco–even after he had left the church. So, Rockwell and Lyman confronted him and told him to turn over the tithes. Brannan of course laughed at them–he told them he'd give them the money only on God's proper written order, otherwise not."

"He'd have been an idiot otherwise," said Drummond.

Lefevre laughed. "Anyway, Rockwell likely believed in his mission, and he found himself frustrated, but he couldn't do anything about it."

"He might have shot him–did he try?"

Lefevre shook his head no.

"So what happened to him next?"

"Well, when he left Brannan, he went to the gold fields and made a small fortune. With his profits he opened a small saloon at Murderer's Bar. And there he almost lost his head."

"What happened?" said Drummond.

"He got into a shooting match with a Boyd Stewart, a Mormon Battalion veteran; and the event was billed as the match of the decade. Rockwell had built a reputation in shooting matches under the name "Brown." He had taken on the alias because most of the miners were from Missouri and Illinois. Anyway, they considered these two men the hottest shooters in California. Hundreds of miners swarmed the place.

"Well, Rockwell won the match and the miners went wild. He

went from hero to criminal in five seconds. They chased him out of town with a hangman's noose."

"Where did he go?"

"Salt Lake City. But when he arrived here he faced even more bad rumors. The tavern locals claimed he'd murdered a J.M. Flake in Utah."

"And?"

"Some people say Flake fell off his mule and died. However, a man passing through here named Nelson Slater wrote a book about it and claimed Rockwell had chased down an immigrant by the name of Flake and–without trial, judge, or jury–cut off his head."

"Could Rockwell have done it?"

"He was in California when Slater said it happened. Non-Mormon immigrants didn't even arrive in Utah till June, 1849, two months after Rockwell had gone to California. But the book is well received there."

Drummond sighed, frustrated, and lit his pipe with quick, powerful puffs. "What did he do next?"

"Brigham Young assigned him full-time to the Nauvoo Legion."

Drummond glanced up curiously from his pipe.

"To track down thieves from non-Mormon wagon trains," said LeFevre, answering Drummond's silent question.

"He kill anybody then?"

"No, it was fairly unadventurous."

Drummond puffed harder. "How long was this for?"

"Two weeks."

"When?"

"February, 1851," answered Lefevre.

"What happened after the two weeks?"

"Brigham Young had more Indian problems and called him back for more help."

"And?"

"He took 30 Indians prisoner for stealing horses in Tooele. But he trusted them too much–he let them keep their weapons and they killed one of his possemen. Lorenzo Custer was the man killed–he had written an anti-Mormon book. So rumors claimed Rockwell killed him instead."

"Is there evidence?"

"None. In fact the possemen were so mad that they killed four of the Indian prisoners in retaliation."

Drummond looked reflective. He was growing impatient with Lefevre, wanting only to hear the facts which could indict the desperado. Additionally, Lefevre possessed a penchant for detail which was beginning to anger his mentor. But Lefevre was too engrossed in his own story to notice.

"Well, he was mad again at Indians–"

Drummond cut in, changing the subject back to the murder. "Yes, but is there proof he didn't kill Custer?"

"All the witnesses–even the posse which was non-Mormon–claim the Utes killed him."

"So what else can we use?" said Drummond. "I need something factual."

"All I can tell you is what happened."

A kerosene lamp reflected off Lefevre's orange-tanned skin and angular, handsome features. Drummond meanwhile only half-listened, absorbed in his own thoughts.

"Brigham Young called Rockwell into his office," said Lefevre, "and sent him back to the Indians once again."

"What for?"

"Missionary work. And then he went back to building his ranch."

Drummond was impatient. "What about his women?"

"Just one woman–she could pass for his daughter."

"And that's all you know?"

"He knew her in Illinois–they've been seeing each other here every day for a week. Her neighbors claim he's on the up and up with her, and that she's mad over him, but nobody knows what he thinks of her. If anything."

Porter Rockwell was shaking. He rode his wagon to pick up Mary Ann for a play. It was January 19th, and he was shivering in the icy winds. But not from the cold. He had a lead part in the play.

Not that he didn't know his lines. Indeed he had performed the same play at Nauvoo years earlier, and was now even playing the same part. But tonight was opening night, and the woman he happened to love would be sitting on the front row, staring straight at him, seeing his every mistake.

As Rockwell arrived at the Neff ranch, he found that, in a yellow dress, with her olive skin and long, dark blonde hair, she looked stunning. He also found himself wishing she had been struck with a mild case of malaria.

"Hurry up, Port," she said, climbing onto the buckboard. He climbed up beside her. "I can't wait to see this," she said.

"Neither can I." He hesitantly snapped the reins and his wagon pulled slowly away from her father's cabin.

Rockwell was dressed as a Spanish soldier. He waited in the shadows behind a stage curtain and peered across the audience. Mary Ann sat on the front row, dead center.

He was building the plans of his life around her, and, upon discovering her at John Neff's ranch, had not let a day go by without seeing her. She lived a quarter day's journey in the sunlight from him, but he found the daily trek well worth his time. His emotions in fact had not given him a choice. He knew she would have to be his. He spend most of his days split between hewing logs in the canyon for the road to his and John Neff's canyon property and building up his own ranch near Point of the Mountain. The days were passing as if in a dream.

Suddenly he heard his cue. He felt his throat tighten. He scuttled self-consciously away from the curtain, directly to center stage. The walk seemed endless. The house was packed. He struggled not to notice Mary Ann, but when he heard whispers, he wondered if they were disparaging and if she had heard them.

Before him stood a Peruvian with a spear. On cue, Rockwell drew his sword. The Peruvian performed adequately–he finished an impassioned speech. Rockwell readied himself for the reply.

He forgot his reply.

He glared at the Peruvian with a face of terror. He broke into a cold sweat. He heard a whisper back stage. The director was attempting to prompt him, but he could not distinguish the words.

Rockwell would rather have faced a thousand screaming warriors, he thought to himself, than to face this.

The director's words came louder. People in the audience began to chuckle.

Rockwell still could not hear him. The director spoke louder. More people chuckled.

Rockwell, still not able to hear the words, decided to do the only thing he could under the circumstances.....he faced the Peruvian and exclaimed, "Excuse me."

He lumbered over to the curtain where the director told him his line.

He then clumped back across the stage to the Peruvian and

declared with boldness, "Another word, grey-headed ruffian, and I strike."

The audience rocked with laughter.

Rockwell gawked blank-faced at the Peruvian. Why were they laughing? It suddenly struck him–not only had the line been unintentionally comical, but his delivery had been melodramatic, and he sounded foolish. He cringed. He sought out Mary Ann's eyes and within them he found sympathy.

And then he forgot what he was supposed to do next. "Do something," said Rockwell to the Peruvian.

"It's your turn."

"To do what?" whispered Rockwell.

The audience now roared. The Peruvian blushed.

Rockwell collected his composure and thought a moment. He was supposed to do something? What was he supposed to do?

He turned to the director behind the curtain and mumbled loudly, "Shall I stick him?"

The audience exploded. Rockwell glowered at the audience and saw Mary Ann struggling for compassion–until she too burst into laughter.

In agony he stood there, frozen. He realized what he must look like, when suddenly, uncontrollably, he also began to laugh.

Backstage, as Rockwell washed off his make-up, he suddenly relived the entire scene–and in anger kicked a table.....and then again he broke out laughing.....

As the crowd dispersed, Rockwell and the other actors greeted them in the lobby. He waited for Mary Ann, anxious to laugh with her over the disaster, but simultaneously wondering if she would even accompany him home.

Then Brigham Young ambled up to him.

Across the lobby walked Simon Lefevre, dressed fastidiously and unescorted. Beside him walked William Drummond, arm and arm with a tall, laughing woman. The woman was noticeably less attractive than Drummond's wife, according to gossip. Drummond's wife, in fact, had just arrived by stage from San Francisco that day. Drummond however had convinced her how tired she was, and had taken this other woman to the theatre. He appreciated the companionship of any good woman, especially one who enjoyed the arts, and he was especially proud of this particular companion. Presently, he spotted Rockwell and Young–and he nodded Simon LeFevre over to Young's conversation.

Lefevre glided across the lobby to Rockwell and Young unobtrusively, and listened to the conversation between Young and Rockwell.

"Get rid of the cattle rustlers," Young told Rockwell. "The outlying settlements are being plagued by them. They say they're bleeding them dry. Bring them in if you can."

"Rustlers don't like being brought in."

"Do it anyway."

"What if I can't?"

Young sighed. "Then do what you need to."

Outside, walking with Drummond and his escort down State Street, Lefevre relayed what he had heard to Drummond.

"We've got our fuel," said Drummond, cooly. "Do what you can to burn him."

Taking Mary Ann home that night Rockwell rode on the buckboard with his arm around her and realized how good–how comfortable and natural–it felt to have the woman beside him.

He told her he would not be seeing her for a few days.

She didn't say anything.

"I know it'll be hard," he continued, "but I'll be back soon."

Again she said nothing.

"I reckon you wonder where I'm going. Well, it ain't to California or nothin'–I'll still be around here."

Still no reply.

"I guess you wonder what I'm gonna be doin'." And then he told her.

She tried to understand, and she tried to fight the disappointment, but she simply did not approve. Certainly someone other than Rockwell could perform the task–particularly a bloody and danger-frought task such as this assignment involved–because, afterall, he had given his whole life to assisting Joseph and then Brigham and now more? If any man deserved to settle down, she figured, it was he. And she was the woman he should settle down with. She caught him studying her.

Not only did she remain silent, she looked down. But finally forced a smile.

After he took her home he returned to his cabin. In the middle of the night, through a deep sleep, he heard a loud knock. He jerked awake. The door flew open and dust whirled inside. He squinted into the darkness and cocked his revolver. Fresh sage filled his nostrils and the breeze cooled the sweat from his face. Quickly he made out the figures of two men in the darkness.

"You Port Rockwell?"

Rockwell was not sure what to do but finally he answered. "I know where he's at."

"We need him right away, if you can direct us to him."

"Who are you?"

"I'm Nick Searle, this is How Chambers." Both men were medium, lean, and appeared to be outgoing. Both hailed from New England and were college educated.

"What do you want?" said Rockwell.

"We're the assistant managers of the bank."

"Good. You didn't answer my question."

Searle, the older man, explained that they had just been robbed for the second time in eight days, and they finally asked, "Where might we find Mr. Rockwell?"

"Follow me."

As they followed Rockwell outside they saw his long hair braided behind his head and falling half way down his back, and they glanced at one another. They knew.

As Rockwell and the two bankers rode in a buggy they passed William Drummond. The judge scowled at the three men.

The two bankers made a remark of Drummond's "bench mistress" he kept in the courtroom. Drummond had found another woman, and had for several days kept her with him during court proceedings and even after hours–both for companionship and to infuriate the locals.

"Who cares about her, really?" said Chambers, still chuckling. "It's his idiot court decisions that riles me. If I was a Mormon I'd be riding him out of town on a rail."

"I don't think he's so bad," said Searle. "He's affable enough in the tavern."

"I don't care if he fights the church–he happens to fight everything that helps local business," argued Chambers. "And that's where it kicks me in the teeth. It hurts banking."

"Yeah, well we're on straight salary anyway–we'll live."

Rockwell meanwhile said nothing.

Three days later Rockwell found the tracks of the five robbers. Riding beside Rockwell, Searle and Chambers were exhausted. The next day they came upon a miner's hut.

"So this is their hide-out?" said Searle. "We'll head back to the city for a posse."

"They'd be gone by the time you get back," said Rockwell. "We'll take 'em now."

"We?"

Rockwell observed their horrified faces. "I'll take 'em."

"It's suicide for you. We'll get a posse."

Rockwell rode down the gully alone, and the two bankers watched.

16

Five of the outlaws played poker while the sixth stood guard outside the hut and shouted to the others.

All six stared in amazement at a man with shoulder length hair approaching the hut so brazenly.

"Whoever gets him in the ear gets his horse," said Rulon Thompson, their leader.

"Naw, he don't know nothin'," said another, "Or he wouldn't be here."

Suddenly Rockwell lurched from his horse and hid behind a

boulder.

Thompson tensed. "I told you we shoulda got him while we could. He knows who we are."

"Don't matter, we'll pick him off soon enough," said Thompson.

The six outlaws loaded and cocked their weapons. They heard the long-haired man's voice echo down the canyon.

"You boys come out and surrender."

Thompson laughed. "Did I hear what I thought I heard?" Three of them began firing towards Rockwell.

The others chuckled.

Gunfire suddenly shattered their chuckling. Two bodies jolted backwards and one spun on impact, as Rockwell returned their fire.

The other three still unhurt aimed directly at Rockwell and fired–but all they saw was a flashing weapon from the man bounding down the hill. One got off a second shot, but seconds later he fell forward with a bullet hole in his forehead.

Rockwell dived into the door and fan-fired six more shots. Bodies jolted and jerked, and soon the remaining three also lay perfectly still.

Rockwell stopped, panted a moment, and viewed the scene. Behind him appeared the two bankers. They stopped in the doorway and gawked. "I think the problem has been taken care of," said Searle.

Lunch that afternoon consisted of bread and jerkey, as Rockwell led the two bankers back to Salt Lake City. Rockwell remained quiet with the two men; all he could think of was Mary Ann..... and then something strange happened in the middle of the night.

He awakened in a cold sweat.

He relived the gunfight.

And to his surprise he was not repulsed by it. He had found in it in fact a feeling of excitement. The dream brought back every vivid moment. He was absorbed by the images he recalled.

He felt somehow worthwhile. He had accomplished something for society. He would report his feelings to Mary Ann. The next day at sunset–with red rays glistening across the snow–he delivered the bankers to their city, and by the following morning he was at Mary Ann's cabin.

There, she studied his face carefully, missing not an expression as he recalled the scene.

She feared what she saw.

He walked to the creek with her and sat on a fallen tree beside the iced-over water. He kissed her cheeks and felt the warmth of her skin on his lips. He could not get the gunfight out of his mind.

In Illinois he had not relived such scenes.....but here, something adventurous caught his imagination about the wind and the mountains and the stars coupled with the badge he now fondled in his hand.

Mary Ann watched him and she trembled ever so faintly.

As the weeks passed, she found him visiting her less often. He visited her once or twice a week, with several weeks where he would not see her at all, and he would report of only some of his adventures. He grew tired of telling her those things which excited him but which only mildly interested her. Actually her feelings were of disgust.

He was on a rampage of killing outlaws.

As hard as she tried, she could not feel the pride he felt. Nevertheless, she still loved him with all her mind. As he loved her.

They spoke little of marriage. She hoped his feelings would change from his work, that somehow he would tire of it.

Due to what she perceived as a growing obsession to accomplish Brigham's mandate and to drive the lawless from the territory–and because of Rockwell's innate pride, desiring no problems in his territory as long as he wore the badge–the remainder of that year she heard of corpses strewn from Tucson to Salt Lake City in a trail of blood and sage, and by autumn's end, her man had created a legend second to none.

Bandits were both curious and superstitious over Rockwell's reputed immunity from bullets. He was the topic of conversation to such extent that they began composing ballads about him.

It was all happening too fast for Mary Ann. Trying to deal with his lifestyle was almost too difficult for her, of course, and for their relationship, yet the stories which swept the communities made her initially proud–but simultaneously jealous–of what he was accomplishing.

Soon, however, she felt she had to compete with his legends. Such that, by Christmas, she was beginning to resent them.

And he didn't seem to slow up. The accolades being poured on him from townsfolk in Salt Lake City and from the desert communities seemed to drive him on.

However, they were mixed. Enemies to Brigham Young and the church called him ruthless, an assassin for Brigham, and used his name to frighten their children into obedience. They labeled him as a destroying angel of punishment. But active Mormons perceived him as something of a folk hero.

Mary Ann meanwhile heard the legends growing daily and was becoming increasingly disconcerted. Eleven months had passed since they had had a normal week together. He was on her mind constantly, and while he was off tracking outlaws, she, too, was in his mind. He assured her each time he'd see her that he would back off from his assignments soon, that the lawless in fact would move out of his territory due to his reputation; yet she perceived the pride he was taking in that reputation. He did not flaunt it, however, nor dwell on it, and for that she was grateful. In fact she was proud of the way he was seemingly building his reputation only to implant within the lawless a fear of the badge, and not for himself. Still, the whole thing bothered her. He was not hers yet.

Drummond heard the legends too–at once angered and pleased–knowing he would have all the brush he needed to burn the Utah hierarchy. Brigham Young meanwhile heard the legends and smiled. The bigger Rockwell's reputation, he figured, the less problems he'd have with the outlaws.

Drummond called a meeting with Simon Lefevre.

"What about the outlaws?" said Drummond. "Tell me everything you know." He knew Lefevre had been investigating with energy.

"He's supposed to be able to kill anybody who gets in his way," said Lefevre. "Ever since he was jailed he has a hatred for anything that persecutes his people. They say he has opened a blood bath on the lawless."

"Who has he killed exactly?"

"Most of the hombres who make their way West and happen to get killed never get identified. Their associates aren't stupid enough to come into the cities to file reports–so a man like Rockwell has basically left a trail like any lawman has–with no names under the gravestones. Neighbors say the Indians respect him because they can't kill him. Anyway, Rockwell believes his legend that he can't die, and that makes him all the more ferocious. He'll walk into any den of desperadoes and cut them down. There are no judges or juries."

"That's what we can nail him on," said Drummond, sitting up straighter.

"No court would indict him."

"My court will."

"Not unless you pack the jury–the folks out here believe religiously in frontier justice–no jury would convict him."

"But if what you say is correct," said Drummond, "Rockwell doesn't bring outlaws back alive, and certainly not that many would oppose him. He must be murdering them."

"Outlaws will do anything to not face prison–they'll always draw on the law rather than be taken–and so far nobody can outgun him."

"I don't know," said Drummond. "He must be sneaking up on them, not even trying for arrests."

"I'm just telling you what I know."

"Do you know how many he's killed?"

Lefevre shook his head. "They say he hunts down bandits like jackrabbits."

"You sure he only shoots outlaws?"

"That's all I know so far."

Drummond perceived something in Simon Lefevre that bothered him. He discerned in his aide's eyes a certain admiration for the killer. "According to talk in the tavern," said Drummond, his voice wavering slightly from emotion, "he kills more than outlaws."

"You asked for the facts." Lefevre noticed Drummond's eyes slightly moist from anger.

At a border tavern in California a dozen and a half outlaws played poker by kerosene light. Whiskey ran free and women roamed both the tavern and the brothel upstairs.

"Nobody can kill the fool," mumbled Ted Shearson, the man dealing the cards.

"Bill Sharky said he could kill him," argued Dan Stewart.

"And nobody's heard of Bill Sharky since," replied Shearson.

Leonard Nuckles looked skeptically at Shearson. "So you believe the legends?"

"I do."

Others in the tavern laughed.

"All right," said Shearson, "Who here has the guts to disprove the legends?"

No one spoke.

"Twenty dollar gold piece here says nobody will do it." Shearson tossed a coin onto the table, sat back, and smiled. Those who had laughed refused to meet his eyes.

The bartender added another twenty dollar gold piece.

Still no one took the bet. Four others threw in gold pieces.

The other twelve men in the tavern had quit laughing long ago. Suddenly from a far corner of the dimly-lit saloon, a stout man with a brown mustache rose and swaggered to the table. All eyes turned to him. He stopped at the table and threw down a gold piece.

"Bartender, you keep the kitty. If anything's lost from it by the time I get back, two bullet holes will be where your eyes once were."

That afternoon the same man was riding north to add another notch to his gunbelt, a notch that would be his most highly prized yet, one that was now worth a small fortune since the entire saloon had taken him on. He thrived on challenges. He already had six notches on his belt from California sheriffs.....and five of them had come from similar bets.....

Mary Ann Neff lay asleep in her cabin when she heard a metallic click on the front porch.

While she wondered if Rockwell would ever slow his legend-making, to the point of settling down to normal and even asking her to marry him, her gut feeling told her to simply be patient.

Whereas she had rebelled against the institution in Illinois, she had with the passing of a few years mellowed somewhat in her views. Although she was still not particularly captured by the idea of marriage and its resulting losses of freedom.....she did happen to love Rockwell.

As she donned a gown to inspect the metallic noises outside she suddenly had the vague impression that a man other than Rockwell or her father was outside. She stepped outside and shivered. Suddenly someone from behind grabbed her.....

She gasped. She was turned to face the man and she beheld his eyes glistening in the moonlight. He quickly pressed her face to his face and before she could pull away.....

She was melting under Rockwell's kiss.

At the Great Salt Lake Saloon, William W. Drummond sat from his corner table staring at the window. It was Saturday night and the place was packed. The tavern was dimly lit and the smoke was so thick it made his eyes smart.

Simon Lefevre strolled up and sat across from him.

"Judge, you ever heard of a Frank Slade?"

"Not that I recall," said Drummond.

"He's got a record, and he's in town asking about Rockwell."

Drummond lifted his gaze from the window to Lefevre's face. "Find him and get him to my office."

After kissing Mary Ann, Rockwell found himself walking her to the creek where they often would sit on the fallen tree and throw rocks into the water. Ripples would spread under the moonlight. And on this night he told her of his deepest feelings. He had just returned from a scouting trip to California, where he had no encounters with outlaws, yet had still felt useful to the territory. He also had felt productive.

She hoped, from his demeanor, that he was ready to settle down and put away his guns. She told him he even looked different. But she was disappointed when he told her he was leaving again.

Nevertheless, he assured her that her impressions of him were not mistaken. He looked different, indeed, and for a reason. The adventure was out of him. She was foremost on his mind. He assured her he would be, as she had dreamed, putting away his guns.

Most of the outlaws had fled the territory, and his perfectionistic desire to rid himself of them all was, as he at last had realized, an impossibility. He was pleased in what he had accomplished, and could hope for nothing more of himself.

He was facing reality. And the foremost desire within that reality now was to settle down with her.

He would now only perform a relatively short assignment for Brigham Young–to find a location for the new penitentiary–which would hopefully only last a week or two–and then he would return.

She was both ecstatic over the prospects and uncertain.

Weeks passed.

At the Neff cabin she waited for his return. One night John Neff carved a wooden totem as he sat before the fireplace.

"One thing, Mary Ann, I gotta hand to ole Port–he did most the ax-swinging himself on that canyon road–and that saved us a lot of money." The county had required a road to be completed before Rockwell's and Neff's canyon could sell lumber. The canyon was under full operation now, and both men were profiting from their investment. Neff managed the operation in his spare time while a foreman actually supervised. Rockwell was merely a silent partner. Mary Ann had found her father encouraging their relationship, and through the months he had advised her not to give up on the man, although she now often wondered if Rockwell were not indeed a silent partner of sorts with her as well. "I can't go on like this forever, Papa."

"Then find yourself another man."

She said nothing. She was frustrated with his long absense and she was angry. "He just can't seem to keep to his plans—if he was even telling me the truth."

"So where do you reckon he's at?"

Certainly Rockwell had completed his location-scouting for the penitentiary by now, she mused, so why hadn't she heard from him?

"I reckon he's gone off to hunt outlaws again," she snapped.

"Honey....." said John Neff, lifting his eyes from the totem and noticing her face set firmly on the flames, "Why do you keep seeing him?"

Mary Ann lay asleep when she was startled awake by a tap at the window.

She looked outside and saw Rockwell smiling up at her.

Outside, she walked hand in hand with him under the moonlight toward the well. She pumped him for answers like she would within seconds begin pumping the well handle.

Rockwell was in a talkative mood. She noticed him rarely inbetween: he was either as open as an hour-glass or as reticent as a wild animal. She further observed that he was usually most sharing in his conversation after long departures, but within days would usually retire into his own mind and there sometimes practically hibernate. The feelings he had for her were every bit as strong as in Illinois, he assured her, and he claimed he thought of her incessantly.

But his new assignments for Brigham Young and its accompanying responsibilities had forced him to face the reality of holding off once again on asking her to marry him.

"What are you talking about?" she said. "I thought you said

you'd given up on the outlaws."

"I have." He promised her that all he needed was the time necessary for their relationship. He wanted to do the marriage right.

She still did not know what he was talking about. "So what kind of obstacle do you have–what do you see? Is the excitement gone?"

His excitement for her was as strong as ever, he told her, and he assured her he needed only to finish a new series of assignments for Brigham Young before he could settle down. But the gunfighting and the danger, for the most part, was gone. What he did not tell her was that another fear had cropped up: he wondered about their future; specifically, if she would retain her feelings for him over the years if other assignments might arrive that could take him away. He could not put himself through the torture of being married to and in love with a woman who refused to support his lifestyle, he told himself. To the very extent he loved Mary Ann, he also feared her.

And deeper: Luana's words still haunted him.....he wondered if he were not indeed an "incurable adventurer." What if, after establishing a life with this woman, and despite all the feelings he had for her, the taste of the wild wind happened to beckon him– like the salt of the air that entices the sailor to the sea? Perhaps he could not stay on a ranch, imprisoned to only his own acres and his children, when he was used to being a free man accountable to and responsible for no one but himself. He had gone through all that with Luana. And maybe she was right.

But perhaps what mattered most was that he loved Mary Ann. She was still a dream to him. And if it came down to choosing dreams, certainly she was the more powerful. He only wondered about the future.....

He also wondered if–when it might come down to his keeping his mind–she would accept him taking temporary freedom–and, basically, if she could simply accept who he really was.

His fears were becoming confirmed by the very next words he heard.

"So why were you gone–and where were you?" she said tersely. "And will you do it again?"

"I found Brigham the best spot I could for the penitentiary. Then he sent me and George Bean off to see the Ute Injuns again."

Mary Ann caught her disfavor and crossed it; she tried to understand the nature of Rockwell's assignment. This time she decided to ask questions, and to try to understand what made the man she loved do what he did.....which was to impulsively seek danger.

Rockwell told her of his problems with Chief Walker. Mary Ann already knew of the infamous chief. Since Rockwell had last seen the Ute leader, Walker had declared war on the whites. It had started when James Ivie in Springville had protected a squaw from being beaten by her brave–and through the tussle Ivie had ended up killing several Ute Indians.

Chief Walker had retaliated and sent several war parties on the Mormon settlements, killing two dozen men and causing hundreds of others to abandon their farms.

The war had been at a crossroads when Rockwell and Bean arrived on the scene.

"So what happened?" said Mary Ann.

"We met with Chief Walker to soften him up for a meeting with Brigham. Before the meeting started, though, ole Chief Walker went into a tantrum to show off his power. He lashed Chief Beaverads across the face with a knife and we had to keep them from killing each other. Because we did save them, Walker was grateful and he agreed to see Brigham. He's waiting for Brigham to come see him now."

"And you take credit for all this?" smiled Mary Ann, chidingly.

"Of course," winked Rockwell. "With a little help from Brother Bean."

"Thank heavens for Brother Bean," said Mary Ann. She knew the Indians loved George Bean. He was a one-armed missionary/ frontiersman who had a way with the red men.

Bean's wife earlier had taught Mary Ann how to plait Rockwell's long hair, and the two women had been like sisters when their menfolk had been away on assignment. This time, however, Mary Ann had stayed home and had not even learned Bean was away, so she had not known Rockwell was off negotiating with the Indians. This was one of the few activities of Rockwell's of which she approved. She placed her arms around his neck and kissed him.

Rockwell knew that despite all the fears and uncertainties he felt about her and about them, he could not survive another month without her. He loved her with too much of his soul. He then told her things she substantially already knew: that she had the "patience of a prairie dog and the love of a she-bear in season." Terms that she would otherwise find insulting had they come from another man, but which, from Rockwell, seemed almost romantic.

She listened of poetry in his life, and soon she found herself trembling as he asked her to "tie the final knot."

Her throat tightened.

17

Frank Slade had more than a small fortune in bets riding on his ability to shoot Porter Rockwell. He also now had a mandate from William Drummond. He had met with the judge and they had drawn up plans.

He slowed his horse near the general store–the one which he had learned Rockwell most frequented. " 'Know where I might find him today?" he said to the proprietor, slapping some change on the counter for chewing tobacco.

"You haven't heard?" said the proprietor.

"I wouldn't be askin' if I had," said Slade.

"He's busy."

Inside Brigham Young's house, Porter Rockwell and Mary Ann Neff stood before the Mormon chieftain and exchanged vows of love and loyalty. Rockwell took her in his arms and kissed her as he never had. The feelings of his wildest dreams were complete. Tears came to her eyes and he wiped them from her cheeks. He finally pulled away from her.

George Bean let out a whistle and Lot Smith began applauding. A dozen Neff neighbors joined in and the cheers became thunderous.

"Didn't think you'd ever stop," said Lot Smith. "And I reckon I'm surprised she's even here."

Rockwell glanced at him curiously.

"Don't feel bad, my friend, it's just that you have the hardest time keepin' a woman liking you of any man I've ever met," said Smith, chidingly.

Rockwell glared at the obnoxious, but nevertheless in his own way, somewhat likeable old scout.

Brigham Young smiled at the unusual proceedings, and soon saw the couple stride out of his house to Rockwell's wagon.

The spring morning invigorated them. The first week of May always had in the new territory.

Across the street was a stranger in their midst, dressed in light brown, leaning against a hitching post, and staring at the couple riding past.

Rockwell spotted Frank Slade and nodded. Slade nodded back. Neither man had met and Rockwell figured him just another admirer.

There was something in the man's gaze however that made Rockwell feel uneasy. He shrugged it off and rode away elated with his new bride.

Slade meanwhile remounted his roan. He would not lose Rockwell from his sight if it killed him. He had strict orders from William W. Drummond, and he knew exactly what he had to do.....

Mary Ann slept soundly while Rockwell stared out the window at the moon. He still could not believe the fact that through all the torture of his life, he was lying beside what to most men would seem a mirage–simply too enthralling, and sculpturally beautiful at that, to be real. The stars he then studied took him, as it were, to other times, other lives, distantly. He was not sure if he were dreaming that, too, when, through the pane outside, he suddenly heard noises.

Rockwell arose with his gun.

Mary Ann asked him not to go outside.

Outside, he stepped towards the well, when he heard footsteps behind him. He twirled and saw a man staring at him, eyes wide with fright.

"Brother Larson, what can I do for you?" said Rockwell.

"Heather–my 15 year old–she's gone."

"What do you mean?"

"With the gold-seekers," said Larson. "She sold feed to a bunch the other day and they was eyeing her over real good."

"Where they at?" said Rockwell.

"The immigrant camp, just outside Tooele." Larson was a light-eyed, light-complexioned, first-generation Scandinavian who had been raised in North Carolina and had converted to the faith. This was his first trial in his six months of Mormon living.

Several months, meanwhile, had passed since Rockwell's wedding. He had not, of course, taken on any outlaw encounters, but rather, at Mary Ann's urging, performed assignments for Brigham Young only to negotiate peace with the Ute Indians. Primarily he had stayed at the ranch and continued building it up, becoming closer and closer to his bride.

Some days, just when he had thought he was perfectly satisfied with the life, he felt that inner urging.....

And now, as Rockwell looked into Larson's eyes, he knew he could not let the man down. Nor could he stay away from the danger. He glanced back at the porch and saw Mary Ann glaring at him. His eyes penetrated hers and he found himself conscientiously up against her will, and, to an extent, her values for the first time yet. Their eyes read each other and finally she knew his decision. She turned back into the cabin.

Frank Slade had performed the first phase of his assignment for William Drummond–he had held Rockwell under surveillance for three continuous weeks after Rockwell's wedding, then had reported to Drummond and waited several months in his hotel room for the next move. All his bills were paid from Drummond's budget. Nevertheless, Slade had grown impatient with Drummond, despite the fact he'd have the protection of the law if he followed orders. He had not counted on months passing, and he felt embarrassed that his comrades at the California border tavern were likely labeling him now as either a corpse or a coward. He further knew they dare not divide up his portion of the bet among themselves until more time passed.

Frank Slade had been planning for months on literally cutting off Rockwell's head and taking it back in a bag. This would not only prove his success and win for himself the plaudits and the money, but it would halt forever the superstitions about Rockwell's legend that rankled him.

Rockwell rode into the night wind. The moon lit a golden pathway in the desert before him, and he followed the tracks of the young woman's kidnappers. He was worrying over Mary Ann, and he hoped this would be his final outlaw confrontation. It did feel good, however.....But he wanted to reassure her that this was only temporary. Certainly he would not be leaving her again.....

And he hoped she would not be too disappointed when he returned. Perhaps she'd forget the incident entirely.

The fact that she was several days away from bearing their first child might mellow her, he figured. He worried about her nonetheless, no matter what he tried telling himself.

He wondered if he should have stayed.

He would get this job done quickly.

By dawn the next day he found the tracks leading over a bed of rocks. Although the kidnappers had taken a route to evade pursuers, he picked up the trail without even slowing his horse.

Seven men ate near a campfire. Forty yards away a bearded chap sat beside Heather Larson, cutting away her clothing.

"Hurry up," called another at the campfire. "I want a turn."

While Heather was staked to the ground, the man leaned forward and kissed her neck, then bit into it. She noted the fellow smelled like horse sweat. He ripped away her blouse.

She loosened a leg and sent her foot into his groin. He lurched backwards and writhed on the ground. She struggled a hand free.

Another man appeared over her, holding a branding iron.

"Go ahead, honey, try kicking again." He slowly moved the branding iron towards her neck.

She could see its red glow even in the sunlight. "Don't....." she said.

The branding iron came slowly towards the curve of her neck.....she felt the heat from the hot metal as it approached her skin.....and just as it reached the point of pain, she heard an exploding crack.

The man with the branding iron dropped over her, and the iron sizzled into the dust. Heather heard another shot and simultaneously saw blood and flesh fly out the front of her attacker's head.

A horseman with long hair came suddenly flying into camp and the remaining six ran for their weapons.

Heather saw the horseman fire–one man was hit and spun on

impact, landing face forward into a scrub oak. Another bullet shot blood from the back of his head–simultaneously flipping him over the tree in a somersault. He fell forward and landed face down in a vat of buffalo dung.

Heather saw two men aim point blank and fire–but the long-haired horseman merely answered with two more shots and both men flipped over backwards with bullet holes through their foreheads.

The other three ran for cover. The horseman casually reloaded one revolver, then took three studious, carefully aimed shots.

All three men were stopped. Two of them, still alive, crawled agonizingly for cover.

Heather saw the horseman take aim again, and with four fast shots he ended their crawling.

The horseman now gazed across the peaceful camp and beheld blood flowing profusely from every corpse. Most of them still had their eyes open. He blew out a sigh and trotted methodically towards Heather.

She could not see the man's face for the blinding sun, but when he stopped over her, his head blocked out the bright rays and she observed his worried expression behind his heavy beard, and then she recognized him.

That night, Porter Rockwell took her home.

He returned to the John Neff cabin at midnight, arriving just in time to see Mary Ann give birth to their first child. Mary Ann clasped his hand. It was March 11, 1855, and in the warm late winter breeze–as the midwife pulled the infant from Mary Ann–Rockwell took one look at the scene–and fainted.

18

Rockwell took care of his wife and child for a solid month. He considered that a lengthy period of time to stay home with domestic chores. It had taken Mary Ann nearly three weeks to recover sufficiently, and now that she had he was ready for a short change of scenery.

He knew she would not be pleased, so he did not tell her his plans. In fact he tried fighting them. Surely because of the feelings he had for her, he told himself, he should not even want to leave.

But he felt hemmed in.

So, when George Bean showed up at his ranch with news that Brigham Young desired him and Bean to renegotiate with Chief Walker, Rockwell was ecstatic.

He tried hiding it, and even acted perturbed that he had to leave his family, but Mary Ann saw through it.

She cried when Rockwell and Bean rode away on horseback.

"I'll be back in a few days," he told her, stopping his horse and looking back at her on the porch.

He could not understand himself. The first night under the stars as he and Bean watched the campfire flames, he said nothing. Bean could tell something was on his mind, and let him alone to think.

Rockwell wondered if he were worthy of such a woman as Mary Ann. Why couldn't he stay on the ranch and be satisfied to make her his entire life? He loved her with all his soul. What was wrong with him?

William W. Drummond was explicit in his proposal to Simon Lefevre and Frank Slade. They sat in Drummond's office and reviewed their strategy. Drummond would continue gaining all information possible about Rockwell and finding evidence to indict him, then would give the signal to Slade to disprove the lawman's "supernatural immunity."

While Lefevre had interviewed local government and church officials to glean what he could of the lawman's assignments–bribing certain record-keepers of both institutions–Slade meanwhile had once again begun following the lawman, and now reported of it to Drummond and Lefevre.

"Rockwell went with George Bean, and I followed him off and on for several days. First thing they did was see Chief Walker. Rockwell wanted to prepare the chief for negotiations with Brigham Young. Young was coming in just a few hours to see the chief. So Rockwell slipped the chief a bottle of whiskey to soften him up. But the plan backfired. Rockwell got the chief stoned out of his brain."

"So what did he do next?" said Drummond.

"Him and Bean visited Walker again and nearly got themselves killed," said Slade. "But they escaped and later talked the old chief into trading with the whites again."

"Where did Rockwell go from there?"

"Him and Bean saved eight Mexican Indian slaves owned by the Utes from being butchered by the Utes. Rockwell and Bean gave the slaves their freedom. That's as far as I followed him, and then I come back here."

Drummond blew a smoke ring. "Rockwell interfered with slave trading? That's illegal."

"Why's it illegal?" said Lefevre.

"James Calhoun, Superintendent of Indian Affairs, has approved of Indian slave trading with the Mexicans," said Drummond. "And it's none of the Mormons' business. We can nail Rockwell on that alone."

"You need something bigger," said Lefevre, who, in some ways

still felt somewhat sympathetic towards Rockwell, but attempted
to hide it from Drummond. Nevertheless, Lefevre knew a promo-
tion was in the wind, and that it was based on his ability to perform.
As Lefevre understood it, though mistakenly, Drummond alone
possessed the power to recommend him to a district office in San
Francisco, away from this puritanical desert. And for that Lefevre
was itching to help Drummond any way he could.

Rockwell returned to Mary Ann and his child. His daughter's
name was Mary Amanda Rockwell, and he was pleased with her
more than he had even imagined he could be. He felt, however, the
more he had thought about it, that he had the right to leave the
ranch if he wished. He should not have to feel imprisoned, and
Mary Ann should feel secure in his love for her enough to allow him
to leave anytime he needed to, for no matter how long.

He was therefore somewhat resentful when he found her quietly critical of him when he returned.

When he announced to her that he would be leaving on two
more short trips–for several days each–he expected her to again
silently seethe, but he was instead surprised to find her encouraging him in these assignments.

She had attended church and heard sermons from the lay ministry that spouses should support each other in whatever occupa-
tional or church assignments the other was given. Rockwell's
seemed to overlap: for both territorial and church service. She felt
it her obligation to support him, and attempted to take on a new
attitude. She fixed him his favorite meal–steak and potatoes and
vegetables, and her luscious brown bread with fresh butter.

He knew however as they spoke in bed that night that she was
trying to cover her real feelings. Despite her obligations, she was
the kind of woman who needed him home, she realized, despite
what she had learned in church. She had fairly warned him of that
before their marriage. And he had gone into the arrangement with
that full understanding. Therefore, she grew in her resentments
the more she thought on the matter. Rockwell could not sleep,
sensitive to the fact that something inside her did not settle right.

When he tried pointing out to her the necessity of his two up-
coming assignments, she nodded as if to understand. Rockwell
told himself that she did understand. But as the night wore on, he
was not able to sleep beside her, sensing her still conscious, although she was feigning sleep, and worrying, yet not willing to talk.

He arose and walked outside.

Under the moonlight he strolled and thought to himself. She presently came outside and put her arms around him. He kissed her and they went inside and embraced. She knew what she felt for him and she would work from there.

Drummond sat in his office with Slade and Lefevre.

"So where did he go on his first assingment?" asked Drummond.

Lefevre was proud that he had the answers. He had interviewed numerous church and state government clerks to find the answers, and had even "casually" met a few women in general stores –after having followed them for blocks–and flirted with them while shopping to learn what their husbands knew. He was proud of his charm and now of his information.

"Pahvant braves had killed eight Pacific Railroad crewmen," began Lefevre.

"I heard about that," said Drummond. "How can we use it?"

"Captain Gunnison, the crew boss, once wrote a book critical of the Mormons. In the taverns here some people think Young sent Rockwell to take care of Gunnison."

"Did anybody else have a motivation?" said Drummond.

"Two Pahvant braves had just been killed by Missouri immigrants, so the Pahvants themselves did have as strong of a motivation as Rockwell had for the retaliation."

"But there's no proof?"

"None."

"What did Rockwell do next?" said Drummond.

"He went to Fort Bridger to give James S. Brown a license from Young to trade with the Indians." Brown was one of seven Mormons of the nine white men at Sutter's Mill who had discovered gold. "Then, Rockwell came back here and spent a few more days with his wife."

"Only a few days? I heard the man was ridiculously in love with her."

"I don't know what's going on in his mind," answered Lefevre. "But U.S. Army Colonel Steptoe next hired him to search out the best route to California. I know Rockwell had told her before he accepted both assignments that he was going, because she had told some of her neighbors. I don't know how well that set with her, but at least she knew what he was up to. I talked to her neighbors and to the colonel's quartermaster, Captain Rufus Ingalls. According to him, Colonel Steptoe thinks Rockwell is the best guide in the West. But when Rockwell returned to his wife again, I think he found a rift in his marriage."

Rockwell arrived at his ranch just before dawn–to find the cabin deserted. He went outside and called for Mary Ann, then noticed in the dust an arrow pointed to George Bean's ranch.

He galloped off to the Bean ranch and got Geroge Bean out of bed.

"I'm afraid she hasn't been feelin' too good, Port," said Bean.

"Is that all she said?"

"Yeah, and that she's gone back to her folks awhile till she feels better."

Rockwell knew exactly what she meant. Bean didn't know; Mary Ann wasn't the type to spread dirty linen before the public, although she was known to share with them her concerns–only tastefully, and not in a manner that would cast aspersions on her husband's character.

Rockwell immediately mounted up and rode off to see her.

"I'm afraid she doesn't want to see you," said Neff's wife, Mary Ann's stepmother.

"Well I'm her husband and I can see her if I want."

"Not according to her," she said. "I'd advise you to stay out of here."

Rockwell began opening the door to march in to see her, when Mrs. Neff informed him Mary Ann wasn't there anyway.

"Then where is she?"

"She doesn't want you to know."

Rockwell sighed and relaxed. She could be anywhere–shopping for material, visiting, or hiding at any friend's or neighbor's home, he figured. And then he realized–if she didn't want to see him, why should he force the issue? If she loved him, she'd come back to him.

He rode away, angrier than he had been in years. He had not planned on accepting the assignment because of her–in fact he had turned it down– but now he rode off to see Colonel Steptoe and announce that he had changed his mind.....he would guide Colonel Steptoe personally to California.....

When Rockwell returned from a three month journey to California he spent two weeks visiting George Bean before mustering the courage to actually return to his cabin.

When he did return to his cabin, he found she was still gone. He discovered painfully–and to his surprise–the impact of the feelings he had tried to dismiss. He had been angry at her criticalness, her not vocally confronting him on what bothered her, her leaving him, and her attempt to impede his freedom, he had figured, but now he felt only one dominent emotion: the fear of losing her.

He rode away from his still-deserted cabin to the Neff ranch in Mill Creek Canyon. He dismounted and strode to the door.

"She's not here," said her stepmother again.

"Where' she at?"

Her own cabin."

"Where's that?" said Rockwell.

"Her father's building it for her over that knoll."

Rockwell galloped across the knoll and reined in at a crude cabin under construction. Mary Ann was helping her father haul wood to the site. Her child, Mary Amanda, was fenced nearby and crying. When Mary Ann beheld Rockwell, she stopped and stared.

Rockwell's head was practically bald.

John Neff also gloated in amazement, then quickly excused himself and left for his cabin.

"I'm sorry I was gone so long," said Rockwell.

"That's something new for you," she said.

"Being gone so long?"

"Apologizing," she said.

"But I did come lookin' for you."

"Before you took off for three months?" she added, still upset. "I was just getting away from you for about two days. I think there's a difference."

"I'm sorry–I shouldn't have." He noticed her staring at his shaven head.

"I guess you wanna know what happened to my hair."

As she gaped at him the additional disappointment of his hair being gone was obvious. "I guess what Joseph said about your hair protecting you don't mean a whole lot to you anymore," she said.

He refused to address her comment. He peered off at the horizon, not knowing what to say. "Should be a good season for cherries, don't you think?"

"So you got Colonel Steptoe safely to Carlifornia?" she said, trying to hold back her feelings. "At least that's what Brigham said you did."

"Yeah, I reckon I was there."

"What did you do there?"

"Visited."

"Who?"

"Folks."

"What folks?" said Mary Ann.

"All kinds of folks."

"Why'd you cut it?"

"Felt like it."

"Why?" she said, sensing something deeply wrong had happened.

"For a woman."

"You cut your hair for another woman?"

"It was only Agnas Smith," said Rockwell. "She had typhoid fever and her hair had all fell out–so I cut my hair off to make her a wig." Agnas was the widow of Don Carlos Smith, a brother to Joseph, and now living in California.

Mary Ann did not know how to approach the question, so she almost left it unsaid.

"You fond of her?"

Rockwell shook his head.

"Then why'd you do it?"

"Felt sorry for her–why would you do it?"

Mary Ann was at once proud of her husband and jealous.

"Frankly, I wouldn't have. Not from what Joseph said to you." She looked him over curiously. "You sure look different without your hair."

"Thank you."

"It looks awful."

"I thought you hated the hair."

"Only sometimes," she said, trying for some levity to cover her deep-seated emotions, "like when I choke on it at night." But her feelings quickly surfaced. "I wonder if you'd have done it for me had I asked."

"Of course."

"I don't think so."

"Maybe you're right."

That night they slept in separate quarters–she in her parents' cabin, he in the new structure. The next morning they argued over where they would live permanently. He demanded they live in the cabin he'd already built several miles away. She demanded they live in the new structure a hundred yards from her parents.

He suggested a compromise. So they compromised. They lived a hundred yards from her parents.

"You call this compromise?" he said.

"If you want to keep living with me, it's compromise," she said.

Rockwell felt grateful she was taking him back so forgivingly. "She's a good woman," he told his horse. "Deserving of better than me." He felt the resurgence of love he had felt on their courtship. By the second night she was pouring her affections over him.

Several nights later he went to a party of city officials, including Almon Babbitt. They sat around a fire on October 20th in Big Cottonwood Canyon, sang, cooked pancakes, and told stories with two visiting Frenchmen–Jules Remy and Julius Brenchly. The two French writers liked Rockwell. He offered to take them to California for no pay, but they refused. They enjoyed his wit and laughed until dawn at his stories.

He continued patching things up with his wife for another couple months. In so doing he did not take on any assignments that would draw him away from the ranch for more than a day. She felt he was making improvement–devoting more time to the family. But during that time she encouraged him on something else he was asked: Brigham Young recruited him as a public speaker.

On January 9th, 1856, Rockwell took the stand with Young and other church brass to talk the Legislative Assembly at Fillmore into funding a new mail system. On January 26th and February 2nd Rockwell went with Young to the Tabernacle and spoke again. Then Brigham got him to travel up and down the Wasatch mountains to preach and ordain church Seventies. Rockwell would return to his wife every other night, and though even that was difficult, she accepted it. But then came a strike that drove the most painful spike of all into their relationship.

"Why do you have to go?" said Mary Ann, nearly in a state of shock.

"I don't know." Rockwell didn't know–but he knew somebody had to lead Almon Babbitt eastward. Babbitt, despite his recent excommunication from the church for adultery, had been recently appointed by Brigham Young as Territorial Secretary, and now Babbitt seemed possessed with a burning desire to return to Washington, D.C. His mission: to obtain for the state capitol several wagon loads of supplies. Rockwell knew he was the one to lead Babbitt eastward. Perhaps it was because Babbitt had saved

Rockwell at Galena–or perhaps because Rockwell merely now smelled the salt in the air.....

Mary Ann loved him that night as always, the impact of the news not having fully settled in. But by the time he would leave the next day, she would confront him.

"If you make it back alive, you must never leave us again. Not for more than just one day.....ever again.....am I clear?"

Rockwell was certain he needed just this one last bit of adventure to clear himself of whatever it was gnawing at him. He kissed her with all the feeling he had, which was now even deeper than that which he'd known in his courtship, and he made her a promise.

"I won't cross the Mississippi River. I won't even go anywhere near it," said Rockwell. "I'll even stay at Fort Kearney while Babbitt goes to the East with the others. I'll just get them across the mountains and across the plains. Don't worry about me. What could possibly go wrong?"

The next morning he began his journey eastward.....and she watched him until he disappeared around the Point of the Mountain, with tears flowing from her cheeks.

William Drummond was about to learn the pivotal piece of information needed before taking action against Rockwell.

Before him once again sat Frank Slade and Simon Lefevre. They had not met in several months but were now anxious to resume business.

Drummond was impatient and turned to Lefevre, "So what about the Babbitt mission? What did Rockwell do?"

"I think we've got what it takes to nail both him and the church in the coffin."

Simon Lefevre suggested they walk from Drummond's office to the tavern; Drummond and Slade complied, and the three men soon found themselves seated at Drummond's favorite corner table, assiduously staring out the window at passing wagons and horses. Drummond had always enjoyed this view most, and from this site he would now learn what would obviously be Rockwell's downfall.

"Rockwell led Almon W. Babbitt, Rockwell's old lawyer friend from back in Illinois, and 36 other Mormons, eastward on April 22nd," began Lefevre. "And in the party were some Mormon missionaries heading to Europe."

"How far did he go?"

"Only to Fort Kearney, for some unknown reason. And he stayed at the fort while the party went farther East. But soon they were all involved in the middle of a plains war."

"What happened?"

"A Danish Mormon wagon train had gone through Miniconjou country and one of their cows had wandered off. A brave found it and butchered it. The Mormons mentioned it to the Army at Fort Laramie, and the Army was anxious to punish the Indians. They sent a platoon of 29 cavalrymen to arrest the brave that killed the cow. They found him but he refused arrest. So the soldiers got in a fight with the Indians—and all the cavalrymen were massacred.

"That made General William S. Harney madder than a wildcat. He rode to the Sioux camp and slaughtered 80 men, women, and children. From that battle he got the name 'Squaw-killer Harney.' And he forced the Indians into a shaky truce.

"That all happened just before Rockwell, Babbitt, and the Mormon bunch had arrived."

Drummmond leaned forward, anxious to hear the remainder of the episode.

Lefevre paused as he regarded his two listeners. He did not know what was going on in Slade's mind. Frank Slade had kept himself busy writing letters to his Mexican wife, to whom he prided himself on remaining faithful. He had also procured for his four children a bag full of carved crafts, purchased directly from local artists and Indians themselves. Although promised immunity from justice, he was growing resentful of the laborious, methodical manner in which Drummond was exercising his plan. Lefevre was meanwhile nervous over Slade bungling things—like killing Rockwell before they could uncover needed evidence. Little did Lefevre know, but Slade was contemplating going after Rockwell soon.

Lefevre continued. "Babbitt finished his business in Washington and got his supplies. He started back to Fort Kearney to rejoin Rockwell. But on his way, the supply train was attacked. His teamsters and a woman and her child were all killed, but Babbitt made it through safely—he was riding a buggy several miles back.

"When Babbitt did make it to Fort Kearney, he hired Rockwell to take his supply wagons on to Salt Lake City. Babbitt announced he would go on ahead with only a driver and a guard to the city. But Rockwell and Captain H.W. Wharton of the Army tried to talk him out of it. Babbitt would not listen. He took off in his buggy, never to be seen again."

"What happened to him?" said Drummond.

"A few days later the Indians came to the fort to sell his effects at the trading post. They praised Babbitt. They said he had fought 'like a bear.' They also said he had run out of ammo and had taken to swinging his rifle at them, but there were too many for him. One Indian had finally snuck up behind him and tomahawked him."

"Where was Rockwell?"

"Off getting Babbitt's five supply wagons and oxen. But by the time he arrived back at the fort, gossip was rampant: the non-Mormons were claiming Rockwell had assassinated Babbitt."

Drummond's mind was reeling.

"Well, immigrants passing through Salt Lake City here later repeated this gossip about Rockwell murdering Babbitt," continued Lefevre. "But nobody–I repeat nobody–back East knows any difference."

"And Rockwell's motive for the murder?" asked Drummond.

"According to the immigrants, Young simply wanted Babbitt 'out of the way.' "

"What for?" said Drummond.

"Because Babbitt had threatened to return territorial government money to Congress. But that's a whole different story. Nobody who knows Brigham Young well thinks he'd actually call for Babbitt's death, but then nobody back East would know that."

Drummond sat back and gazed on Lefevre thoughtfully. "We've got our fuel."

Frank Slade meanwhile stared into his drink. Lefevre continued.

"Rockwell went only so far as Fort Laramie with Babbitt's supply wagons, and there he stopped for the winter. But several Mormon handcart companies wouldn't listen to him and decided to keep going to the valley. They got caught in a blizzard. Hundreds were killed. But Rockwell waited till the worst weather passed, then came on to Salt Lake City November 4th."

"Where did he go from there?" said Drummond.

"His wife had given birth again three months earlier, so when he arrived home he decided to settle down with his family."

Drummond sighed, feeling victorious; he sat back casually. "Get word to Rockwell that I wish to see him. Slade, I want you on his trail night and day. When you find your best shot, take it. He doesn't need to see it coming."

"I don't know what you're expecting," said Slade, "but not from the back."

"Just do what it takes," said Drummond. "He can see you, but not know what hit him."

"Don't worry," said Slade, "he won't."

19

Rockwell's return to Mary Ann had found her ecstatic. She had faith in Rockwell's promise to go no farther than Fort Kearney, and she further knew he would never again leave her. She had proudly presented her new child to Rockwell. Rockwell was shocked to see that the child, Sarah Rockwell, looked exactly like him.

"Poor critter," he said, chuckling to himself.

He was proud of his wife. They talked for hours his first night back. He had initially enjoyed being out in the wild, but after several weeks had begun deeply missing her.

It was out of his system, he told her.

She wondered for how long. She pushed the thought from her mind and merely celebrated the days following his return.

One week after his return he was repairing the corral gate as Simon Lefevre rode up with a letter.

"I can't read this," said Rockwell, who was still illiterate, which half the population was for the day.

"Then let your wife read it," said Lefevre, who quickly rode away.

William W. Drummond lay asleep beside his favorite woman when the door crashed open.

Moonlight beams shot onto his face and he squinted. A darkened figure shuffled up to the foot of his bed.

Drummond flushed, and shouted at the man. "Who are you and what the devil do you want?"

"I'm Port Rockwell and what the devil do you want?"

Drummond stared at him, baffled. "What time is it?"

"Full moon–what time did you think it was?"

Drummond cleared his throat and felt his heart racing. "I'm not armed."

"I didn't say you was," said Rockwell. "I got a letter saying you wanted me–now what do you want?"

"To warn you."

"That's awful nice of you....." Rockwell began walking back to the door.

"You don't wish to hear what I have to warn you about?"

"Not really," said Rockwell. "I can take care of myself."

"I can keep you from getting in real trouble if you dictate something to me," said Drummond.

Rockwell stopped at the door and glanced back curiously.

"Dictate what?"

"Your life's story."

"It'd never sell," he said, heading out the door.

"Wait a minute."

He stopped again.

"You need only 'confess' your murders to me. And if you do– you'll save yourself and your people a great deal of grief."

"That's real thoughtful of you–being concerned about my grief and all, but, let's face it, I always have enjoyed dodging trouble, and so have my neighbors, now if you'll excuse me....."

"Wait. I've got paper and quill pens on that desk. You stay here all night and dictate to me what you will, especially, shall we say, what you have done in the name of miracles." Rockwell had by now grown most of his hair back. Drummond was looking at the hair as he spoke. "Especially, shall we further say, what you feel I would need, and you could be a rich man. Especially regarding Almon W. Babbitt. You can name your pile."

"I've heard that before."

"Your not cooperating won't alter history one bit, but your signature could help your own."

"I read everything you're saying, but I don't think so."

"That's quite a feat for an illiterate man," smirked Drummond.

Rockwell tipped his hat to the woman.

"Mrs. Drummond."

The woman replied, "She ain't in town this month. She headed back to California for a visit." To Drummond the woman asked softly, "Honey, do you know when she'll be back?"

Drummond was impatient with her remarkable stupidity. He quickly turned to Rockwell. "I think you know where the door is."

Rockwell walked away, leaving the door swinging in the breeze. Drummond and his mistress stared at the open door.....

The next day William Drummond pounded his gavel to end his day in court. He wondered where Frank Slade was. His eyes had been turned to the door all day, waiting for Slade's return. Slade was supposed to have eliminated Rockwell by now. Drummond was surprised at himself for his nervousness, particularly in light of the fact Slade had both a record and a passion for successfully killing whoever he wanted—even skilled gunslingers. Then an odd thought went across his mind: he wondered if perhaps Rockwell and Slade were not off somewhere sharing a drink or two—if Slade had not been somehow charmed by the desperado as Lefevre had been. He pushed the thought from his mind and wondered when Slade would return.

At the south end of Salt Lake Valley, meanwhile, Rockwell rode his wagon through the pass at Point of the Mountain and saw a familiar face on horseback.

"Excuse me, Mr. Rockwell."

Rockwell glanced at him curiously.

"I mean to talk to you."

"Yeah?"

"My name is Frank Slade."

"What can I do for you?"

"Well I've come clear from California to settle something with you. And I've been following you longer, off and on, than I care to admit."

"Oh? Why's that?"

"No particular reason—just to kill you."

Slade pulled a revolver from behind his hat on the saddle horn.

Rockwell held back his surprise and kept his voice casual. "Why do you want to kill me?"

"A lot of people want to see you dead."

"Is that a fact?"

"A well known fact."

"Well, I'm flattered," said Rockwell.

"You should be, but I reckon it's been worth my while. The wait, I mean. I'll be financially reimbursed when I return."

"Thank goodness for that," said Rockwell. "I'd hate for you to have been following me around for free."

Slade chuckled.

Rockwell continued, "But I really hate to disappoint you."

"How do you reckon to do that, Mr. Rockwell?"

"With the outcome of this little confrontation and all."

Slade smiled, "I think you'll be the one disappointed, Rockwell."

"Is that a fact?"

"That is a fact."

"Well, now that we have all our facts clear," said Rockwell, "I reckon you can get on with your business.....at least in a minute or two."

"A minute or two?"

"Yeah. Mainly when you're ready."

"As if I'm not ready?" snorted Slade.

Rockwell chuckled softly.

"What're you laughin' at?" said Slade.

Rockwell didn't answer. He just kept chuckling.

Slade fought his disconcert. "Have you ever seen a snake that's been gut-shot? It squirms in the dust for hours before it dies. I reckon I've done that to hundreds of snakes, and dozens of men, and even half a dozen lawmen."

"Well now," said Rockwell, "you oughta be real proud of yourself."

"I am."

"If you've killed half a dozen lawmen, I would make an even seven, ain't that right?"

"An even seven?" Slade laughed. "I kinda like you, Marshal. An even seven. That's good. I do like you."

"Well I kinda like you too, Slade."

"Yessir, you got a sense of humor as loco as mine," said Slade.

"Maybe I am as loco as you."

Slade lost his smile and trembled a little, then suddenly broke into loud guffaws. "Maybe I oughta just shoot you in the head right now for sayin' that and get it over with."

"Naw, that'd spoil your fun," said Rockwell. "Deep down you wanna gut-shoot me like that snake you was tellin' me about." Rockwell could see Slade trembling again.

Slade broke into a sweat. "I reckon you're right. When you're dead, with your face twisted from the pain and everything, that's when I'll take off your head and put it in with my bag."

"Sounds like a great idea," said Rockwell. "And besides, what's another snake's head?"

Slade broke into louder laughter. "That's right! That's right!" He then gasped and panted.

"So when you're ready, let me know," said Rockwell.

"What're you talkin' about?.....I am ready!"

Rockwell laughed and slapped his knee. "No, you're not."

"Don't tell me if I am or not."

"Well it is impossible to kill me, didn't you know that?"

Slade angered even further.

Rockwell was, moment by moment, capturing his curiosity such that Slade could not yet kill him; Rockwell was both stalling for time to think of a strategy and playing with Slade's mind–and Slade knew it.

Slade fought his emotions but was unsuccessful. He almost choked on it. He spat out his words. "Frankly, I don't believe in your long hair protecting you–so don't tell me it's impossible to kill you."

"Actually," said Rockwell, "I wasn't referring to the hair protecting me–there's another reason you can't kill me."

"Why's that?"

Rockwell stared at Slade's pistol. "You can't kill a man without a firing pin!"

Slade's face flustered with panic. He glanced down at his pistol. Rockwell was wrong! There was a firing pin! Slade, pleased, looked up again and found himself staring straight into Rockwell's revolver.

Simultaneously, he found himself staring at the flash coming from the revolver.

Momentarily, he saw nothing but barren desert dirt and blood soaking into the sand, draining from his own face.

He was lying face down, sprawled across the road.....And within ten seconds he was dead.

Rockwell tipped his hat up with his pistol barrel, and sighed. It seems he just couldn't even take a peaceful ride in the country anymore, he mused, without some obnoxious idiot bothering him.

And then he rode home.

20

A knock sounded at Rockwell's door. Mary Ann was the first to awaken, when suddenly she saw outside, silhouetted against the dawn, Brigham Young.

"May I come in?" said Young.

Rockwell rolled over and opened his eyes to Brigham standing at the foot of his bed.

"That was a plain, stupid move, Port."

"What plain, stupid move was that?"

"Threatening Judge Drummond."

"Is that what he told you?"

"You should not have seen him."

"He ordered me to see him."

"Next time clear it with me."

" 'Won't be a next time," said Rockwell. "He bores me. I don't bother visiting people a second time who bored me the first time."

"You're right about one thing," said Young, "there won't be a next time. He's left the territory."

Rockwell smiled, "What for?"

"You, partly. But mainly cause hise wife wrote a letter to the newspaper complaining about his mistress. The non-Mormons got as fed-up with him as we did, and finally I reckon he felt the pressure and left. But he claimed you were a big part of it–no telling what he'll tell the Eastern press."

"No telling."

"I mean about you threatening him and all."

"Threatening him?" Rockwell awakened more. "You believe that?"

Young gazed on him a moment, his facial muscles relaxing, and then he apologized to Rockwell. "But I need you for another assignment, Port."

Rockwell gave a glance to Mary Ann, who looked away, confused, crushed.

Rockwell was chosen to man Brigham Young's new mail service from Salt Lake City to Laramie. John Murdock was to man the second leg–from Laramie to Independence, Missouri.

Mary Ann took some consolation in the fact that her husband was to be gone only a short while on each excursion, but she did not know how many runs, nor for how many years, nor how often he would be gone. And the fact he would be riding deep into Indian-infested wilderness each time, coming just off the Indians plains incident just a bit further east, did not set well with her.

She worried constantly while he was gone.

When Rockwell returned from Laramie with a wagon full of mail, he was cheered in the streets of Salt Lake City.

He had no idea what he was riding into, but the *Deseret News* had made an event over it, and he was embarrassed at all the attention.

At least when he had built his legend as a killer of outlaws, they didn't throw parades in his behalf, he mused.

At his cabin Mary Ann greeted him with a hug, but in her kiss was the shadow of uncertainty. The uncertainty stemmed from her defenses she was erecting–an emotional barrier to buffer her from the inevitable fear she felt overtaking her. The fear of losing him. She tried driving from her mind that such a possibility existed, but she was unsuccessful. She found herself constantly fighting the depression overtaking her. She knew he would eventually be killed.

"You going to the big to-do at Oakley's barn tonight?" she said.

"I'd just as soon rest."

"Been years since we danced," she said.

Rockwell studied her and understood. "If you wish, yeah, let's go."

"Not unless you want to."

"I want to," said Rockwell, not wanting to.

"You really want to go?"

"Yeah, I really want to go," he said, really not wanting to go. "What dance is it?"

"It's the celebration over your bringing in the mail–and I reckon it's mostly over the fact Drummond's really gone."

"Yeah," said Rockwell. "I guess I do really feel like dancing."

He said that, suddenly really feeling like dancing.

Carriages and horses were tied in front of Oakley's barn at the south end of Salt Lake Valley.

Inside, Rockwell twirled Mary Ann until she laughed with dizziness. But the laughter wasn't from pleasure. It was like the laughter of drunken souls trying to forget their pain. The music finally ended. Rockwell walked over to the sidelines.

Brigham Young ambled up and placed his arm around his shoulder. "This is not the best news you could hear."

Rockwell peered at him.

"William Drummond's arrived in New York."

"That's as good a news as I've heard in a long time," said Rockwell.

"He wrote a letter," continued Young, "and it's been published in all the New York City newspapers."

"About what?"

"He resigned as federal judge here, and he listed a few reasons."

"Like what? That I threatened him?"

"No, he claimed you murdered Almon Babbitt."

Rockwell was caught with the wind out of him.

"Where is Drummond–I'll kill him."

Later that evening, after returning from a long walk, Rockwell rejoined the barn dance. It was nearly 2 o'clock in the morning. Brigham Young was rarely up that late, but was still enjoying the festivities. He approached Rockwell and gave him another assignment.

"Forget Drummond, he's just another hound barking at the caravan," said Young. But now I need your help with the mail service again. I've given complete autonomy to Hiram Kimball over the mail service, and he wants you to take a second trip to Laramie."

"A second trip already? What's he want to do–ruin my marriage?"

Rockwell stared at Mary Ann now dancing with Lot Smith, his old neighbor from Nauvoo whom he had always argued with more than he had ever conversed civilly. They had scouted together occasionally for Brigham Young but had never seen eye to eye on anything–and both were stubborn men. The fact Lot Smith was dancing with Mary Ann made Rockwelll uneasy. Smith was clever with words: she would laugh at Smith–more so in fact than at Rockwell's humor which men seemed more inclined to take to.

And women seemed to take to Smith anyway. Like most Mormon men, Lot Smith was not a polygamist, although he could have afforded a second wife. Polygamy was an issue which amused Rockwell. As writers had done with his own name, they had made fortunes off books about polygamy, writing on a topic they knew nothing about. Rockwell believed the Bible that Abraham, Isaac, and Jacob had practiced it, and he was therefore amazed by all the criticism his people received even though only five percent of the Mormon population practiced it.

But tonight he wondered if Lot Smith would consider taking Mary Ann to wife if something happened to him.....

And he further wondered if, with the increasing distance Mary Ann seemed to be displaying towards him, she would take to Smith emotionally as much as he suspected.

Rockwell had always found it a compliment of sorts that men would take a second glance at his wife, but something about Lot Smith bothered him. He realized it was because his wife liked him back–he could see her expression as she and Smith danced–and then he caught himself smiling at his jealousy. He eyed Smith again and found himself admiring a man who could charm the women. It reminded him of himself in earlier years.

Unknown to Rockwell, three-quarters of the women in the barn were attracted to Rockwell. And Mary Ann was simply momentarily enjoying other male attention–she was hopelessly addicted to Rockwell's charm and often hated herself for it; Rockwell had always been able to manipulate her with it, yet he was strangely unconscious of it.

"Brother Brigham," joked Rockwell. "I just got back from my first journey to Laramie last night! And if I know Hiram Kimball, he will probably want me leaving again tomorrow–just to get back at me."

"Get back at you?"

"Yeah," said Rockwell.

"What for?"

"A little fist-fight."

"What little fist-fight?"

"About 12–13 years ago in Nauvoo," said Rockwell. "That's the last time I ever saw him. I can't even remember what it was about, but I whipped him into the dust." Rockwell smiled at the memory.

Suddenly he felt a tap on his shoulder. He turned and saw Kimball deliver a mouth full of fist into him. Rockwell went crashing to the wall. The music stopped and all eyes turned.

Kimball stared down at him and smiled as big as a frog. "Now I reckon we're even."

Rockwell arose from the floor, staggered slowly to Kimball, and stopped. Rockwell glanced at Mary Ann, who scowled at him, then at Young, who glared, and suddenly he extended his right hand to Kimball and shook hands, then muttered, "I reckon we are."

Outside, Rockwell rode out of the barnyard with Mary Ann beside him on the buckboard. He glanced up at the moon, rubbed his jaw, and mumbled, "He's good."

On the ride home, he informed her of his newest assignment– the mail load to Laramie next week. She refused to speak to him. He informed her of Drummond's letter to the New York press, and of the accusation of him murdering Babbitt.

She looked off, distraught. If he had just not confronted Drummond so boldly, she figured, Drummond would have left him alone. But her comment went unsaid; she felt it useless to argue with a veritable rattlesnake beside her. She had long ago learned that she couldn't win an argument. Despite all his kindnesses to her he was a man that could not be crossed.

"All I want to know," said Rockwell, reading most of her thoughts, "is what the harvest will be like this fall." He was afraid to say what he really felt. He really wondered if she would be around when he returned–or if she would be back at her parents. He knew it would be asking perhaps more than she had to give– for him to be leaving her and the children seven of every eight weeks, for what could be an indefinite period—and he did not have it within himself to drop the assignment: deep down, once again, he was looking forward to wilderness travel. He still felt she should accept that about him. He had forgotten how much he craved leaving civilization where dangers of elements and Indians ever threatened, and the exhilaration he felt from it. He couldn't wait for this second journey, he mused, despite what he now told Mary Ann.

And she sensed it.

Yet he was torn over leaving her. Nevertheless, he felt such confidence in her love for him that even though she might be off with her parents again when he did return, she would, of course, have him back.

Still, it bothered him that such a stress still existed between them. It had kept him awake some nights on his last journey. But underneath it all, he hoped—even figured—that she would grow used to his adventurous nature—so he could have both her and his freedom whenever he needed it.

Afterall, she did love him, he figured. Why shouldn't she change? As much as he tried pacifying his conscience on the matter, he knew she was more deeply troubled than she cared to express. But he just wasn't ready to make any permanent changes himself. He had tried. He wasn't ready. He wondered if he ever would be.

At least it was not a matter of losing her. He loved her too much, and could never survive that.....

Rockwell rode the mail wagon towards Laramie.

Mary Ann, back home, stewed. This time, she figured, the press would be 20 times worse against him than it had been in Illinois—it was the national press. The *New York Times* serviced hundreds of state and territorial newspapers with national news.

Rockwell had a knack for bringing on himself half of what happened, she noted, yet she wondered why she couldn't have kept him home the night he insisted visiting Drummond at 3 A.M.

She pushed the thought from her mind and refused to blame herself. She glanced at his picture then forced her eyes from it.

She stared out the window, also wondering if she would be home when he returned.

Not forty miles from Fort Laramie, Rockwell saw two horsemen coming. He cocked his shotgun.

He heard his name called. He set down the gun. The men were Abraham Smoot and Jason Stoddard, two Salt Lake City officials returning from the East. They were tall, suntanned, middle-aged, and dignified-looking. They galloped up to him and reined to a halt.

"Port—turn the wagon!"

With the mens' horses added to his team, Rockwell rode towards Salt Lake City, Smoot and Stoddard seated beside him. Over the bumpy, dusty trail Smoot told his story.

"President Buchanan saw the newspapers—he read Drummond's letter—and he is sending the Army to invade Utah! Twenty-five hundred cavalry, infantry, and artillery are coming to arrest you and replace Brother Brigham with Drummond as governor!"

The three men arrived in Salt Lake City.

The town was deserted.

They drove to the Post Office. The Postmaster informed them everyone was celebrating their ten-year anniversary 25 miles east, up Big Cottonwood Canyon.

They rode to the party. American flags snapped from a dozen peaks and the valley was filled with six brass bands, a company of infantry, and thousands of applauding pioneers. The smell of barbecued beef filled the air.

Rockwell jumped from his wagon and bounded to the speakers' platform. He wondered if Mary Ann were among the celebrators—he knew her well enough to realize she was probably at home, dutifully watching the children. But wondered if by chance she had brought them there and had her eyes on him that very second. Brigham Young was seated, preparing his address.

"You can sit up here, Port."

"I've got to see you privately."

"After the speech," said Young.

"Now."

As Young saw the sobriety in his demeanor he was struck with curiosity. Smoot and Stoddard joined Rockwell. "Can we see you in your tent?" said Smoot.

Young gazed at all three men and took them back to his tent. The bands stopped their music and the people waited for Brigham Young's address. When he emerged from his tent they beheld his heavy countenance. The mood of the crowd shifted. Young strode to the podium. His stocky frame stood erect.

Rockwell, Smoot, and Stoddard stood behind him. Young hesitated, thinking, then cleared his throat.

"When we arrived in these valleys, I said, 'Give us 10 years of peace and we will ask no odds of Uncle Sam or the Devil.' Now, 10 years later, God is with us and the Devil has taken me at my word."

Outside Brigham Young's home in Salt Lake City, Mary Ann slowed her buggy. Twilight had settled in. The war council would soon begin.

Mary Ann stared at a shadowy form as it approached on horseback. She continued studying it, remaining silent.

It stopped and gazed at her curiously.

"So will you be home?" said Rockwell, remaining horseback and staring at her.

Her face was stone, revealing nothing. She finally turned and rode away, down a moonlit Salt Lake City street.

Rockwell followed her with his eyes. His eyes shifted to the moon, which, to Mary Ann, might never look the same again. He wondered.

PART V

THE WAR

21

At the war council in Brigham Young's home, Rockwell sat in buckskins. Attending were a dozen uniformed officers, all listening to General Daniel H. Wells.

"Finally, gentlemen, the leader of the infantry portion of the U.S. Army's invading force against our Mormon community, Colonel Alexander, wrote this letter to us and I quote it, 'Never have a people had so many odds placed against them as you have. We, however,' continues Colonel Alexander, 'have the flower of the American Army–2,500 cavalrymen and artillery.' That's the end of his letter.

"So I replied to the colonel with these words: 'We have perhaps a hundred men to fight you at any one time. Therefore, I see the obvious predicament. So, I plead compassionately for terms of surrender.' "

Wells glanced at his officers, "Unfortunately, gentlemen, he was extremely unreasonable. He refused to surrender."

All the men burst into laughter. Rockwell chuckled but his thoughts were on Mary Ann. Despite his love, he would not beg for her as he had Luana. And he was certain now that he could no longer be or act like something he wasn't.

Yet he suspected, deep down, if he were not losing her.

He could not let that happen. He was not sure what he would do.

But he knew at the moment he had to force Mary Ann from his mind. It seemed easy when he thought of the injustice of the invasion. Still, he wondered, what was she thinking? She would not allow herself to lose him, he figured. But was she to that point in her mind? Certainly she wasn't, he pondered.

Or was she?

Brigham Young stood, somber, and faced the officers.

"The Army seeks to drive us into submission. They plan to make us an example of rebellion. Our spies have already found scraps of songs they wrote on their trail bragging of their intentions. Leading the force is Squaw-killer Harney."

Rockwell winced–he remembered the general's massacre while at Fort Kearney.

"For 25 years now we have been scorned, held in derision, insulted, and betrayed. We have had no privilege of defending ourselves, and once again we are condemned unheard. But this time, gentlemen, we shall resort to the great first law of self-preservation and stand in our own defense!"

Rockwell felt his blood rush, and at the back of the room he arose and leaned against the wall.

"Nevertheless," continued Young, "my orders to you are, un-equivocably, to *shed no blood.*"

A murmur spread among the officers. Rockwell's eye twitched.

"Details will be forthcoming from General Wells," added Young. "You will see, brethren, that the Army has taken on more than it can chew."

Several officers looked off, doubtful of their chances. Rockwell however slowly tightened his fists behind his back.....

"Finally, I wish to read you a letter," said Young. "They do not know of my mandate to shed no blood, so it will work to our benefit. Following is a letter I just penned to Colonel Alexander: 'In the name of Israel's God we will have peace, even though we be compelled by our enemies to fight for it. We have, as yet in our persecutions, studiously avoided the shedding of blood. But you can easily perceive that you and your troops are now at the mercy of the elements, and that we live in the mountains, and that our men are all mountaineers. This the government should know, and also should give us our rights and then let us alone. Both we and the Kingdom of God will be free from all hellish oppressors, the Lord being our helper. But if you persist in your attempt, you will have to meet a mode of warfare against which your tactics furnish you no information. We, for the first time, possess the power to have a voice in the treatment we will receive. And with us, *it is the kingdom of God or nothing.*"

Brigham Young's officers stared at him silently. He lifted his grey eyes from the letter and gazed across the room. His men were grave. His eyes rested upon Rockwell, who suddenly winked at him.

In that, Young found a certain spark of courage to arouse his soldiers. He broke into a smile and said, "Let's get 'em!"

Rockwell was the first to raise his voice, and all the men broke into a cheer.

Three days east of Salt Lake City, Rockwell and his dozen soldiers sat on horseback atop a mountain and studied a wagon camp below.

"That's the advance patrol," said Rockwell's assistant, Henry Ballard, a short, bull-like individual whom Rockwell found remarkably efficient.

Rockwell saw several infantry officers parting from a campfire and disappearing into tents. As the hundred soldiers drifted asleep, Rockwell peered at the moon and pondered. He studied the camp with a hand telescope. Moonlight glittered off the guard's canteen. The guard finally drifted asleep.

Rockwell sent his men all across the mountainside with torches, then regrouped them hours later and gestured them to follow him. They eased their horses down the mountainside behind Rockwell.

Soon, he and six of his dozen guerrillas went charging through camp, clanging bells and pans, shouting, and firing weapons.

The infantrymen emerged half-dressed, when they discovered to their dismay Rockwell and his men stampeding the horses.

An Army officer shouted, "Grab your arms and commence firing!"

"Sir....." An aide said, nodding toward the mountainside. The officer peered up and saw 500 campfires dotting the mountain. "Sir, I think we're outnumbered at least 10 to one."

The officer shouted to his men, "Don't touch your weapons!" The soldiers stood as still as sheep while Rockwell and his men herded their hundred horses through the canyon and away.

Rockwell's aide, Henry Ballard, turned to him again, "When they find out the campfires on the mountain are unmanned–what do you think that officer will do?"

"Wish I could hear him," said Rockwell. The Army had Rockwell's guerrillas outnumbered 15 to one.

"But I reckon the fun ain't even started."

Rockwell and his men herded the horses to camp headquarters. There he sat on a boulder beside the company look-out, Corporal Daryl McMillan. McMillan had beady eyes and stiff protruding lips that reminded one when he spoke of a talking oyster.

The corporal scanned the distant, moon-lit horizon with a telescope. "Captain Rockwell, the general has a message for you, sir." He handed Rockwell a paper.

"You think I can read this, son?" said Rockwell. "First of all, it's dark; second of all, I can't read."

"I took the liberty, sir, to read it."

"You could be court-martialed for that, corporal, but I'm one who rewards a soldier for his curiosity. Go ahead, tell me what it says."

"Squaw-killer Harney was replaced," said the corporal.

"That's good."

"By Colonel Albert Sydney Johnston."

"That's bad."

"Why is that, sir?"

"Quit calling me sir. Port's good enough for me–it's good enough for you."

"Yes, sir."

Rockwell looked at him and shook his head. "First of all, Johnston's a rabid Mormon hater. Second of all, I wanted to confront Squaw-killer Harney myself–he's a ruthless, witless fool and I wanted to humble him."

"I'm sorry, sir."

"I'm sorry too, corporal. A horrible evening this is turning out to be," said Rockwell, tongue in cheek.

"Johnston's a good general, I hear."

"Thank goodness for that. At least there's some consolation in this war. It will make it more challenging."

Neither man said a word the next ten minutes as Rockwell pondered, observing the broad valley below. He struggled to keep his mind from Mary Ann. But what was she thinking? The look-out continued spying the valley with his telescope.

"Are the trenches all dug yet, corporal?" said Rockwell.

"Yes, sir, and the breastworks are built. Plus, they're rolling boulders to the precipice of the cliffs. As you see, sir, the canyon road down there passes directly beneath those cliffs."

"Are you sure the Army will stay on the road?"

"Yes, sir. We've dammed the river. They have to stay on the road."

"Is the water deep enough?"

"It's not the depth that matters, sir. It's the quicksand we've created." The corporal smiled. "It's beautiful quicksand."

Rockwell smiled also.

"So once we keep them on that road," continued the corporal, "we can rake them from all our positions–smash their wagons to splinters with those rocks. The trails up to these cliffs are these-cret– only we know where they are." The corporal pointed as he spoke.

"Somehow," said Rockwell, "I don't think they're going to win this war." The corporal sat back and beheld Rockwell silently chuckling. "No, sir," continued Rockwell, "I don't think they'll even reach Echo Canyon here. I think we can do a lot more damage before they even get here." Rockwell strode to his men at the bonfire and ordered them to mount.

"One other thing, sir," called out the corporal to him, now a hundred feet away, "General Wells ordered you to recruit 40 men from Major McAllister's company and drive off the Army's cattle."

"Like wheat in the old mill," said Rockwell, "it's as good as done."

Rockwell and his new recruits arrived at the Army's second camp, farther behind the lines. His plans were to stampede the cattle. But, upon arriving, he was frustrated. Corporal Henry Ballard turned to him.

"Looks like they second-guessed us."

"I don't see a problem," snapped Rockwell. His mind began searching for a solution.

"Sir, they've got the cattle behind all the infantry–hose cattle are protected well," said Ballard.

"You think that's a problem?"

"We can't touch them."

"Who needs to?" said Rockwell.

"Aren't those the orders?"

"They can be changed."

"Anyway you look at it," said Ballard, "the Army's got their cattle and we can't get at them."

"Corporal," said Rockwell, after reflecting on the scene, "the cattle have to eat, don't they?"

Ballard glanced at him curiously.

Rockwell ran with a torch. He lit the field directly in front of the Army. His 40 men followed, also putting their torches to the field. As the dried grass went up in blazes, he noticed artillery turned on them, and he shouted for a retreat. The spreading fire caused the large herd of cattle to stampede across the field and into the nearby woods. The Army, he figured, would never be able to find most of the cattle.

Shells began bursting about, and Rockwell and his men ran to their horses.

They pounded down a narrow canyon and away from the artillery's range. Finally he halted his men and took a quick count—all 40 were unscathed. They were, in fact, laughing.

Rockwell gazed back at the camp; the sky reflected the burning fields.

Meanwhile, Lot Smith led his men toward 75 Army wagons. Darkness shrouded his force as they came upon the civilian teamsters.

Their captain, Bill Rankin, stepped forward. Rankin was tall, stoop-shouldered, and gruff.

"What do you want?"

"Nothing much," said Smith. "Just for your train to turn the other way until you reach the States."

"By what authority do you issue such orders?"

Smith pointed to his men. "That's part of it. The others are up there."

Rankin did not know how many men Smith had; he could see only a few guerrillas, the rest trailed off into the darkness. Rankin was thus left to his imagination as to how many Mormon guerrillas actually did surrounded him. He feared several hundred. Smith actually had 20. Rankin grumbled but complied; he turned his train around.

Smith and the 20 guerrillas disappeared back into the darkness and rode south. They came upon another supply train.

"Where's your captain?" said Lot Smith.

Philip Dawson stepped forward. He was wide and overweight,

with very large, liquor-induced puffy cheeks and a red, bulbous nose. "I'm your man."

"I have a little business with you," said Lot Smith.

"What's the nature of it?"

"To order you and your men to get your private property out of the wagons."

"For what reason?" said Dawson.

"I mean to put a little fire in them. Is that reason enough?"

Dawson was nonplussed. "For God's sake, don't burn the trains."

"It's for His sake that I am, my good man," said Smith. "Now you and your men can stack your arms over there."

"And if we refuse?"

"We'll load you full of buckshot. Any more questions?"

Smith and his men rode from wagon to wagon with torches, and they lit the canvas.

James O'Marty, Lot Smith's Irish assistant, shouted, "By St. Patrick, ain't it beautiful! I never seen anything go better in all my life!"

"Dawson!" shouted Lot Smith. "Before we fire up your rear wagons– take some provisions out for my men."

Lot Smith next came upon Randolph Simpson, another supply wagon captain, a half mile away. Simpson was short and resembled an animal because he had so much hair. Though 30, he could pass for 50, and his face had a surly look.

"I'm here on business," announced Lot Smith.

Once again Smith was met with the question, "By what authority?"

Smith smiled and pointed his index finger towards heaven. "Now hand me your pistols."

Captain Simpson said nothing.

"You realize how much I hate doing this," said Smith, tongue in cheek.

"Yeah, I bet you do." said Captain Simpson.

"But I'm afraid you don't have any choice, so I reckon you better just get your men to hand over their pistols and hand me yours while you're at it."

"Sir," said Captain Simpson, "no man ever took them yet, and if you think you can without killing me, go ahead and try."

"I admire a brave man," said Smith.

"Good, because you've met one."

"But I don't like blood. And you insist on my killing you—which will only take a minute."

Simpson thought about Smith's words. He complied and disarmed his men.

Smith then shouted to his own men, Leave two wagons for the enemy's provisions. And burn the rest!"

Simpson shouted back at Smith, "Don't burn the train—not while I'm in sight!"

"Why not?"

"It'll ruin my reputation as a wagonmaster."

"What the devil does that have to do with anything?" said Smith.

"It's my life."

"If it burns, man, it burns. If your reputation goes up with it, it goes up with it."

"I've done this for twenty years!" shouted Captain Simpson.

"We don't have time to be ceremonious," mumbled Smith. "So just watch and enjoy the sight."

Smith's guerrillas set fire to the wagons. Simpson refused to watch
and peered off at the woods in anger.

The next morning Rockwell and his men rode along the mountainside. Bill Hickman reined in and announced to him that the Army had three prisoners of war at the heavily guarded main camp, but that the Army's cattle camp happened to be practically unguarded.

"Where"" said Rockwell.

"Ahead at Ham's Fork," said Hickman.

Rockwell and his 52 men galloped ahead and found five miles before the camp Lot Smith and his 20 men.

"Rockwell, you codger, what the devil are you doing here?" said Lot Smith. "It's good to see you but you're in my way!"

"Smith, you old fool, you're in my way!"

After five minutes of bantering, they finally agreed on a strategy: they would take their combined forces to the Army camp and there decide what to do.

When they arrived, they spotted the herd of 1400 army cattle on the bottom lands below.

"Rockwell, we will take those cattle immediately."

"That's just like you," said Rockwell. "Without even exploring their security, you would just move right down there and take them, is that it?"

"That's it."

"I bet them cattle was put there just for you as a trap," said Rockwell. "The troops found out what a half-wit you are, and that you would stick your fool foot into that kind of a trap. I bet them willows over there are chocked full of artillery. And the minute you expose yourself they'll blow you and your command higher than Gilroy's kite!"

Lot Smith pulled out his glass and surveyed the scene. He tucked away the scope and began riding down the bluff.

"Smith," yelled Rockwell, "come back here!"

But Smith kept riding and his men followed.

Rockwell was furious and commanded his men to follow. He caught up to Smith in a rage, shouting at him for going so fast and also yelling at his own men for going so slow.

"Wait for them to catch up, you fool!"

"No time to wait!" said Smith.

And Smith was right. They had two miles to reach the cattle, but by the time they did arrive, the Army guards had yoked up several teams.

Rockwell and Smith hid behind a boulder and surveyed the flatlands. Suddenly Smith shouted at his men to, "Charge!"

Rockwell was taken off guard; he sat staring, stunned. Smith and his 20 guerrillas went bounding out of the ravine, while Rockwell shouted at him again. Then Rockwell noticed the Army guards in a panic. They had caught the Army completely by surprise. Rockwell whirled on his own men.

"What are you waiting for! Catch up to them!" At which point his 52 men went galloping over the ravine, thundering down the hill, onto the guard's camp.

They held the guards at gunpoint while Smith's men unyoked the cattle.

"Hurry up!" said Rockwell to Smith. Rockwell knew several hundred infantrymen could just as easily be marching towards them from around the bend as not. "Smith, didn't anybody ever teach you how to unyoke a steer?"

"Shut up, Port, and do your job!"

"I am, Smith, which is more than I can say for you. Look at your men, they're funbling like they're all drunk!" He was engaged in good-natured chiding with Smith but the Army guards were amazed, not understanding the rapport the two men had with each other.

The head guard, a sergeant, presently walked up to the two Utah officers, "Are you going to take our stock?"

"It looks a little as if we will," said Rockwell.

Captain Jesse Roupe, small eyed and large faced, strode up to Smith. "Can I have enough cattle to take my wagons to camp?"

"How many do you need?"

"Nineteen."

"Take 20," said Rockwell. "You and your men can have steaks tonight. You've been through a lot–what with us thundering down on you all the time and what-not–you deserve them."

Rockwell and Smith mounted their horses and rode away.

As the guerrillas followed their two leaders, Rockwell turned and shouted down the hill to Captain Roupe, "By the way, you can tell Colonel Johnston at the main camp something for us."

"What's that?"

"Tell him we will kill every man he's got if he doesn't liberate our three prisoners of war."

"Yes, sir," said Catain Roupe. His men immediately mounted and rode off back to the main camp.

Rockwell and Smith ordered their men to divide the cattle into suitable herds, and they quickly drove them away.

As they rode into the darkness together, a quarter mile ahead of their 60 men and 1400 cattle, Rockwell reflected on the day's events. He repeated to himself what he had said to the guards, and he chuckled over their discomfiture.

A few minutes later Rockwell struck on an idea. He informed Lot Smith of it, then rode back to his own men and ordered them to remain with Smith.

Rockwell rode again past Smith, whom he patted on the back.

Smith smiled, "I hear from Mayor McAllister that our officers were scared we couldn't get along–but we proved 'em wrong, eh, Port? You're more fun than I thought you'd be."

"Yeah, all we need's a war," said Rockwell, "and we can get along just fine."

"Maybe we'll be lucky and have another war," said Smith.

Both men laughed, and Rockwell rode ahead to Fort Bridger. Rockwell's admiration for the man had been further confirmed. He knew why Mary Ann liked him.

He then wondered how she was faring. He feared the direction in which her emotions might be riding, but he could do nothing about it. He would decide what to do about her–and perhaps about himself–later.

He felt pleased he was no longer a prisoner to his passions as he had been before in his life. Nevertheless, a slight twinge of uncertainty haunted him–he pushed the feeling from his heart and he made his mind up to think of the war.

Now with 72 troops under his belt, Lot Smith felt he could take on the entire U.S. division.

Riding through a canyon he and his men came on the trail of a U.S. Cavalry detachment. He decided to follow it.

"We'll figure out some kind of problems to give them," said Smith to James O'Marty, his assistant.

Suddenly they came on a large force of cavalry–several hundred strong–and found themselves precariously close to them.

They halted 40 yards away. Lot Smith peered across his men and read their faces. He saw in them what he felt within himself–apprehension. He rode forward and met U.S. Army Captain Randolph B. Marcy halfway. Marcy was stocky, 40'ish, greying, and thick-limbed. He radiated well his authority, and could, in fact pass for a colonel.

"I suppose you are Captain Smith?" said Captain Marcy.

"Yes, sir."

"These soldiers under my command are United States troops. What armed force do you have?" said Marcy with a smirk.

"They're from Utah."

"What is your business out here?" said Marcy.

"Odd.....everyone keeps asking me that." Smith's men chuckled at their leader's audaciousness. They were clearly, vastly outnumbered by the Army.

"So what is your business?" said Captain Marcy.

"Watching you. What's your business?" said Lot Smith.

Marcy sighed and realized Smith was playing games. Marcy felt the man was not as clever as he thought he was.

"Looking for a way into Utah."

"Nonsense," said Lot Smith.

"What's nonsense about it?"

"Two reasons, sir, with all due respect."

Captain Marcy glanced back at his troops, who chuckled at Lot

Smith, thinking him unintentionally amusing.

"Well?" said Marcy.

"First of all, you'll never make it into Utah."

Marcy glanced back at his own men again and they laughed louder.

"Second of all," said Smith, "you're off course!"

Smith's men then burst into laughter. Suddenly, however, Lot Smith noticed that, while they had been talking, a number of Marcy's troops had formed a long line to the sides and behind Smith's men, nearly surrounding them. Smith realized there was no way to escape but up a steep hill to the left.

Captain Marcy read Smith's eyes and suddenly shouted a command. His troops began thundering down on the guerrillas and closing the circle.

Lot Smith shouted an order to his troops–and within seconds they charged up the slope. While galloping up the hill, Smith was surprised to find a ravine. His men followed him and before the infantry realized what was happening, the guerrillas had cut back down the hill in the ravine, leaving the soldiers up on the mountain, watching them, disconcerted. The small band had escaped through their fingers, as it were, like butter. The ravine was a dangerous ride. The soldiers gave up their chase.

Lot Smith dismounted and sat on a rock. Hours had passed and he gazed across a creek at the Army and imagined how chagrined Captain Marcy must feel. Suddenly one of his lieutenants came riding up, shouting, "The troops are upon us!"

Smith turned and saw forty troops behind him–they had snuck around the guerrilla force and now were taking aim at the Utahans. Smith shouted his command: his guerrillas remounted and took off in a gallop.

Eighty shots were fired by the Army–but none took effect, although one did pass through the hat of one private, Mark Hall, of Ogden. Two Mormons' horses however were shot, and the troops shouted exultingly, thinking they had hit the enemy.

Smith and his men answered with a cheer and rode around the hill to safety, unscathed.

Porter Rockwell, meanwhile, arrived at Fort Bridger. The Mormons had bought the fort months previously, paying Jim Bridger with gold. It held strategic importance of which Rockwell was quite aware. On the way to the fort Rockwell had picked up several volunteers and now he gave them an order.

"We've crippled Johnston's Army," began Rockwell, "but they can travel northward here to the fort and settle it unless we do something about it." Rockwell then rode forward and put his torch to the wood. His men stood back and watched the fire soon turn into a maze of towering flames. Rockwell watched the flames also, and finally pulled away from the sight and led his men on to Fort Supply.

On the night they arrived, he confronted a small crowd of Mormon settlers.

"Colonel Alexander is on his way here now," said Rockwell, "though most of the Army is further south in the canyons. How many of you are willing to let the Army settle here?"

John Fredericks, a tall, intense mill owner, spoke up, "Well I ain't letting them drive me out again–even though it took me five years to complete this mill and my house, I'll put my own torch to it first!"

Rockwell stared at him, finding some difficulty speaking. "How many else of you would do the same?"

Suddenly every man and woman at Fort Supply raised his hand in unison. They held torches by which to see, and, upon removing their valuables, immediately applied the torches to their homes and businesses, then backed away from the massive fire.

Rockwell winced at the sight; he turned away from the crowd, feeling moved.

When Colonel Alexander arrived at Fort Bridger, he exploded. His 400-man detachment were chagrined to see what they had hoped would be their retreat for the winter now merely a huge pile of ashes. Colonel Alexander dismounted, took a few steps toward the ashes, grabbed his hat, and hit it against his leg.

Rockwell meanwhile rode with his men to City Supply where they burned 15 more buildings. They warmed themselves by the flames and rode towards the southern campaign for their final confrontation with the Army.

Colonel Albert Sidney Johnston emerged from his tent. He was a husky, bright-eyed officer who spoke with a southern accent. His pride was in the union and his life was the military. He knew if he performed well in this campaign, the title of "general" would be his. He yearned to whip the Mormons in line. He was dark complex-

ioned and had fine, brown hair and dark eyes. He scanned the
mountainside for enemy. The sun had set and the moon was hidden by a mountain.

Captain Jesse Gove rode to him and dismounted. "Sir, Colonel
Alexander has settled at the fort."

Johnston mumbled, "His last message said it was burned."

"Yes, sir, he has another message for you here, sir."

Johnston squinted at him impatiently. "Read it."

" 'Dear General Johnston,' " read Captain Gove, " 'we are powerless to effect any chastisement of the marauding bands that are
constantly hovering about us, yet the elements of nature combined, as it were, against us is what concerns me most.' " Captain
Gove beheld Johnston's smirk.

Johnston commented icily, "Is the intrepid colonel haunted by
Brigham Young's ludicrous threats?"

"Certainly not, sir....." Less emphatically: "I don't think so, sir."

"Read the rest of it."

Gove hesitantly returned his eyes to the letter. He wore thick
spectacles, which gave one who spoke to him the feeling they were
looking into the eyes of a reptile. " 'Not only is the weather here the
worst I have seen,' says Colonel Alexander, 'but even our own
mules are now attacking us.' "

Colonel Johnston grabbed the letter, wadded it up, and threw
it into the mud.

Across the same camp, at the base of the mountain, Rockwell
and five others ran from a boulder. They hid behind a wagon.

Inside another wagon, fifty yards deeper into camp, three Utah
prisoners of war were tied securely, feeling desperate.

Rockwell noticed the guard looking the other way. Rockwell ran
forward and stopped 20 yards ahead. He hid behind a wagon. The
guard glanced back, saw nothing, and resumed staring at the
mountainside. Rockwell ran to another wagon, 10 yards closer to
the prisoners. He stopped at still another wagon and studied the
guard. Then he took off again.

He finally arrived at the prisoners just as the guard turned.....

22

Rockwell pulled a bowie knife and jumped into the wagon. The guard had turned but had not seen him. The three prisoners gaped at Rockwell. Within seconds he had their ropes cut.

He allowed them to stretch a moment, then he helped them back to the edge of camp. As they ran their last 20 yards, the guard spotted them and shouted. The Army was alerted.

Rockwell's men had been waiting at the boulders; they ran forward a few yards, grabbed the prisoners, and helped them make it to safety amidst flying bullets. A dozen infantrymen fired repeatedly at them.

Suddenly, across camp, four guerrilla horsemen came charging through camp. All the camp's guards were occupied shooting at Rockwell and the escaping prisoners, so the four horsemen had momentarily free rein: they galloped with torches straight to the munitions wagons.

General Johnston and his officers were stunned. When they heard the first explosion, they perceived yet another problem: they whirled and saw still another group of horsemen–seven in number–galloping across the far side of camp, tossing torches into other munitions wagons and shouting,taunting the soldiers.

Johnston swore. One wagon after another exploded and sent meteoric showers into the night.

Infantrymen ran through camp in a panic, some hopping about with trousers half on. Johnston saw huge forking flames shooting to the canvas covers of dozens of other wagons.

Johnston shouted to his men to abandon camp. Officers relayed the message, and Rockwell observed the massive havoc he had unleashed.

He stared from behind a boulder across camp and began chuckling.

Outside camp General Johnston stood, gaping at the sight. The last wagon caught fire, and he scanned the panoramic view of several dozen blazes. In anger his eyes searched the mountains. He presently heard a voice echoing down the canyon. All the soldiers heard it, stopped, and stared, most half-dressed, at the direction from which it boomed. It was the voice of Porter Rockwell.....

"General, I don't mean to talk for Brigham Young or nothin', but I suggest you may as well head to that big pile of ashes once called Fort Bridger–'cause you ain't ever gonna bother us again. We fly the stars and stripes proudly. I just wonder what the devil you think it stands for."

The general and his men stood staring at the mountainside, unable to see the source of the voice. Meanwhile, the flames of the burning wagons soared high into the midnight sky.

Rockwell surveyed the vista, beholding the red flames' reflections dancing off two thousand soldiers' faces. And he smiled.

23

As Porter Rockwell rode with most of his men back to Salt Lake Valley, he helped herd 624 steer and 104 mules.

At the entrance to Immigration Canyon he stopped his horse and gazed at the silver-colored Great Salt Lake. It was late afternoon. High clouds shadowed the valley, and the sun shot filtered fingers through the clouds, bouncing crystal-like beams off the shimmering lake's surface.

Rockwell ordered his men to ride on. For an hour he sat atop his horse and stared, thinking and alone, realizing that although the war had pushed his problems with his woman away momentarily, he had no recourse now but to face them head-on. He loved her as he never had before, and he realized that if she really would have him back, he would simply have to make a few hundred more compromises.

He had lived as a free man long enough.

His independent, willful spirit had practically destroyed their life together, and he realized essentially for the first time that what he had resented–her criticalness of him and her not accepting about him what he thought should only be natural in a man–was not her fault. He realized fully that he had been a devil to live with and that she had been an angel.

"That's a good mix," he mumbled to himself. "Except it don't

work." He spurred his animal and rode down into the valley, as uncertain about her feelings now–and if he would even have another
chance–as he had ever been about anything in his life.

Just after dawn he arrived near the south end of Salt Lake
Valley. He discovered Mary Ann leaning against the well, gazing at
the shadowed mountains. She still had not decided about him. But
when her eyes rested on him, watching him approach on horseback, she perceived a different countenance in him than she had
ever before seen, and she came to an immediate decision. The next
thing she noticed was his smile.

Then, as he stopped in front of her, she stared a minute into his
blue eyes as if they were open windows.....

EPILOGUE

Porter Rockwell resumed marshaling and built a ranching empire. Brigham Young negotiated a peace with President James Buchanan, and the Army was forced to settle 40 miles outside Salt Lake Valley.

William W. Drummond never succeeded in replacing Young as governor. Drummond was later convicted on two counts of fraud, and eventually became a sewing machine salesman in St. Louis.

He died as a vagrant in a Chicago asylum.

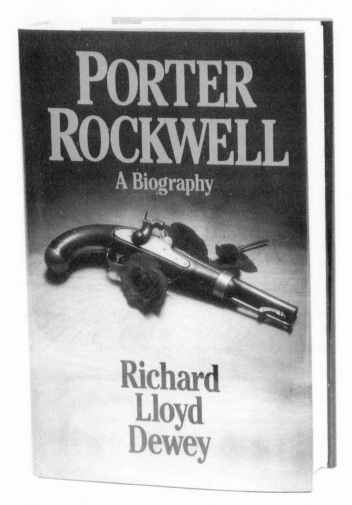

PORTER ROCKWELL
A Biography
Richard Lloyd Dewey

The epic biography that traces Porter Rockwell from turbulent Eastern beginnings to battles with Mid-western mobs to extraordinary gunfights on the American frontier. Quotes hundreds of journals, letters, and court records. Illustrated by western artist, Clark Kelley Price.

592 pages. $19.95, plus $1.75 shipping. Prices subject to change. Send check or money order to Paramount Books, Western Distributing Office, P.O. Box 1371, Provo, UT 84603-1371.